DELAY
of GAME

Tracey Richardson

BELLA
BOOKS

2017

Bella Books, Inc.
P.O. Box 10543
Tallahassee, FL 32302

Printed in the United States of America on acid-free paper.

First Bella Books Edition 2017

Editor: Medora MacDougall
Cover Designer: Judith Fellows

ISBN: 978-1-59493-526-8

Other Bella Books by Tracey Richardson

Blind Bet
By Mutual Consent
The Campaign
The Candidate
Side Order of Love
No Rules of Engagement
The Song in My Heart
The Wedding Party
Last Salute

Acknowledgments

Thank you to all the women I've had the pleasure of playing hockey with over the years. The game, the people who play it, the fans, have all enriched my life tremendously. This book would never have been written without the encouragement of fellow author Chris Paynter, who simply told me I *had* to write a hockey-themed romance and wouldn't let me off the hook. I want to thank my local writers' group (ASCRIBE Writers) for their ongoing friendship, support and encouragement and for making our monthly meetings fun. Thank you to Bella Books and their awesome staff for their unmatched dedication and professionalism. As always, I'm indebted to my favorite editor, Medora MacDougall, who *gets* me and my books, and makes my books, and me, better. And last but not least, thanks to my partner Sandra, who's helped make it possible for me to indulge in this passion called writing full time.

About the Author

Tracey is a two-time Lambda Literary award finalist and a first-place (RWA) Rainbow Writers winner. Retired from a twenty-six-year journalism career, Tracey enjoys golf, hockey, guitar and kayaking (when not writing, of course!) in the beautiful Georgian Bay area of Ontario.

Author's Note

All characters and events in this novel are fictional. The 2010 Winter Olympic Games were held in Vancouver, British Columbia, and the scores of the Olympic women's hockey games in this novel are correct, but all other details and information about the Olympics, the hockey games, the individuals and the teams in this novel are products of the author's imagination.

CHAPTER ONE

Interference

August, 2009

Niki Hartling's first instinct was to ignore the two sharp raps on her office door. There was precious little time for interruptions with the start of the new semester eleven days away and the mountain of curriculum work that lay ahead of her.

A third knock forced her out of her chair. *Fine*, she thought with fresh exasperation. She'd make them go away quickly, especially if it was a colleague wanting to grumble about course loads and schedules. Or worse, a student begging to get into one of her already filled classes or perhaps wanting a teaching assistant's job. Or God knew what else.

She pulled open the door and stepped back in surprise. "Lynn O'Reilly, my God, woman! What are you doing halfway across the province?"

Lynn, a tall woman whose leanness had given way to a muscled stockiness in the years since her hockey-playing days, wrapped Niki in a bear hug, squeezing the breath from her lungs. "Nice to see you too, Nik." Her grin was as wide as a watermelon split in two. That was Lynn, wearing her emotions on her sleeve, whether it was her temper or her cheer. "I bet I'm about the last ex-teammate you'd expect to see standing in your very impressive university office after all this time, eh?"

No, Niki thought as a blade of sadness bit into her heart. The last former teammate she'd ever expect to see standing in front of her was a woman she'd mostly given up thinking about a long time ago. A woman she'd once loved with the naîvéte and abandonment that could only come with being in love for the first time, where every feeling, every moment together, dwarfed all else. But eleven years had sailed by. Eleven years in which Niki had married, become widowed, was left with a child to raise alone. Eleven years in which she had grown up and been through more than most people endured over the course of decades. Seeing Lynn again only reminded her that she didn't have the time or the inclination to think about the old days. Not when there was so much in the present to worry about.

"Jeez," Niki said, rubbing her face by way of giving her emotions a reset. It wasn't Lynn's fault that so much had changed, that so many things in her life had become hard. "It's been a long time, hasn't it?"

"Hard to believe it's been over a decade since we shared the same ice. But you haven't changed a bit. You look like you could still strap 'em on and give 'em hell on the score sheet, the way you did in '98."

Nagano 1998. The first Olympic Games to include women's ice hockey as a medal sport, and a bittersweet silver medal for Niki, Lynn and their Team Canada teammates. The memory was as clear as if it had happened yesterday, that moment when the silver medals were prominently placed around their necks. When all of the players but Niki and Lynn cried tears of frustration and disappointment and anguish. Their team had been the favorite to win gold, but Niki and Lynn, the team's *de facto* leaders, had known better than to buy into all that sanctimonious, head-swelling hype. It was the underdogs who were blessed with the advantage, with the mental edge in sports, Niki tried to counsel her teammates then, because the underdogs were almost always hungriest and played with the least amount of pressure. But her advice—and the goals she scored almost single-handedly—hadn't been enough. It was in that moment when the silver medal was draped around her neck that Niki knew it was time to hang up her skates, because she, too, had ultimately come up short in matching the Americans' desire to win. She'd given it everything and it hadn't been enough. The wanting was there but the result wasn't. Ultimately she'd failed her team, failed herself, and knew that as a player it would be impossible to want—and to come so close to achieving—anything like that again. When you tried your best but couldn't quite reach the top of the mountain, there came a time when there was nothing left but to turn around and go back down.

Niki swallowed, deciding it was too long ago and too painful to dredge up their playing days. Little could come of this little stroll down memory lane. "Speaking of the Olympics, congratulations, by the way."

"Thanks," Lynn said, whistling under her breath. She would be the assistant coach for Team Canada's entry into the Vancouver Olympics six months from now. But there was a current of worry in her voice and the way she was shuffling her feet. "I don't know, Nik."

"There's nothing not to know. You're up to it. They wouldn't have picked you otherwise." Niki was deeply familiar with the pressures Lynn faced, because she had been an assistant coach to the national team in the 2006 Olympic Games in Turin, Italy, where Canada had claimed gold against the Americans, exactly as they'd done in Salt Lake in '02. But the golden glow was short-lived. Six weeks later her wife Shannon was diagnosed with pancreatic cancer and given only months to live. Niki had not coached a game of hockey since.

"It's not that, Nik, but thank you for your confidence."

No, it wouldn't be a lack of confidence, not with Lynn. Lynn was capable, was brutally ruthless at times. Or at least, when it came to winning. She wasn't afraid of making decisions, wasn't afraid of doing whatever was required. A bull in a china shop, as both a player and a coach.

"Got time for a walk?" Lynn asked with a hopeful lilt to her voice.

"Of course." Anyone who'd traveled the four hours down the clogged Highway 401 from Toronto to the University of Windsor campus deserved a few minutes of her time, curriculum be damned. And for Lynn to show up unannounced after all these years, well, whatever she wanted to talk about had to be important.

The campus was deserted, as it would remain until the semester started. It took only minutes for Niki and Lynn to reach the Detroit River and the meandering, paved walking path along its shore. Summer still hung hot and humid in the air, autumn giving no hint that it was poised to take over. But that would change in a few weeks, when the leaves would begin their costume change and a damp chill would deepen its claim on the days.

"Not that I pretend to know much about it, but I guess you're getting ready for the new semester?" Lynn said. She'd never gone to college or university. Right out of high school, she had joined the professional women's hockey league—the National Women's Hockey League. The professional part was a joke, though, because it only paid a few hundred dollars a month. Lynn had slogged in a factory making bicycle parts to augment her income, then made the transition to coaching in the same league a few years ago. It was a big step up for her to join Hockey Canada's coaching ranks, just as it had been for Niki four years ago.

"You'd think I'd have the curriculum down cold after all these years, but I like to tear it down and rebuild it every year."

Lynn laughed. "You would. Biggest perfectionist I've ever seen."

Niki taught sports management in the university's business school. Her classes were popular, especially with professional and semi-professional sports becoming bigger and bigger business in North America. And yeah, she was a taskmaster as a teacher, expecting her students to exhibit the kind of drive and ambition they'd need to get ahead in their work life. Schools were insular, protective. The real world, whether it was business or sports, was a snake pit.

"Which," Lynn continued, "is why you were such a damned good coach. Your attention to the smallest details, for one."

They stopped to gaze out at the river, gray today beneath the lightly overcast sky. A lake freighter inched toward the skeletal-like, murky shadow cast by the Ambassador Bridge, the ship's mammoth steel hull so close that Niki could probably have thrown a stone and hit it.

"Ever miss coaching?" Lynn asked, and something in her voice told Niki the question wasn't entirely rhetorical.

"I don't think about coaching anymore. Haven't in a long time." It wasn't a lie. Hockey was no longer on Niki's radar because other, much more pressing things claimed her attention. Like making a living. Like being a single mother.

"You playing at all?"

"Recreational pickup once a week. It's about all I have time for. Look." Niki knew Lynn wasn't the type to beat around the bush. Nor was she here for a friendly catch-up session. They were friends, but they were hockey friends. Lynn hadn't even made the trip to attend Shannon's funeral three years ago. "Why are you really here, Lynn? What's on your mind?"

The look in Lynn's brown eyes was forthright. "Hockey Canada is going to fire Coach Rogers next week."

"What? Why?"

Mike Rogers was head coach of the women's team and had been for the past two years. Niki knew it was highly unusual to start fresh with a new head coach six months away from an Olympics. In fact, it was pretty much guaranteed suicide for the team. The planning, the strategy sessions, the selection camps and meetings, would all have been taking place for months now. It would be like switching jockeys in the start gate of the Kentucky Derby.

"I'm not high enough on the ladder to know all the whys. But there are rumors."

Niki considered pressing Lynn, but decided it wasn't her business. Nor did she really care what was behind the firing. She was about to ask Lynn why she was telling her all of this when it hit her like a two-by-four across the shoulders. "Oh, no no no. No, you don't, Lynn O'Reilly."

Lynn didn't try to deny anything. A small smile tugged at the corners of her mouth, and one dark eyebrow posed a question.

Niki turned sharply and began walking quickly. It took only seconds for Lynn, with her longer strides, to pull even with her. "You're here on a recruiting mission, aren't you? Well, I'm afraid you've wasted your time, Lynn. Would have been cheaper and quicker if you'd just called, you know."

"I was in the neighborhood."

"Yeah, right."

They walked in silence for another minute, Niki fuming inside that Lynn didn't know her better than all this. Didn't know that there was no *way* she'd even consider taking on a coaching job with Hockey Canada. It was about as likely as joining the astronaut program.

"You're pissed at me, aren't you?"

Niki stopped, fixed Lynn with a look that contained no forgiveness. She felt used. "There are at least ten good reasons why I won't return to coaching, but only one that matters. To me, anyway."

Lynn's expression softened. "How old is Rory now?"

"She just turned ten this summer. She's young, Lynn, just a kid. A kid who's known more upheaval and heartache than a kid her age ever should."

Dread and grief and anger formed a hard knot in Niki's stomach. Most days, she muddled through, doing her best to maintain a stable environment for Rory. Routines had kept her sane and Rory secure while they waited for grief to dissolve into something more tolerable. They'd recently begun to get a little comfortable with their new normal, but it was a process. A slow process. She'd kept everything the same since Shannon's death. Same house, same Sunday dinners at Shannon's sister Jenny's house, same two-week-long vacation at a Lake Huron rental cottage every July. Even if she were interested in coaching Team Canada—which she wasn't—she would never pack up Rory and move her to the team's training center in Calgary for the next six months. It'd be far too selfish. And way too hard.

"Look," Lynn finally said. "They're going to be calling you in the next couple of days. I only wanted to give you a heads-up."

"And to feel me out?"

Lynn shrugged, wouldn't meet her eye for a moment. When she did, there was no apology in her stare. "All right. Here's the truth. Hockey Canada wants you for the head coach's job. They know your track record, know you're a proven winner. You helped the team to gold at the last Olympics as an assistant coach, and before that you won two CIS titles coaching Windsor here. You're money in the bank, Nik. Rogers has been losing his grip on that team for months. 'Course, doesn't help that he's been screwing one of the players."

Niki blinked. Such unprofessionalism was absolutely forbidden these days in sports, even among consenting adults. The stakes were too high. "I don't even want to know who."

"No need. She'll be quietly separated from the flock after Rogers is let go. The mothership wants all its ducks in a row before they cut Rogers loose."

"And I'm one of those ducks."

"You're their top choice. And mine too. Not that I have much say, but I respect you, Nik, more than anybody in the game. There's no other coach I'd rather serve under."

"Thanks, Lynn. I mean that. And if things were different, I'd think about it." She spread her arms out for emphasis. "But Rory's my priority. And I won't uproot her for the next six or seven months or put her through my long days at the rink, days or weeks of being on the road with the team."

The hours would be ridiculously long. There would be meetings, practices, videos and notes to review, scouting other players and teams. There'd be exhibition games in and out of town, then of course a month in Vancouver for the Olympics. Rory liked it here, Windsor was all she knew, and her aunt and uncle and cousin were here. No, this was where she—they—belonged right now. "I'm afraid you've wasted your time."

Lynn relaxed her shoulders, as though she'd fully expected Niki's rejection. "How are you doing these days, Nik? I mean, really doing?"

Niki bit her bottom lip to keep it from quivering. People had mostly stopped asking her, as if after a certain number of years went by, all the bad stuff had magically evaporated or been forgotten. And so Lynn's question threw her. "I'm doing okay. Rory and I have each other. And Shannon's sister Jenny and her husband Tim have been great." She didn't much feel like explaining further. There was no way to accurately encapsulate her life or her feelings to someone she hadn't seen in years.

"Well," Lynn said. "Hockey Canada is still going to call you, no matter what I report back to them. You've got a couple of days to think about it."

"I don't need a couple of days to know I'm going to turn it down."

Lynn could have pressed her, could have tried different angles to get her to change her mind, but she didn't, and it was a relief.

"Are you still in Toronto or have you made the move to Calgary yet?"

Lynn fished a business card from her shirt pocket. "I've been out west a lot this summer preparing, but I'm officially moving there next week. This card has an email address that never changes. Keep in touch, all right?"

Niki pocketed the card, knowing she'd probably not make use of it. They'd had some fun times when they were teammates all those years ago, but a lot of things had changed since then. Niki had changed. Hockey wasn't much a part of her life anymore. Well, except for her women's scrimmage group that played once a week and hauling Rory to practices and games for her atom girls team. She barely even watched hockey on TV anymore.

"Come on," Niki said after a moment in which neither seemed to know how to fill the silence. "I'll walk you back to your car."

"Sounds good."

They changed direction and headed down Sunset Avenue, the silence growing more awkward. The two women had little between them anymore, nothing else in common, except for hockey and the old days. And Niki didn't want to revisit the old days. "So what do you think is the ticket to beating the Americans in Vancouver, any idea yet?" The US had finished second to Canada at the last two Olympics, but they were an ever-growing threat and had been getting better and better every year since. They'd won the previous two world championships against Canada, including a 4-1 spanking four months ago in Finland. The likelihood of Canada winning a third consecutive gold medal appeared less and less likely.

"The Americans are going with youth," Lynn replied. "So they'll be fast and eager, but we're more disciplined and experienced. If our legs can come close to matching theirs, we'll do fine. And we do have a couple of really good up-and-coming youngsters we're developing."

Niki thought about the two teams' contradictory approaches—Canada bringing along their younger players more slowly, the US seemingly throwing their rookies into the deep end right away. It worked sometimes, because the younger players were fearless and didn't know what it was like to lose to Canada. But she'd not been paying much attention to the two teams since the last Olympics, since Shannon died, and she only asked Lynn out of politeness. "Sounds intriguing, but the US must have at least some older veterans on their team, right?" A team full of rookies and sophomores wouldn't cut it.

Lynn flicked her a sideways, unreadable glance. "Just one. She'll take all the leadership on her shoulders, looks like. But I'm not sure her body will hold up. In fact, I'll be shocked if she's still in the lineup by February."

"Who is it?" Even as the words left her mouth, Niki's heart somersaulted as she realized her mistake.

The look on Lynn's face confirmed what she already knew, though Lynn obliged with an answer. "Eva Caruso."

Niki had to slam her eyes shut for an instant. Hearing Eva's name jarred her, made her dizzy. And it pissed her off that it should have such an effect on her. Eva had been many things to her—a college teammate at Wisconsin, an adversary at the Nagano Olympics, and most of all, her lover. They'd been each other's first loves, and in the years since, Niki had accomplished many things. She'd married, had become an instant parent, had turned to teaching. But nothing she'd done had been so simple, so pure, so consequential, so overpowering as loving Eva. In all the ways that mattered, Eva was like the first buzz from alcohol or the first high, and one that was never again to be replicated by another sip or another puff. Loving Eva was a feeling she'd never quite shed, like the tongue constantly worrying the divot where a tooth had once been. Gone but still there in some imaginary form. Eva had left an imprint in her soul, even after all these years.

But she didn't want to talk about Eva, not to Lynn, not to anybody, and not now. She was past thinking of Eva, oh yes she was. So past her, that her rapidly beating heart was from the spicy burrito she'd had for lunch, she told herself. She didn't give a shit what Eva did or didn't do, whether she would prove to be Team USA's hero or its fallen, pathetic star clinging to the past. No way. She would *not* think about Eva because Eva had nothing to with her life anymore and never would again.

Niki shrugged and affected a casualness that was entirely false. "Well, no matter who's on their roster, I know you guys have got this, Lynn."

CHAPTER TWO

Breakaway

The crunch of steel carving ice, the air so chilled that puffs of her breath rose in wispy white clouds before her, raised an exhilaration in Eva Caruso that was every bit as new and magical as the first time she'd ever laced on skates and glided onto a frozen pond. She'd been a fast learner back then, trading candy bars to the older kids if they'd show her how to skate backward, how to turn on a dime, how to get off a wrist shot. She was ten before her parents finally agreed to sign her up for organized hockey—a boys' team on which she was the only girl. She'd taken her lumps that year, figuratively and literally, on her way to becoming the team's second highest scorer. From there it was high school hockey, then NCAA in Wisconsin and playing internationally for Team USA, and finally, professionally for the National Women's Hockey League and then the Canadian Women's Hockey League before taking a leave of absence from hockey a year ago.

The easiest time in her hockey life, the most gratifying in many ways, were those pond hockey days. The memories flooded through her, eliciting nostalgia for the joy of simply playing, of simply skating, and they masked any worries about the present or the future. Any worries about anything, really. When she strapped on her equipment and gripped a stick in her hands, nothing but that moment existed in her mind. Scoring, making a tape-to-tape pass, riding an opponent off the puck—those were the only things she cared about. But now, as she cut a hard turn left, then right to test her damaged knee, she questioned yet again if returning to hockey was the right decision. And not just hockey, but taking a final run at Olympic gold. The 1998 Olympics produced her one and only gold medal. Salt Lake brought silver, then a torn ACL in her left knee had kept her out of the Turin Winter Games in '06. Her age was against her now—thirty-six—and so was her body. Her hunger too had waned, or at least the level of hunger required of an elite athlete to burn through the physical pain, to grind out the personal sacrifices, to put everything on the line to play the game she loved. Her once full tank was little more than fumes now. Until the past week, she hadn't even skated in nearly a year. But dammit, she wanted to leave hockey on *her* terms, not on the terms dictated by her knee and by her age. If she could try one last time for gold, there'd be no future regrets. She could go out on top of the world.

Eva stopped suddenly, sending a spray of ice chips arcing into the air, then took off in a running start. She sprinted to the other end of the ice, her blades digging in for power before each stride, raced back again. She cursed the burning in her lungs, the quick lance of pain in her left knee. She wasn't in good enough shape yet, not even close, and if she were a betting woman, she'd wager her chances of even lasting to the opening of the Olympic Games were about fifty-fifty at best. But Eva Caruso wasn't scared of having the odds stacked against her.

She stopped in front of the Home bench to catch her breath and to wrestle her doubts into submission. She didn't really need a second gold medal or a second silver either if that should happen. She didn't need the grueling months ahead of her, didn't need the pain that would accompany pushing her body to the limit, didn't need the financial hit of taking a leave from her lucrative business of managing pricey home renovations and constructions in Traverse City, Michigan. She had nothing more to prove. She'd reached the pinnacle of women's hockey and was talked about in the same breath as legends Cammi Granato and Haley Wickenheiser. Nothing to prove, but she had much to give back, and that too fueled her return to the game.

She wanted to mentor the young players with their kamikaze energy on the ice and their wide eyes that glinted like those of an addict chasing their favorite drug. Eva wanted a legacy that was about more than her on-ice accomplishments; she wanted also to pass on the things she had learned in her years of competing at the highest level of women's hockey. She was duty-bound to save the young players some of the pain and heartache she'd endured. And they would be giving back to her as well, whether they knew it or not. She'd need to feed off their excitement and boundless energy if she were to survive the next few months. Hockey would, she hoped, once again become the nourishment and joy her soul craved.

"How's the knee feeling?"

Eva looked up sharply. She hadn't noticed Alison Hiller, head coach of Team USA, climb into the bench from the stands. Alison was the bitter pill she'd have to swallow in returning to the team.

"Fine," Eva said, still gulping air like a swimmer who'd stayed under too long.

"Liar," Alison said, exacting a thin smile. Eva knew the long-time coach couldn't care less how she was feeling, as long as she was able to perform. "Think you're ready for a full practice tomorrow? Or should we yellow jersey you for a couple more days?"

Yellow jerseys in practice meant the player was injured or rehabbing, and the other players were to go easy on her. Against her better judgment, Eva said, "I'll be ready."

Alison's eyes narrowed skeptically, but she nodded once. "Good. I want to see you put in a good practice, then we'll have a sit-down."

By design, Eva had avoided Alison as much as possible

these last few days. But that would need to change, as the team began working more closely together and more intensely to prepare for the Olympics. Their first exhibition game, against the University of Minnesota women's team, was less than three weeks away.

"Fine," Eva said.

Alison turned to go, then leaned back over the boards, something perversely pleasurable in her expression. "How's this for some juicy gossip?" She didn't wait for Eva to reply. "Team Canada's announcing tomorrow they're firing Rogers as their coach."

"Good for them," Eva snapped, not giving a shit what her rival team did or didn't do.

"Guess who's replacing him?"

Eva sighed impatiently. "I don't know, Wayne Gretzky? No, wait. Mickey Mouse? Spiderman?"

"More like Wonder Woman." Her laughter was like nails on a chalkboard. "Your old flame, in fact. Niki Hartling."

Eva's heart stilled and she shivered in spite of the layer of sweat collecting beneath her shin pads and shoulder pads. *Jesus!* She hated that the mere mention of Niki made her feel like she'd just seen a ghost. Inwardly she collected herself, refusing to give Alison the satisfaction of a reaction. She skated as fast and as far away from her coach as her trembling legs could manage.

* * *

Eva lay down on her narrow bed with an ice pack taped firmly to her knee. It was a relief to have been assigned her own room at the training complex. Being a veteran player had its perks.

As her knee throbbed, her heart revisited that old familiar ache. Hearing Niki's name—even thinking about her—was a knife that always sliced her deep and sharp and clean, before pulsing into a dull hammering pain that took minutes and sometimes a drink or a pain pill to sweep away. It shouldn't be like this after so many years, Eva told herself, angry that it was. She and Niki hadn't been a couple in eleven-and-a-half years, hadn't come face-to-face in about six. Their parting, on the eve of the '98 Olympics in Nagano, had been messy, ugly, complete with yelling, the smashing of trophies, the tossing of a lamp and the scattering of clothing from a dresser in their shared apartment until the place resembled the aftermath of a tornado's destruction. They couldn't get away from each other fast enough, couldn't wait, days later, to go hard and reckless at each other in the final game for Olympic gold. It was a collision in the neutral zone with Niki that had sprained Eva's knee for the first time, beginning its slide into the taped up, sewed up, glued together excuse for a knee she had now.

In the years since, they'd both carefully and intentionally ignored one another in the few instances they crossed paths. It was as though they'd never shared a bed, never shared their lives for nearly four glorious years where they were inseparable, where their love had consumed every ounce of their awareness, every minute of their time and energy outside of hockey and school. In those days, Eva couldn't draw a single breath without feeling Niki right there in the center of her chest. To go from that to a big fat nothing between them, a black hole, was a whole new kind of pain. Eva had decided a long time ago that she had to stop caring if she ever saw Niki again. Had, in fact, to stop thinking about her. But all of that, it was now clear, was a joke. Niki was the one absence in her life she would forever feel.

Niki rejoining her national team couldn't have come as a bigger surprise to Eva. And not as an assistant coach this time, but as its head coach, if Alison was correct. Of course, Alison wasn't exactly the perfect model of honesty and morality. Years ago, she had taken pernicious pleasure in firmly placing the wedge between Eva and Niki that ultimately led to their undoing as a couple. Alison had been Team USA's assistant coach then, and her task, which had come all too naturally, was to make sure her team had worked up a hateful lather for the Canadians. You can't merely dislike your opponent, you must hate them, she had warned her players more times than Eva could count, calling their rivalry a war and all kinds of crap that, over the course of the months leading up to the Olympics, had worn away at Niki and Eva's relationship like a grinding wheel to a stone. The final straw was a couple of floppy disks, clearly labeled as Team USA property, secreted in a pocket of Niki's hockey bag. Eva had been rummaging for a roll of tape one evening and discovered them. The minute she was alone, she shoved the disks one at a time into her old desktop computer and examined them long enough to realize they were her team's detailed notes on its players and strategies. A digital playbook, as it were, and it was devastating in the hands of an opponent.

Eva shook her head as she remembered Niki's impassioned denials that she had stolen the disks and then her own refusal to believe Niki. It was evidence of how far their relationship had eroded, of how much their love had evaporated in the face of such pressure, of such fierce competition, of such construed hatred for the enemy. To Eva's horror, she discovered months later that Alison had planted the disks on Niki as part of some sadistic and misguided strategy to ramp up the hate between the two teams. And of course, to drive Niki and Eva apart for good. The damage was irreversible. Niki had moved on, unwilling or unable to forgive Eva for not believing her. And Eva, well, Eva hadn't tried to repair things between them because in her heart she knew they'd begun drifting apart long before that stupid stunt of Alison's. She'd justified her casual attitude by deciding their love wasn't worth fighting for, that Niki would never love her again, that there was no point in trying to reconcile. Somewhere along the line, she'd begun believing it, especially when it seemed Niki had no intention of reaching out either.

Eva rolled over, shook a Percocet from her bottle on the nightstand. She swallowed it with one gulp of water. It was only one pill. Normally, it was an Advil or two at bedtime, but tonight, with Niki on her mind and the prospect of Alison taking center stage in her life for the next few months, an Advil wouldn't be nearly enough to kick her spirits into something resembling happy.

Eva closed her eyes, wondering not for the first of many times, what the hell she had gotten herself into.

CHAPTER THREE

Power Play

Niki had never been so nervous before the media. Not as a player in those first Olympic Games in '98, not as a university coach at the national championships and not even in Turin three-and-a-half years ago as Team Canada's assistant coach.

She flicked a hand through her short, blond hair—a habit all her life, even though her hair had enough body to perpetually hold its shape. She stared at a spot on the wall behind the reporters as Hockey Canada's president, Dan Smolenski, praised her and the team. When her turn to speak came, she kept it short. She wasn't the expansive type anyway, but what was there to say? She didn't know the team, hadn't yet met with the players, although she'd begun to do her homework on each of them. She didn't know what to expect come February, what their chances were of earning gold. It was all brand new to her, and besides, everybody knew she'd been parachuted in after the sudden and unexpected firing of Coach Rogers. What she would do, she told the reporters, was nothing short of her best for the team and for the country.

Silence, followed by audible grumbling, told her what the reporters thought of her vague platitudes. It took only seconds before they turned their single-minded attention to Smolenksi. Why had the previous coach been fired? Why make a change five months before the Games? How would it impact the players, their strategies, their preparation?

Niki caught a smile of encouragement from Lynn, who sat at the other end of the long table. An array of microphones sat before them. The lights from the cameras were hot and blinding and relentless. *You wanted this*, she reminded herself. *You knew what it would be like*. But it wasn't enough to make her feel better, and again she wondered what the hell she was doing.

She thought about Rory, and her heart cracked. The little girl had been so brave in urging her to take the job, so mature beyond her (barely) ten years. She wasn't old enough to know Niki as anything other than a mom, as a teacher to big kids at the university and as a recreational hockey player who was so much better on the ice than the other women she played with one night a week at the neighborhood arena. But she wanted Niki to be famous, to go to the Olympics, to win a medal, to teach those girl hockey players how to be awesome! Rory wouldn't take no for an answer, and to see her daughter's eyes shine with brand-new admiration and pride for her gave Niki the sudden desire to do whatever she could to please her. She never wanted to see those big brown eyes full of tears again, never wanted to see them so laden with that wrenchingly awful sadness that, for a long time, had paralyzed them both. And so she did what Rory asked.

The family conspiracy didn't stop with Rory. Jenny—Shannon's sister—had urged her to take the job as well, confiding in her how Shannon felt guilty that her illness had stolen her away from coaching. She never wanted you to leave hockey, Jenny told her. The clincher was when she said she and Tim would be happy to take Rory into their home as one of their own for the next six months.

Days of soul-searching followed, of carefully talking to Rory to make absolutely certain the kid knew what it would all mean and of asking herself if she could handle being away from Rory for weeks, months, at a time. They'd see each other over Christmas, and Rory would spend the Olympic Games in Vancouver with her, but that might be all. She might not even make it back for Halloween, which coincided with what would have been Shannon's fortieth birthday.

A reporter's question, asked with calumnious impatience, propelled Niki back to the present. Why was *she* chosen as head coach? Hockey Canada's president smiled like he had all day and answered that Niki had been the team's assistant coach at the last Olympics, a proven coach at the university level and an elite player herself, probably even a future Hockey Hall of Famer. But why, the reporter continued, choose someone who'd been away from the game for more than three years and had never been a head coach internationally? Surely, he suggested in a tone bursting with judgment, there were other more qualified candidates.

Smolenksi again recited Niki's qualifications, effusively stating his confidence in her, and Niki had to force herself to sit stone-like, to school her expression into one of bored disinterest. But inside, her thoughts warred with each other—outrage that they could dissect her like she wasn't even there and ultimately resignation that such an inquisition was deserved, coming with the territory as it did. It was natural that her appointment would be criticized and questioned by the media. She'd been away from the game for a long time, especially at this level, and a ton of work lay ahead of her. Of course people were going to be skeptical about her abilities, as they would be about almost anyone plugged into this role so late in the game. But like she'd always told her players, believe in yourself first and forget what anybody else says. The locker room chalkboard was a jungle of smeary inspirational quotations. Things like "Negativity breeds failure," "Hard work beats talent every time," "If you fail to prepare, you're prepared to fail" and "Sports do not build character, they reveal it." As a coach, Niki had to walk the talk, and so she raised her chin and hardened her stare.

When she was asked what would be her first priority as coach, she elected for something vague enough to still be the truth. "To start preparing my team to win the gold medal in Vancouver."

"Want to tell us how?"

"No."

"Will you win the gold medal, Coach?" another reporter asked.

"I wouldn't be here if I didn't think so. I have every intention of winning gold on our home turf. Nothing less will do."

"Jesus," she said to Lynn minutes later as they took refuge in Niki's office. It was a cinder block room with red wall-to-wall carpet, as big as the locker room, at the Olympic Oval arena at the University of Calgary's campus. The conference table was a large, round monstrosity that sat ten. There was a flat-screen TV on the wall nearest the table, a wooden desk in the corner with two chairs facing it. Behind the desk were a couple of wooden puck racks mounted on the wall, where pucks autographed by the world's best women hockey players perched. Niki had only moved in a day ago and had not yet unpacked her framed picture of Rory and another of herself, Rory and Shannon posing in front of Niagara Falls the year before Shannon died.

"You haven't had to do a presser in a while, eh?" Lynn said, taking a seat at the conference table.

With the back of her hand, Niki wiped away the slick film of sweat from her forehead. "Remind me next time to only invite the nice reporters."

"Ha, nobody would show up if that was the case."

Niki hadn't had to deal with too many sports reporters over the years. At least not the cantankerous know-it-alls that had, moments ago, put her through the meat grinder. As a player, the reporters had mostly gone easy on her, acting more like fans than interrogators. Coaching at the university, she'd mostly dealt with student reporters and the occasional reporter from the local paper. In Turin, she'd been the national team's assistant coach and, as such, wasn't required to be a talking head.

"Well, it is our national religion after all. And the first time we've hosted the Winter Games since 1988. And the first chance to win women's gold in hockey on home soil." It was a big deal and they both knew it. Niki sat down opposite Lynn and watched as her assistant coach slid a binder as thick as a Bible in front of them. "Guess I can't blame them for being a little intense."

Lynn's eyes were twin laser beams. "If they're that intense now, wait until the Games actually begin. You sure you're up to all this pressure? It's a lot more than the usual, and the media—hell, the country—won't settle for less than perfection."

It was true. There was everything to lose, with expectations that were enormous and unforgiving. She knew, with a profundity that came from having lost her wife, that she never again wanted to revisit the desolation that came from wanting something so bad, of trying so hard to change what was predestined and, ultimately, not achieving it. "I'm not doing this to win silver. And neither is anyone connected with this team. That," Niki said in a voice as chilled as the snow-capped mountains in the distance, "is all that matters."

Lynn nodded, her eyes trying to calculate something unstated. "Then let's get to work, shall we?" She flipped open the binder. It was the complete roster of Team USA, players and staff. It contained everything Lynn and Hockey Canada knew about their number one adversary. It was the book on Team USA, as prepared by Hockey Canada's staff of scouts, analysts and managers.

"Biggest weakness?" Niki shot a glance at the binder.

"Youth and inexperience."

"Biggest strength?"

"Youth and inexperience." Lynn's smile was her exclamation point, and Niki knew exactly what she meant. The young players would have infinite energy, would be highly motivated, and their inexperience meant no preconceptions, no sense that there was anything to lose. But their lack of experience meant emotion often filled the gap, and with fervent emotions came mistakes.

"Their biggest unknown quantity?"

"That's easy," Lynn said, flipping to another page in the binder. "Eva Caruso."

Niki swallowed. "How so?" She had her own opinions but wanted to hear Lynn's.

"Great player, great leader, but her body's giving out. Potential is there to lead this team on the ice and off, to cushion the team's transition to a younger crop of players. Knows what it takes to win, but if she's not healthy and can't be a leader on the ice, her leadership abilities will likely be neutralized."

Succinct but accurate, Niki thought, finally letting her gaze drop to the eight-by-ten portrait shot of Eva. She was stunning, even more so as a woman in her mid-thirties. The shoulder-length black wavy hair, the olive Italian complexion and big brown eyes gave her an exotic, Mediterranean look that, Niki knew from experience could and did turn women (and men) into stuttering fools. She had the killer body too. Tall, muscular, as fit as a marathoner. But none of those things was enough to make Niki forgive her, and they certainly weren't enough to draw her interest beyond the clinical appraisal by a coach of a rival player. No. Any emotional link to Eva was in the past—exactly where it should be. There was only the business of hockey between them now.

"So if she can't lead this team on the ice, you think it will directly affect the Americans' chances?"

"Absolutely. Like I said, find a way to neutralize her, and the kids will be running amok out there on the ice."

There was something about Lynn's tone Niki didn't like. "You know I will *never* condone 'neutralizing' another team's player. Are we clear on that?"

She'd seen it happen before, though never on her watch, where an opponent was intentionally injured. If you had to resort to such unprincipled antics, you didn't deserve to win, Niki firmly believed and had said many times.

"Of course."

"And that's both on the record and off the record. I'm not going to say one thing and mean another."

Lynn shrugged. "Can I ask you something? Between me, you and the walls?"

Niki nodded.

"How are you going to feel when you see her face-to-face? When she's out there playing against us?"

"Are you asking me if I'm going to lose my ability to coach my team? Become some kind of blubbering, sentimental fool?"

Lynn spread her hands out on the table but didn't say anything.

"Come on. You know me better than that." She didn't need to spend any more time talking about Eva. She knew the way she played—hard. Knew she took no prisoners on the ice. She reached across and flipped to another page in the binder. "Let's talk about Coach Hiller."

Lynn rolled her eyes. "Still a first-class bitch."

"How badly does she want this?"

"Like a starving cat chasing a mouse. We've embarrassed them for two straight Olympics now, and Hiller wants to avenge their gold medal loss in Salt Lake more than she wants to breathe. We beat them on their home turf, now she wants to beat us on ours."

Niki settled back in her chair. So Alison and Eva would be their biggest threats, but for different reasons. Niki knew both women all too well. "I want you to keep an eye on Alison. Keep track of any news about her you can find. Media interviews, anything anyone is saying about her. I want to know what she's up to. I'll do the same with Eva."

A skeptical eyebrow rose from Lynn at the mention of Eva.

"Yes, you heard right. I'll keep an eye on Eva's progress, and yes, I'm up to it. That ship has sailed." Eva would not be a conflict of interest that would trip her up. They were both professionals, or at least Niki was. "I just want to know what they're up to, how they're handling things, how they're doing, what their next moves are. Keep notes, report back."

"Does that mean the occasional road trip for us?"

"Absolutely. We'll catch a few of their exhibition games, and as soon as possible." Niki liked to rely on herself as the team's best scout. "I have some catching up to do."

Lynn nodded. "I'll see that everything's booked."

Yes, Niki thought with a finality that gave her comfort. *It'll be all business between Eva and me, with absolutely no room for emotion or nostalgia or anything else.* Eva was just another rival hockey player. Nothing more, nothing less.

CHAPTER FOUR

Line Change

It took several moments of the alarm clock jackhammering into her dreams before Eva gained enough consciousness to smack the damned thing off. She loved game days but hated that they had her getting up at seven in the morning. First it was to get something in her stomach, then to give it a couple of hours to settle before reporting to the rink for the hour-long on-ice practice that started at eleven sharp. Which really meant getting to the rink no later than ten so she could stretch and warm up. After practice, there was another half hour of warming down, followed by a massage or an ice bath or whatever mending her body needed, a quick meeting, lunch, then a short nap. She'd start the routine of eating, stretching and warming up all over again well before tonight's seven o'clock start. And while game days were far more gratifying than practice days, what she really wanted to do was go another round in the sack with Kathleen Benson, maybe a few more minutes of sleep after that and a lazy shower.

Kathleen groaned beside her, slowly rubbing the sleep from her eyes. "Shit. Guess that's me too."

Another orgasm was fast becoming more fantasy than reality. "You better get back to your room before the Wicked Witch discovers you've spent the night here," Eva quipped.

Kathleen was the team's athletic therapist. It hadn't taken more than a few days at training camp before she and Eva decided to hook up for a no-strings relationship that wouldn't stray beyond the physical. It was going to be a long few months ahead of them, a few months in which outside relationships were not encouraged and, frankly, not wanted. Eva had witnessed many romantic liaisons succumb to the pressures of the Olympic Games, including hers and Niki's all those years ago. She'd never be that stupid again. Nor would she ever lose her focus again when so much was on the line.

Eva pinched Kathleen's ass as she rose, naked, from the bed that was too small for the two of them. "Same time, same place, tomorrow tonight?" Tonight's exhibition game against the University of Minnesota women's team, the Golden Gophers, meant there'd be no time, or energy, for sex afterward.

Kathleen yawned as she pulled on jeans and a sweatshirt. She was a couple of years younger than Eva, as tall but slimmer, less muscular. Kath wasn't an athlete, but she was one hell of a good trainer. Her skills at taping, massaging, mending would be indispensable in keeping Eva in one piece until all of this was over and the gold medal was hanging around her neck. Kathleen gave her a wink, said she'd see her at the rink later.

The morning skate was less demanding than an off-day practice, with the idea of the players saving their legs for the game. The stripped-down practice was more about sharpening their hand-eye coordination with passing and shooting drills, loosening up, maybe getting a feel for line chemistry, drilling down to any last-minute details they would need to incorporate into tonight's game. In the locker room, Eva slipped on her red practice jersey, noting immediately who else was wearing red. Linemates, or lineys, for the immediate game tended to wear the same colored jerseys in practice. Sometimes it was the only way to know for sure who you were skating with that night.

Eva's first clue that changes were afoot was the red jersey being pulled over Dani Compton's head. Dani, like Eva, was a center. And two centers never played on the same line unless it was for a power play or killing a penalty, in case the first center was kicked out of the faceoff circle.

Her first act on the ice was to skate over to Alison to ask her what was up in a tone that left no doubt about her displeasure. Eva had always been a top line center, since back before high school. She could understand being dropped to the number two line because of her creaky knees, but if she wasn't going to be a center at all, then she—or the coach—was far more deluded than she had allowed for.

"You're taking left wing," Alison said, turning away abruptly so as not to entertain any other questions—or complaints— from Eva.

Eva was too much an old pro to let her simmering anger infect her attitude on the ice. She carried out the drills with her usual attention to detail, her customary missile-locked intensity. She watched in judgmental silence, however, as Dani lost more than half her faceoff draws. Dani was a young player who might have a future at the national level, but she wasn't there yet. She certainly had no business taking Eva's job at center, nor playing in the top six.

In the locker room after practice, slipping off a jersey that now smelled like a horse barn, Eva eagerly glanced at the large chalkboard near the door. The lines for tonight's game were scratched out, and sure enough, there was Eva's number seventeen on left wing, with Dani at center. On the second line. *Okay, calm down. It's not quite October yet.* These meaningless exhibition games were simply a chance to get the younger players more ice time and to let Eva get back to her old self as a number one center.

A sticky note was tacked to her change stall. *Lunch in my office—A.H. Good*, Eva thought. A chance to have it out with Alison over these crazy line changes. She hadn't come back, putting her livelihood on hold and risking her body, to be a glorified cheerleader.

* * *

Alison had never fooled Eva. They weren't friends, not even close. As a coach, Alison was cutthroat and would do whatever it took to win, including, back when she was an assistant coach with the team for the Nagano Games, coming between her and Niki. Eva hadn't forgiven Alison for that, but then, her expectations of her in the morals department were extremely low. And it wasn't like Alison pretended to be the pure and honest type. She was a first-class bitch and wore the title like it was a worthy accomplishment. Everything about her demeanor screamed "I dare you."

Alison motioned for Eva to grab a sandwich from a platter in the middle of the round conference table in her office. It was good to have a buffer between them, Eva thought, in case she got the irrational urge to leap across the table and strangle her.

Eva saw no sense in delaying the obvious. "So. Was today an experiment with Dani at center?"

"Yes and no." Alison leaned back in her chair, arms uncompromisingly folded across her chest. "We'll see how she does, but I expect you to help mentor her, get her comfortable there."

Eva took a bite of her turkey sandwich, which held no appeal. It tasted like mushy cardboard. "Fine, I'll help where I can. But when do I get back on center?"

"You don't, most likely."

With effort, Eva swallowed the gluey lump of congealed bread and turkey caught up in her throat. "What?"

"You're on wing for the foreseeable future. It's where you need to be. For your own sake, for the team's sake. And I'm not going to argue with you."

"I'm a center, Alison. I've always been a center. And I'm damned good at it." Wing was for players who weren't the best skaters, who (usually) couldn't play defensive hockey worth a crap, who only had to worry about mucking in the corners, playing a north-south game, and getting the puck to their center. This was an outrage, and Eva fought to keep her voice and her red-hot Italian temper from exploding.

"Correction. You *were* a center. You're not up to it anymore, not at this level, and the sooner you face that fact, the better."

Her ears ringing, Eva thundered, "Then what the fuck am I doing here? Anybody can play wing. You don't need me."

A smirk played at the corner of Alison's mouth. "My, my. I see your ego hasn't shrunk any over the years. And unfortunately, we do need you or you wouldn't be here. You're the only one on the team with the experience and leadership qualities this team needs. The kids need you, and they need you to show up every game. If I put you on center, you'll be in the training room more than you'll be on the ice."

Conceding didn't come easy to Eva, especially with something as important as this. "I didn't sign up to come back as a winger. It's bullshit. It's like asking Beyoncé to sing backup vocals."

"Beyoncé you're not. And it's not bullshit. You know I'm right. Besides, when you signed up for this, you said you'd do whatever the team needed. I'm not asking, Eva. This is what the team needs from you."

Eva threw the remains of her sandwich back on the paper plate in front of her before shoving her chair back roughly. "Fine. Whatever you want, *Coach*." She spat the word out like it was part of the remaining bits of sandwich in her mouth.

Both women stood, their gazes as hard and unyielding as the table between them.

"And drop the attitude, Cruzie, or you'll find yourself on the fourth line."

In the empty hallway outside Alison's office, Eva leaned against the cinder-block wall and let its rough, cold surface lightly scratch her cheek. She might as well be the fucking mascot, she thought, her blood boiling that she, a legend on this team, a future Hockey Hall of Famer, could be treated this way. It wasn't right. It was downright insulting, and she should probably shove it back down Alison's throat by quitting.

Turning her back to the wall, she slid down until she was resting on her haunches. She wasn't a quitter. Never had been. Her nature was to fight. Well, except that one time. She quit on Niki all those years ago, but Niki had quit on her too, and it was that convenient splitting of the blame she used over and over to let herself off the hook. Their breakup was easier to accept if the blame went both ways.

So, she thought with a sense of dejection that was rare. *This is what it's like to lose something.* And this time, there was no one else to blame, because as much as she wanted to lash out at Alison, she knew, with excruciating clarity, that the coach was right. She wasn't the same player she used to be. She wasn't here to be the star anymore. It hit her like a punch to the gut.

CHAPTER FIVE

Offside

Niki and Lynn chose seats in an upper corner of the rink, removed from anyone else so they would be left alone. And hopefully left unrecognized. They'd taken the two-hour flight from Calgary to Minneapolis to watch Team USA's exhibition game against the Golden Gophers. It was a scouting mission and totally within the parameters of ethics. Both the Americans and Canadians scouted one another at every opportunity. Nevertheless, the two women didn't want to draw attention to themselves during the game because they were here to work without disruption. Niki remembered scouting a game before the previous Olympics where she had to put up with a drunken fan in the next row who thought it was perfectly acceptable to trash talk her about her team's chances against the US. She'd kept her mouth shut until, her patience finally expiring, she offered to refund him whatever he'd paid for the ticket, "Because," she told him, "clearly you're not here to watch the game."

Now she did a double take at the pregame roster sheet. "Wow."

"I noticed it too," Lynn said beside her. They often spoke in verbal shorthand. "Eva must have pissed in Alison's cornflakes to be demoted to wing. And on the second line."

It wasn't uncommon for a coach to demote a player to a different line or position or to bench her altogether as a way to send a not-so-subtle message. She wondered if that was the case with Eva, or whether Eva was no longer up to the rigors of playing top line center minutes.

The players burst onto the ice for their ten-minute warm-up. Niki's eyes locked onto Eva from the instant she took her first step, watched as her dark wavy hair poked out of the back of her helmet, lifting in the breeze generated by her speed. She circled tightly, cut straight up the middle to accept a pass and took a booming wrist shot on her goalie. Watching her move gracefully, powerfully, efficiently with those long strides, unleashed something in Niki that rumbled like a tiny earthquake, spreading out from her core, leaving her a little breathless. Eva looked the same as she had a decade ago: lithe, agile and like she owned the rink. That poise alone made her stand out from everyone else; Niki would have recognized her from the farthest seat in the house and with one eye closed.

Shannon hadn't been as strikingly beautiful as Eva, not by half. It was part of what had attracted Niki early on, those average looks—short brown hair, eyes the color of over-processed milk chocolate, an unremarkable mouth, a body that was neither tall nor short, neither thin nor overweight. It was almost as though, having been burned once by a fire so hot and formidable, she was afraid to go near anything like it again. Because with Eva's beauty and the sexual chemistry that crackled between them came a volatility that Niki did not want to revisit in her next relationship. No. As exciting as life with Eva had been, she had *so* had enough of it.

Closing her eyes, she could instantly summon those soulful, almost black eyes of Eva's that seemed bottomless. And with that memory came more—a hunger for each other that sometimes couldn't wait for the bedroom when any surface would do, epic battles that would peak with screaming and sometimes throwing a nearby object. The highs were matched by the lows, the rapture equaled by the despair. *God*, she thought now. They were so young and so capricious, each cocky in thinking she was right about everything, each willing to scorch the earth without warning or reason.

The game underway, Niki and Lynn silently took notes. It was their first opportunity to see some of the young Americans in game action, but it was also a chance to scout the team's set plays: how they ran their power play, their penalty kills, how they broke out of their zone, how they defended their own and how strong was their goaltending. Team USA didn't play the same puck possession game as the Canadians, Niki noticed right away. Instead they relied more on speed and individual skill. It gave her fresh hope that, with quick accurate passing and smart plays, her team could beat this younger and highly skilled one.

Whenever Eva was on the ice, Niki tracked her every move. There was no need to watch her so closely, because she was already intimately familiar with how Eva played, but she couldn't help herself. She wanted to see how she managed wing instead of center, wanted to see if she still had the goods to be a threat on the ice. The short answer was that Eva still possessed elite skills. She wasn't as quick as she used to be, but her puck sense, anticipation and creativity were as sharp as ever. She knew where to be on the ice, was a great passer and set-up player but could also score seemingly at will. The remaining question was Eva's stamina. Would she be able to handle the rigors of sixty-minute games, the bumps and jostling she'd need to withstand in the corners and in front of the net, week after week leading up to the Olympics? And what of the grueling practices? The travel? The pressure to win gold again?

It was early in the third period when some of the answers began to reveal themselves. Eva took a slash to the back of her legs while providing a screen in front of the net. She lay on the ice for a minute, then rose to her knees as the trainer came out to check on her. She skated off on her own power but headed straight for the locker room.

Lynn shot Niki a knowing look, slowly shaking her head. But what Niki knew better than anyone else was how tough Eva was. She was a fighter, and it would take a lot more than a dirty slash to keep her out of a game.

* * *

In the locker room, Eva gingerly removed her gear in the same order she always did: gloves, helmet, jersey, elbow pads and chest protector, followed by skates, shin pads, pants, socks, protective cup.

Kathleen leaned against the cinder block wall with a watchful eye. "She got you pretty good, huh?"

"Yup."

"There's a table next door. I'll rub you down. Ice bath when you get back to the hotel."

Ice baths were the worst; the thought of one immediately made her teeth hurt. Minutes later, she lay down on the massage table and let Kathleen knead her back and legs, as though she were dough and Kathleen's hands the rolling pin. It was painful, and she had to clamp her molars tight to keep from crying out. But it helped, and after ten minutes she could walk without the pain she'd had when she hobbled off the ice.

She left her gear stowed in her hockey bag, which would be picked up and tossed in the bus for her later. She slung a small duffel over her shoulder as her team began straggling into the locker room. The women whooped and high-fived her because they'd won by two goals. Alison had her usual scowl; she was never happy unless they tromped their opponents by at least half a dozen goals.

"See you all on the bus," Eva said, shutting the locker room door behind her and along with it the loud, exuberant chatter of her teammates. Someone had turned on a radio or iPod, because Lady Gaga's "Just Dance" boomed from within. It was going to be a long four months if she had to listen to that kind of music in the locker room. She chafed at the thought of Rihanna and Britney too. Throw in some Pussycat Dolls and she'd for sure slit her wrists. Bon Jovi or Bryan Adams she could handle.

Distracted, she rounded a corner toward the lobby and was halted by someone's shoulder clipping her bicep. "Sorry," she mumbled before lifting her eyes from the floor.

"My fault too."

Eva gasped. "Niki."

For a moment Niki wavered as though she were unsure whether she should stop or keep walking. Flee, more like. But she stopped, and where Eva expected there to be ice in those stark blue eyes, there was a melting sincerity that surprised—and nearly flattened—her.

"W-what are you doing here?" Eva mentally slapped herself for the lame question. And the stuttering…that was smooth.

Niki held up a three-ring notebook as if it explained everything. It did.

"Congratulations," Eva said without smiling. "Your team's lucky to have you as coach."

"Thanks. And I hope you're right."

"I am." This, Eva thought with satisfaction, was so much more civilized than the last time they were in the same place together. It was nearly six years ago, at a charity auction for women's hockey at the Hockey Hall of Fame in Toronto. From across the room they had speared each other with glares. Glares that were almost malicious, with hurt and anger every bit as fresh as the day they'd broken up. After that unpleasant exchange, each of them had spent the evening pretending the other didn't exist. It was also the first and only time Eva had ever seen Niki's wife, though they were not introduced. Briefly, Eva wondered now if she should offer condolences about the woman's death—she'd heard about it through the grapevine. But it'd been two or three years ago, and this new and unexpected civility between them left her almost mute.

"You took a nasty cross-check." Niki's pale eyebrow rose questioningly.

With a bravado Eva didn't feel, she smiled and said, "Don't worry. I'll still be able to give your team all it can handle when we play you in two weeks."

A flicker of a smile crossed Niki's face. "Guess we'll see about that."

And then she was walking away without so much as a goodbye. Same old Niki, Eva thought. *Walking away without a look back.*

Eva walked a few more feet, but once she was sure Niki was long gone, she stopped and bent over, hands on her knees as if catching her breath. She slammed her eyes shut, the lingering scent of Niki's mild perfume or body wash—something citrusy with a hint of sage or rosemary—tickling her nose, unearthing distant, shapeless memories from long ago. Her heart didn't know what to make of this sudden thaw in their relations. They hated each other, didn't they? Hadn't that been the common thread that had bound them all these years? And yet it had never felt right hating Niki, especially once it became clear that there'd been no betrayal after all. But by then Eva hadn't known how to bridge the gulf between them, how to apologize. Starting over again became more daunting as the weeks and months slipped by, and before she knew it she was off to play pro hockey in Montreal and Niki was off to...wherever it was, grad school somewhere. Boston College, perhaps.

If nothing else, she no longer had to dread seeing Niki behind the bench for the first time as head coach of her rivals. That would happen in a couple of weeks, when the two teams met in Calgary for an exhibition game. Having seen Niki now meant she could concentrate fully on the game.

CHAPTER SIX

Game Misconduct

"How's your hockey team doing, sweetie?" Niki smiled into the phone as Rory described her team's latest victory and gave a play-by-play of how she scored the winning goal. Niki never expected Rory to become the little athlete she had. Shannon hadn't an athletic bone in her body, leaving Niki to conclude that Rory's ability must have come from her biological father. They didn't know much about the donor; Shannon and her former lover had picked him out of a catalog. How unexpected that ten years later, neither of Rory's two early mothers were in the girl's life. Shannon's partner Diana deserted them shortly after Rory's birth, the wakeful nights and dirty diapers enough to convince her that she preferred life without kids. Niki was the only parent Rory had now.

"I miss my girl," Niki said. "You know you're my number one, right?"

Rory was only two when Niki and Shannon got together and four when Niki and Shannon married and Niki officially adopted her. Becoming a parent wasn't something she'd planned or ever given much thought to, but Rory had been a gift. A gift to make her appreciate the little things in life, like watching her in a school play, helping her with math and reading, teaching her the rudiments of hockey. She remembered the first time she'd taken Rory to a live hockey game when Rory was four and how she couldn't understand why a penalized player had to go sit all by himself on the other side of the ice and how shameful the timeout must have been for him. Niki still chuckled to herself every time she watched a player make the trip to the penalty box. *Shame, shame.*

"Okay, Mom, I miss you too. When can I come and see you?"

"I don't know, sweetie. It's been really busy, but I'm going to ask your Aunt Jenny if she can bring you to Toronto in three weeks. I'll be there for a tournament we're playing in. We'll all stay in a really nice hotel and we'll get to spend lots of time together, okay?"

Rory's voice trembled, piercing Niki's heart. "Okay, I guess."

"I love you, sweetie, and I think about you every hour. I'll talk to you again tomorrow, okay?"

"Okay. I love you too, Mom. Bye."

Niki held the phone to her chest for a long moment. She'd known it was going to be hard being away from Rory—for both of them. And though they had both been in agreement about the head coaching job, it didn't make the reality of their time apart any easier. Over the last three years, they'd come to rely on each other, to be teammates in their journey through grief, but now they were each flying solo. *I've made a commitment to this team,* Niki thought, trying to convince herself—again—that she'd made the right decision. *I can't back out now, no matter what.*

Moments later she found Lynn in her office poring over scouting reports for tomorrow night's exhibition game against the Americans. "What do you say we go out for dinner together?"

Lynn's quizzical expression softened to one of understanding. "Sure thing. I'll bet it's hard being away from home sometimes. How about Jimmy's down the street?"

Jimmy's was a roadhouse well known for its chargrilled burgers and steaks and microbrewery beer. It brewed its own beer in giant copper vats along one side of the restaurant. Niki had only eaten there a couple of times, but because of its proximity to the University of Calgary campus, the place was a beehive of activity and always loud with boisterous conversation. Students, professors and athletes all frequented Jimmy's and treated it like a second home. A game of darts or billiards was always on the go.

"Want to talk about it?" Lynn offered as their beer and burgers were deposited in front of them.

"Not really." Niki smiled to lighten her tone. She'd spent a lot of time with Lynn lately, but it didn't mean she wanted to bare her soul to her. She liked to keep her own counsel.

"Well, would you look who's here," Lynn whispered urgently, jerking a thumb toward the bar area.

Niki glanced sideways, trying not to appear too obvious. She quickly gave up the pretense and stared. It was Eva, sitting at the bar shoulder to shoulder with another woman—the medical trainer for Team USA, if she wasn't mistaken. The two were laughing and chatting like intimate friends, each sipping on a glass of beer. A moment later, the trainer's hand crept to Eva's thigh and gave it a lengthy squeeze. *So that's how it is.*

"Huh," Lynn said. "I didn't know those two were a having a thing."

Jealousy caught like a flame to dry tinder in Niki's gut. She'd never forgotten the feel of Eva's strong thighs beneath her own fingers or the feel of her thick, wavy hair against her cheek during the times she leaned close to whisper something in her ear. Exactly like this woman was doing. *Jesus*, Niki thought, pissed off at herself. She couldn't begin to understand the reasons why it was so difficult to ignore Eva Caruso and the feelings she ignited in her. Why the hell, after all this time, couldn't she forget about the crazy love they'd shared, the heart-stopping passion, the insane lovemaking, the fierce arguing that sometimes burned them both up in a conflagration of hurt feelings and indignation? It was pleasure and pain, bitter and sweet, and even now it was so intense as to almost be unbearable. Back then they were young colts bucking at the gate, and now as she watched Eva share a lusty kiss with Kathleen, she wondered if little had changed with Eva. Was she still the irrepressible, irresponsible young stud she'd once been?

"They're both adults," Niki said with strained indifference. "They can do what they want."

Lynn shook her head in condemnation, like Eva had done something as heinous as gotten behind the wheel of a car while drunk. "Same old Eva. Can't keep it in her pants. And can't ever seem to grow up."

The venom in Lynn's voice surprised Niki a little. "Are you trying to make me hate her? Because there's really no need."

Lynn smiled. "Good. I was worried you might be letting bygones be bygones with her."

"What's that supposed to mean?"

"It means she treated you like crap. She hurt you, Nik."

"I'm a big girl. It was a long time ago, and I was as much of a jerk as she was when it came to our relationship."

"Well, at least you stopped being a jerk and grew up." Lynn flicked another glance at Eva and Kathleen, snuggling together as though there was no one else in the room. "Doesn't look like she's learned a thing."

Niki had heard a lot of rumors about Eva over the years, mostly having to do with a long string of girlfriends. She waited until Lynn's gaze swung back to her. "Does it matter? To us and what we're trying to accomplish, I mean."

"It does, at least until the Games are over. Then I could give a shit about her."

"Don't tell me you've been going to Alison Hiller's school of hating your opponent. Because if we need *that* to motivate us to win, we're in trouble." Alison had been a thorn to Niki and Eva all those years ago, ultimately leading to the nuclear explosion that was their breakup. And while Alison had really only been the match and not the gasoline, Niki swore she would never treat her charges like they were pawns to be used in a sport that was equated to war. Her players were people first, second and third. And she had no right to try to manipulate their feelings toward anyone. Hate was a weak motivational tool anyway.

Lynn's face colored a little. "The stakes are high, Nik. That's all I'm saying. This isn't some little game of shinny in somebody's backyard rink. Alison will be looking for every edge she can get, and frankly, so should we."

Niki didn't care for the direction their conversation was taking and began to gather up her things, what was left of her food having turned cold. "Well, we're not her. We're going to run this team like a machine. A machine without emotion, because that's how you win games. We're going to be better than them at every little thing, even the smallest things, because the minute you let emotion overrule your behavior, you'll lose. We're surgeons, Lynn, and the hockey rink is our operating theater."

Lynn stood to go too, but Niki waved her back down. "Stay and finish your dinner. I'm sorry, but I think I've lost my appetite. I'll see you at the rink tomorrow afternoon."

She counted out forty dollars to cover her share and purposely chose a route farthest away from the bar area. As she was closing the distance to the door, Eva turned from across the room and pinned her with those haunting, dark eyes. The moment was over before Niki knew it, but there was something in Eva's look that said she was sorry. About all the things she'd never actually apologized for, Niki imagined. But she propelled herself forward, not wanting to expend any more emotional energy on Eva. As she opened the door, Alison Hiller barged in.

"Excuse me," Niki said.

"Well, well. Plotting strategy for the big game tomorrow night, Coach?" Alison's eyes gleamed with undisguised malice.

Niki smiled. "Nope. No need for last-minute cramming. See you at the rink tomorrow night, *Coach*."

* * *

Eva adjusted her hoodie, trying to cover the untamed mass of hair that she hadn't felt like dealing with this morning. She slid on sunglasses too to avoid being recognized on the outdoor ice rink at the edge of campus. Normally she didn't mind the attention from hockey fans. Posing for selfies and signing autographs came with the territory of being one of the most recognized women hockey players in the world. But it was game day and she wanted to be left alone to not, as most people might suspect, concentrate on tonight's game, but rather to empty her mind. A leisurely skate, feeling the ice beneath her blades and the cool breeze against her face, was all she wanted.

She stepped onto the ice, gliding slowly at first to test its consistency. It was a bit soft, which wasn't unusual for outdoor rinks in late October. There would be pipes underneath to help keep it frozen, but whenever the air temperature was above freezing, as it was today, it was a nearly impossible task to keep the ice as solid as cement. She'd be careful to avoid grooves made by other blades; she didn't need to tweak anything. Tonight's exhibition game against Team Canada would undoubtedly be trench warfare, as it always was.

She skated counter-clockwise around the rink, pleased that there were only two other people, a guy and a girl, college students by the looks of them, skating hand-in-hand at the other end. Plenty of space without the worry of somebody cutting in front of her or crashing into her. No drills, no coach barking at her, no teammates whizzing around her, nobody expecting anything of her. It was refreshing to have no stick, no protective equipment encumbering her.

Skating, it occurred to Eva, was the one constant in her life that made her feel free. Alive. Happy. It was like being the pilot of her own plane in a big, wide open sky, her contrails the scratches her blades left behind on the ice. She could go as fast or as slow as she wanted. She could deke, twist, turn, reverse, spin. Anything she wanted. Especially without a stick and a puck, which, she didn't mind admitting, too often turned her into a demon. When she played hockey, she wanted to win, wanted to pummel the other team, wanted to be the best. When she skated as she did now, she could relax and breathe, dissolve into anonymity.

The couple at the other end were talking to someone, their voices chirpy and amplified enough to insert speed bumps into

Eva's random, floating thoughts. She shot them a look more of irritation than curiosity, tightened her hoodie around her face, kept her distance from the three skaters—a woman in jeans, hockey skates and a hoodie nearly identical to Eva's had joined the couple. Eva skirted around them, did a double take before stopping hard enough and fast enough to send a jet of icy mist into the air.

"Niki?"

Blue eyes widened, narrowed again. A slight nod that was barely polite.

"What are you doing here?" Eva knew she should have continued skating past Niki, but it was too late now. She'd opened her big mouth.

"Skating. Same as you."

The young couple took the hint and wobbled away on their ill-fitting skates, wishing Niki a final good luck for Team Canada tonight. They hadn't recognized Eva as one of the enemy.

"Skate with me?" Eva asked before she had time to think about her offer. Being around Niki unleashed a spasm of feelings in her, most of them confusing, some of them diametrically opposed to one another and all of them aggravating. Yet ignoring Niki did not feel like the thing to do either. After all, they couldn't avoid each other forever and would, in fact, be seeing a lot of each other the next three months. There was so much history between them. So many things left unsaid. And so many things said that had left scars. Perhaps it was finally time to talk, to somehow find a way to make sense of their hostile parting all those years ago. If she were to end her hockey career once and for all after this season—and she was pretty sure she would—closure with Niki felt like a necessary part of the process.

Niki turned and slowly skated away, but Eva wasn't ready to let her go. *I should let her go but I can't, dammit.* In three strides she was at her side.

"Is it because of the game tonight?" Eva asked.

"What?"

"The reason you're giving me that I'd-rather-you-were-dead look."

Niki's lips quivered like they were about to erupt in a smile. "I wouldn't go that far."

"Hmm. So it's not your game face?"

"I'm not Alison. You know that."

"Ah, then you hate me all the time, not just on game days." Eva wasn't entirely kidding.

Niki slowed her speed. She was graceful, had always been a natural and effortless skater. She was one of those people who never truly understood how good she was. She was the antithesis of the athlete who thought they were greater than they actually were, who harbored a tricked-out, buffed-up vision of themselves that held little truth. Niki could have been the best woman hockey player in the world, perhaps of all time, if only she'd wanted it bad enough. But she'd never quite wanted it the way Eva had.

Niki sighed impatiently. "I don't hate you, Eva."

"Then shouldn't we try to be friends?"

Niki stopped skating, faced Eva. The ropey muscles of her jaw were visible. "Are you serious?"

"Yes. Why wouldn't I be?"

"You're forgetting our teams will most likely be playing each other for the biggest prize in hockey in little more than three months. What, you think we should go out for a drink? Or a bite after the game tonight? Really?"

Niki's tone was a scalpel slicing neat, sharp slits in Eva's heart.

"You said yourself you're not Alison."

"No. I'm not. But I'm not your buddy. Or your girlfriend. You seem to have that base covered anyway, by the looks of things in that restaurant last night."

Ah, so the surliness was due in part, at least, to Kathleen. "She's not my girlfriend."

"Forget it. You don't have to explain."

No, Eva thought, she didn't. But she wanted to. "She's just, you know, a friend. With benefits."

A neat blond eyebrow rose. "So not much has changed with you, eh?"

It was meant to be a hurtful, judgmental reminder that Eva had never settled down with anyone the way Niki had. "What do you care?"

"I don't."

Maybe not, but Niki was looking at her like she was judge and jury and Eva the hardened criminal who was guilty of something horrible.

Fine, think what you want. Eva decided that Niki had become very much like Alison. She turned and skated away, her legs pumping as hard as they could. She skated straight to where she'd left her boots and duffel bag. *Screw this. And screw you, Niki Hartling.*

CHAPTER SEVEN

Intent to Injure

Niki took her place behind the bench, ramrod straight as she faced the flags while the two national anthems played over the speakers. Afterward, she wanted to pace, but the space was too narrow. What she *really* wanted to do was to throw something, and her gaze flicked to the water bottles positioned in front of her players like little plastic soldiers. She couldn't shake her disappointment with herself for how she'd behaved earlier with Eva, for revealing her anger, her hurt. What did it matter that Eva continued to flit from woman to woman, like a bee sampling the nectar of every flower? No. It absolutely didn't matter. Eva could do whatever the hell she wanted *with* whomever the hell she wanted. Niki didn't give a rat's ass on whose pillow Eva rested her head at night. And yet her stomach was on fire.

Furtively, she thumbed a Tums from the roll in her pocket and slipped it into her mouth. Skating this morning was supposed to make her forget how the sight of Eva at the restaurant had made her heart beat like a bass drum in her chest. To run into her at the outdoor rink was the cruelest of tests and one that she'd failed miserably. *Goddamn you, Eva.*

The referee blew her whistle to signify the game was about to begin. Technically, the game was meaningless, but it would give both teams an opportunity to test their game plans, to pit their top players against each other, to gauge firsthand how much of a threat the other was going to be. Niki had told her players to go hard, but not full out. No need to show Team USA everything we've got, she told them. Holding something in reserve would give them the element of surprise later on. For that reason, she scratched her best forward. It had been Lynn's idea, and it was a good one.

"D to D, D to D!" Niki yelled at her two defensemen on the ice, seconds after one of them fumbled with the puck in the neutral zone for too long and coughed it up. She slapped Alycia on the shoulder, her youngest center. "Your line's next, kiddo. Pressure them deep. Don't let them break out, okay?"

She was pleased with her players' hard, accurate passes, which were confounding the speedy Americans. But they needed to consistently play good positional hockey and to show no hesitation or the Americans would pick off those passes. She made a mental note to herself to remind her players to make faster decisions.

Alycia's line took a shot on goal. The American goalie deflected the puck neatly into the corner, where Eva slickly scooped it up and marched it down the ice. Niki's eyes followed her, watched as she deked around one Canadian forward, then another. Eva wasn't the fastest skater on the ice anymore, not by a long shot, but she had hands of gold and razor-sharp instincts that hadn't lost a beat. A third Canadian defender fell victim to Eva's clever puck handling. *Christ*, Niki thought, an end-to-end rush in which nobody was touching her. She snapped a glance at Lynn and the map of frown lines on her face, returning her gaze to the ice in time to see Eva score top shelf.

"All right," Niki said firmly to her players on the bench. "It's okay. Our team is not one player like those guys. We'll win it together. Now come on, let's go! We play as a team!"

After two periods the game stood knotted at a goal apiece. In the locker room at intermission, Niki spoke in general terms. She told her team that while the Americans were coming on stronger with each period, they could be stopped "if we stick to our game plan. They're young but we're smart. Remember that." What she didn't share was her concern that they weren't likely to match the Americans' energy level for three periods. She'd need to work them harder in their fitness training, because as it stood now, a fast start was the only way they could hope to win.

"If they're so young, how come it's their old grandma who's killing us?" grumbled the goalie.

Niki suppressed a smile. Eva would hate being called grandma. "We can take away their speed by jamming up the neutral zone. That means a one-two-and-two defense. Forecheck and backcheck the hell out of them so they run out of room out there. Squeeze them, okay? Force them to make a crappy pass."

The third period was evenly back and forth, both teams getting their chances. Then Eva broke out of a neutral zone scrum with the puck and went in on a two-on-one. Because she'd already scored once, the lone Canadian defenseman and goalie both expected Eva to again shoot the puck. She didn't. Her tape-to-tape pass at the last second ended up off her teammate's stick and into the back of the net.

"Shit!" Lynn erupted from the other end of the bench. A deep flush worked its way up her neck and into her face like a fast-flowing river. Lynn's primary job on the bench was to coach the defensive side of things, and she huddled with the two players closest to her.

When the play resumed, it became clear the remainder of the game would be a chippy affair, Eva's goal having fired up Team Canada. Ideally, Niki wanted her players to keep their emotions in check and play a methodical game. What she saw instead caused her to smack her clipboard against her thigh in frustration. Her players were charging into their opponents, getting their sticks up, flirting with penalties, trash talking. All the things she didn't want them doing. She was seconds away from calling a timeout when her biggest defenseman took a run at Eva, crushing her into the boards. The referee's whistle pierced the air, but it did little good, as players from both sides crowded around, bumping one another chest to chest and talking more trash. By the time everyone dispersed to their benches, Eva lay in a crumpled heap.

Seeing her hurt instantly sent Niki back to the gold medal game in Nagano, where an innocent open-ice collision between the two of them had left Eva with a torn knee. She'd felt sick about it, especially when Eva, her face contorted in pain, shot Niki a look of pure hatred and unadulterated blame. You did this to me on purpose, her black eyes had said. Of course Niki hadn't, but she'd done nothing over the years to dispel Eva's belief, to try to explain. When you played hockey at this level, you didn't apologize for playing hard. They both understood that.

"Aw, fuck," Niki mumbled, and not only because of the five-minute major penalty posted on the clock, but because Eva still hadn't moved much, though she was at least sitting up. Her trainer—the same woman she'd been pawing at the restaurant last night—bent over her, placed a hand on her shoulder, talked to her, touched her knee with her other hand.

Niki clenched her fists behind her back, her chest tightening. She wasn't petty or mean and didn't condone rough stuff on the ice. She wanted Eva to be okay. Didn't want her scoring goals against her team either, though, and didn't want her beating them for Olympic gold, but she did want her to finish out her playing career on her own terms, same as she herself had done after the Nagano Olympics. Any injuries sustained now, with three-and-half-months to go, would be disastrous for any player. Especially a thirty-six-year-old in the twilight of her career and who already had a bum knee.

She stole a glance at Lynn, who had a self-satisfied smile pasted onto her face. With it came the sick realization that the hit on Eva had been intentional, meant to take her out of the game or at least to teach her a lesson. And Lynn, judging by the glee on her face, had given the order.

Goddammit! Lynn knew that type of play was forbidden on Niki's watch. Her ire wasn't because it was Eva who'd gotten hurt; she didn't want her players gooning anybody. She wanted them executing the game plan. Wanted them executing the game plan with emotionless precision—machinists building a win one piece at a time. The minute you got sucked into a gong show, you were finished.

Eva finally limped off the ice with the trainer's assistance and headed straight to the locker room. Niki paced, successfully fighting the urge to go check on her. It wouldn't do for the coach to leave the bench to check on an opposing player. She watched the rest of the game play out, a 4-1 loss for her team, then briskly followed her players into the locker room.

"That," she said in her harshest tone, "was an embarrassment. We let them dictate the pace. We let them do whatever they wanted. We rolled over and let them have their way with us. Our positional play was terrible, and worst of all, we didn't want to win bad enough. When we started losing, we let ourselves become totally unglued." She drilled her eyes into the defenseman who'd taken Eva out. "And then we get a major penalty for taking out their best player? What kind of beer league bullshit is that?"

Lynn cleared her throat and looked away. Niki would deal with her later.

"This had better be the only time we lose to this team this winter." Niki settled her gaze on each player in turn. "Trust me. Losing to the Americans can become a habit if you let it. A very bad habit. If any of you aren't up to the task of beating them, then I'll gladly show you the door. The decision is yours, women. This is a team of champions, not failures, and the sooner you figure that out, the better."

She didn't enjoy being a hard ass, but sometimes it was the only way. She let her message settle like ashes after a blistering fire, then turned on her heel and strode out. Lynn followed her like a lost dog.

Sharply, Niki said to her, "I'll talk to you tomorrow."

* * *

Eva winced at the pain in her knee. It felt like the blade of a serrated knife had been jammed in there. She'd had an X-ray, but the results would be a few more minutes. The ER doctor's simple manipulations sent her memory hurtling back to her previous ligament replacement surgery and the many arthroscopic missions before that and the despair that always accompanied the procedures for days and sometimes weeks afterward. Every time she got hurt she worried her career was done.

"I suggest you have an MRI when you get back to Minnesota, but I strongly suspect it's only a sprain." The doctor, a woman about Eva's age, offered an encouraging smile. But no simple gesture was going to keep Eva from feeling that her Olympic dreams were being flattened like a penny on a train track right now.

"I'll be back in a few minutes with your test results," the doctor said, giving Eva a reassuring wink on her way out that did nothing to reassure her at all.

"I think she's probably right," Kathleen said. "A month or so off hockey, some physio, and you should be fine. But we'll set you up with an MRI when we get home to be sure."

Eva wanted to cry but wouldn't give her lousy knee the satisfaction. "I'm so fucking sick of my body not being able to keep up with hockey, Kath. Is it too much to ask for a few more months before it craps out completely?"

"To be honest, it was kind of a dirty play. Number fourteen boarded you, and your knee got sandwiched in between her and the boards."

"Ten years ago, hell, six years ago, I would never have been injured on that play. It pisses me off."

"I know." Kathleen patted her thigh. "We'll get you through the Olympics, even if I have to use glue and duct tape on that body of yours."

There was a faint knock on the treatment room door before it opened. Niki stepped in. The shock of seeing her sent another ripple of pain coursing through Eva's knee.

"How are you doing?" Niki said after a nervous clearing of her throat. She displayed none of the ill temper and judgment she'd shown at the outdoor rink this morning. This time, her eyes bore only concern. Maybe even contrition.

"I'll live." Eva failed to keep the sarcasm from her voice.

"Is it your bad knee?"

"No. My good one. I don't know if that's lucky or unlucky. Now I get to have two bad knees."

Kathleen, who'd been studying the two of them like they were part of a science project, made a hasty excuse and left the room.

"I wanted to make sure you were okay. And to say...to say I'm concerned about what happened. And I'll deal with it."

"Concerned about me or concerned about your player's actions?"

"Both." Niki stood stiffly, ignoring the chair near the treatment bed, clearly signaling that she wouldn't be staying long. But she was here, and what that meant, Eva couldn't guess.

"Well, no need to worry about me." Inside, Eva was nowhere near as casual as her words, but she didn't want Niki's sympathy. Or pity. "They say it's likely a sprain. I should be good as new in a month. Six weeks at the outside, I suppose."

Niki was polite enough to look relieved. "Good. So you'll be able to play in Vancouver."

"Come on," Eva said, a fist of anger clamping around her windpipe that caused her voice to sound like gravel under tires. "You don't want me playing in any gold medal game, especially if it's against your team, which we all know it will be."

"No, that's not true, Eva. I know what these Games mean to you. And I think I have an idea of what you sacrificed to be here."

Eva's anger left her as quickly as it had come on. Niki was the one making all the sacrifices to go to the Olympics—she had a kid she'd left behind, while Eva had simply locked up her condo and her business in Traverse City until she returned.

"Your daughter. How old is she?"

Niki blinked at the question before a smile edged onto her lips. "Rory's ten. But of course if you ask her she'll say she's almost eleven."

"Does she like hockey?"

"Loves it."

The unguarded joy in Niki's face reminded Eva of the way she'd looked at her on their second date. Eva was a college freshman then, Niki a sophomore when they'd gone to an outdoor blues concert together. The autumnal evening air had been so bitingly cold that they both huddled beneath Eva's oversized jacket, clutching one another as if each were the other's life raft. The rain, icy and stinging, came at the end of the evening, and they ran to the bus shelter together, still holding onto one another, the soggy jacket held aloft over their heads. They went back to Eva's apartment and made love for the first time, Niki's skin so warm beneath the flannel sheets, it was like she was on fire every time Eva touched her. It was, Eva had long ago decided, the happiest night of her life.

She swallowed, her heart thumping at the memory. The sight of Niki now was no less heart-rending. "I'm glad you stopped by, Nik. It means a lot."

"I also wanted to say...I'm sorry."

"About my knee?"

"Well, that too. But I meant about earlier today. At the outdoor rink. I was out of line."

Niki's outburst had been a little shocking, but Eva had been secretly cherishing it in a little corner of her heart. Niki's jealousy of Kathleen was a guilty pleasure because Eva wanted, she realized, for Niki to still feel something for her. The opposite of love wasn't hate, someone once told her, but indifference. And indifference from Niki was the worst. "About that—"

"No, it's okay. No need to talk about it further." She pointed to Eva's knee. "You take care of that." She backed toward the door exactly at the moment the doctor entered, and the two women nearly collided.

Wait, Eva wanted to cry out. *I do want to talk about it further. I want us to talk about what happened all those years ago, to talk about why we gave up so easily*. There was also the morass of feelings that kept tripping them up, making them both act a little crazy lately. They should talk about that too and about how they were going to handle regularly running into each other now.

"I'll be seeing you around," Niki said, and she was gone before Eva could say anything to stop her.

"Good news," the doctor said, holding a sheaf of X-rays in her hand. She marched over to a light box on the wall and flicked it on.

CHAPTER EIGHT

Faceoff

Niki took another sip of her coffee, but it did little to boost her energy. She'd slept like shit last night. It was losing to the Americans, it was seeing Eva hurt and in the hospital. And then, she'd realized halfway through the night, today was Shannon's birthday. Or would have been.

These days she felt even more adrift from Shannon. Or her memory, to be more precise. She was far away from their home, from Rory, from all the familiar places. And then there was the reemergence of Eva in her life. So many changes lately, which, in her judgment, wasn't necessarily a bad thing because it might finally force her to move on, the way everyone told her she needed to. The problem was that she wasn't yet committed to moving on. Shannon had been her rock—safe, predictable, dependable. Not a pushover, but calm, laid-back, always took a minute or two to answer a question while she thought it over, rarely overreacted to anything. Yet if Niki were honest with herself, there were times she wished Shannon had been more spontaneous, more expressive, less independent, less introspective. She'd shared so little sometimes of her true feelings and had accepted her cancer diagnosis with a resignation that infuriated Niki. Shannon had been a quiet fighter and not the ballsy, take-no-prisoners combatant Niki was used to in the world of high-octane sports. Too often it had left her angry, afraid that Shannon wasn't trying hard enough to beat the cancer.

She glanced at the framed photo on her desk of herself, Shannon and Rory posing before Niagara Falls on a family vacation. They looked happy, they always did, everyone said so. The perfect couple. But they hadn't been the perfect couple. Shannon kept so much to herself, and Niki overcompensated with her smothering, expressive instincts. She was constantly attempting to hug and kiss Shannon, crushing her with physical affection. It was her insecure need to prove to herself that Shannon loved her and that she loved Shannon, she realized later—too late. Without the lightning rod of passion in their lives, Niki was sometimes unsure about the depth of their love. But never had she verbalized her feelings to anyone, including her wife.

A knock interrupted her brooding and Lynn edged into her office, looking like she too hadn't slept well.

"Come in," Niki said. "Coffee's on if you want any."

"Thanks but I've already had a pail of it this morning." She took a seat across from Niki's desk.

"About the game last night." Niki captured Lynn's eyes and wouldn't let them go. "Did you ask or order Samantha to take Eva out of the game?"

Lynn's nostrils flared in a quiet show of defiance. "Of course not."

"I'm asking because I saw you huddled with her on the bench before that play."

"I told her to close down the lanes, to not let anyone by her, especially Eva. But I did not tell her to take her out."

Niki had already talked privately with her defenseman. Samantha was evasive about the episode and admitted there'd been no intention to injure Eva or anyone else.

Niki sighed. Without evidence to the contrary, she had no alternative but to accept the two women's explanations. "All right. But we've got to find a way to make sure our players maintain their discipline. I'm going to bench Samantha for our next game. Show her that she won't get ice time if she doesn't play disciplined hockey."

"It'll leave our D corps a bit short."

"I don't care. We'll manage. We'll move Stanners from forward to D if we have to."

Lynn cleared her throat, glanced away for a moment. "I heard you visited Eva in the hospital after the game."

There was something about Lynn lately—the mounting pressure of the approaching Games, perhaps—that Niki didn't care for. With every passing week, her assistant coach seemed more stressed, more competitive, more cynical, less cooperative. "How did you hear that?"

"Word travels, that's all. It gives me concern."

"About what? That I'm consorting with the enemy? Look. I know I asked you to keep an eye on Alison Hiller, but please tell me you're not *becoming* Alison Hiller." Niki rubbed her throbbing temples. "Can't we act nice and coach this team to victory too?"

"I don't know," Lynn said, her face and shoulders collapsing a little. "You're right. Alison's a first-class idiot. And if you want to be friends with Eva, there's no reason why you shouldn't. I know you're a professional, Nik."

"Whoa. Who said Eva and I are friends?"

Lynn smiled without pleasure. "You were lovers, after all. And you're both single, or at least, I don't think she's involved seriously with that athletic therapist. As long as you kept things discreet, of course, and kept the two things apart, I don't really see a problem."

Lynn's about-face was another example of her erratic behavior lately. She was up, down, quiet one minute, unable to contain herself the next. "C'mon. That's not going to happen. Eva and I are barely civil toward one another." That wasn't exactly true. They weren't lions circling each other in a cage anymore, but they were not friends.

"You sure about that?" Lynn's smile dissolved. "You were pretty upset last night when Eva got hurt."

"I was. But I was upset about our lack of discipline."

Lynn stared at her for a long moment, everything about her suggesting she didn't believe Niki.

"There's nothing between Eva and me except for ancient history." Niki pulled a three-ring notebook from her desk drawer and laid it on the desk. "Let's go over the game last night. I made a lot of notes this morning."

She flipped open the book, her mind wandering to Eva. Dammit, Lynn was trying to make her feel guilty about Eva, and it was working. Was she caring more about her ex than she should? Was the ice around her heart cracking a little? *No*, she thought, *I don't have time for this.* She forced her attention back to her notes and to the task at hand. If she didn't quickly find a way to reverse her team's fortunes against the Americans, it was going to be a damned slippery slope ahead of them.

* * *

Eva set the barbell on the rack and sat up. Sweat dripped along her temples and streamed down her neck and chest. The knee sprain was keeping her from most of her lower body workout, but she could and did work on her upper body. Battles along the boards and in the zone in front of the goal crease required her to keep her core and upper body strong. It didn't often come through on television, but the contact in women's hockey was almost as prevalent as it was in men's. A well-timed shoulder could send a player flying, there were endless scrums along the boards, there were whacks and hacks and hard shoving in front of the net. If you weren't strong, you were on your ass and out of the play.

Kathleen handed her a bottle of water. "You're pushing it pretty hard today. What do you say we finish up with a swim and a sauna?"

"In a while. I want to work on my abs next."

"It won't get you back on the ice sooner."

Eva toweled the sweat from her neck. She wouldn't be game ready for at least three more weeks and would miss the two exhibition games in Toronto in a couple of weeks. Team USA and Team Canada would each play a team of Canadian university all-stars before facing each other in a one-off. It was like a mini-tournament that would take place from Friday through Sunday. Eva would accompany her team and practice as best she could, but she wouldn't play. She'd be in the stands and would watch all the games and prepare a report on what she observed. It sucked and was no replacement for playing; she'd never aspired to be a coach or a scout. She'd never forgotten the old saying that people who couldn't play, coached. It didn't apply to Niki, however, so maybe it was just bullshit. Still…

"Kath, to be honest, I'm worried. What if I'm done? What if I can't get my knees back to where they need to be in time?"

"C'mon, don't start doubting now. They'll get you through."

Eva had tossed and turned the last few nights thinking about her future with Team USA. The knee sprain was another strike against her, another nail in the coffin of her playing days. She hadn't been willing to admit it earlier, but Alison had been right to demote her from center to wing. The next stop was a demotion to the third or fourth line, where she'd only see a few minutes of ice each game, and if that happened, she was as good as done.

"I'm not the player I used to be. Not by a long shot. And when I come back, I'll be even less so."

"Bullshit. You'll be as good as you were before the sprain, and it'll still give you seven weeks before the Games begin."

Eva took a long drink of water. "No. Alison was right. I don't belong at center anymore and I don't belong on the first line."

Kathleen narrowed her eyes at Eva. "There's no need for you to lose your confidence like this. You were playing amazingly well in that game right before you hurt your knee. You were the best player on either team."

"I was the best player that night in spurts, but I'm not the best player or even among the three best players night in and night out anymore. I'm being a realist, Kath."

"So what are you saying?"

Eva moved to a thick mat on the floor and lay on her back. "I'm saying I'll crawl to the finish line, do whatever I can do to help the team win. But I'm not under any illusions anymore. I know I'll be lucky to make it to the gold medal game intact."

Kathleen joined Eva on an adjacent mat and began doing the same stomach crunches, although at a slower rate. "And how do you feel about that?"

"A little like I've been beaten before I've even started. But I'm not giving up." Even to herself it was a hard thing to admit that her ego may have tricked her into thinking she could do this and do it well. But she was here now. And she would finish what she started.

"Good." Kathleen paused before beginning another round of crunches. "And since we're on the subject of how you feel about, er, things, how did you feel about running into Coach Hartling at the hospital?"

Eva lay back on her mat. Of course Kathleen knew about her long-ago relationship with Niki. They'd never talked about it, but it wasn't a secret; she assumed everyone associated with the team knew about her and Niki. But Kathleen's question seemed to be more than academic, judging by the sudden rosy tint to her cheeks.

"Why are you asking?"

"Honestly?" Kathleen shrugged. "Because I have a feeling maybe you never stopped being in love with her."

Eva resumed her crunches, averting her eyes this time. "Where would you get an idea like that? I've never talked about her with you. I've never said anything about being in love with her."

"I saw the way you looked at her. And the way she looked at you."

Eva halted mid-crunch, swiped at a fresh drop of sweat at her temple and lay back down. "What's that supposed to mean?"

"I saw two people who share something that nobody else can touch. Like nobody or nothing else is there when the two of you share the same space. It's like there's only enough air in the room for the two of you."

Eva's gut reaction was to deny it, but she'd be lying. She sat up straight. "There's nothing going on between us, if that's what you're worried about. I'm not sleeping with anybody but you."

Kathleen's smile had the weight of sadness to it, but her tone remained neutral. "I know you're not. But I think we should stop."

"What? Why?" And what did Niki have to do with anything? She'd been clear with Kathleen from the start that there were no strings, no expectations, that they would be friends who had sex sometimes, nothing more. Was Kathleen wanting more? Was that what this was about? "Are you jealous of Niki?"

Kathleen shook her head. "I'm not jealous. But I do need to get out of the way."

Eva drained the last of the water in her bottle. "That's ridiculous. Get out of the way of what?"

"Of two people who look like missiles heading straight for a midair collision." Kathleen stood up and retrieved her towel from a nearby bench. "And I don't want to be collateral damage."

"Kath, wait."

"I like you, Eva. Maybe a little too much, but not enough to compete with someone you're still in love with." She slung the towel around her neck and winked to show there were no hard feelings. "I enjoyed it. I enjoyed *you*, but just friends is for the best. I'll see you around."

Eva collapsed back on her mat. *Someone I'm still in love with?* No, Kathleen had it all wrong. She'd loved Niki once, fiercely. Would never forget Niki, because first loves were like that. And yes, Niki could still open her emotional floodgates, but she wasn't in love with her anymore. Which was a huge relief, because if she was in love with her, she'd be in for a world of hurt.

CHAPTER NINE

Icing

Is your daughter going to be in Toronto for the games next weekend? I'd like to meet her if she is. That is, if she doesn't mind being introduced to an enemy player. ☺ E.

Niki read the email from Eva a fourth time, because it took that many times to get over the shock of seeing her former lover pop up in her in-box. It came as a surprise that Eva had found her email address. She hit the reply button and bit her bottom lip.

Yes, she will be there. She's very excited about it. I think she will be happy to meet an enemy player, though I'd keep an eye on my shins if I were you! ☺ She's pretty competitive. And loyal. —N.H. P.S. Will you be playing?

Niki hit send before she could second-guess herself and returned to the rest of her in-box. It was only a moment before Eva replied.

I'll keep my shin pads on when I meet her. ☺ I'll only be practicing with the team, not playing yet. ☹ I'll see you guys there! Bring her to our practice session and I can meet her afterward—you'll be there scouting it anyway I assume.—E.

Niki sat back in her chair, needing to digest this new development. So. Eva wanted to meet Rory. She supposed it would be okay, since Rory was such a huge hockey fan and knew who Eva was and that she'd once been part of Niki's past. Rory even had one of Eva's hockey cards.

What was harder to fathom was why Eva wanted to involve herself in this area of Niki's life. Were they friends now? Was Eva looking for something more? Niki certainly hoped not. A superficial friendship might be okay, but such a thing was iffy, especially as the Games inched closer. She didn't want anyone, least of all the media, thinking she was associating with the enemy. It was a risky little game Eva seemed to be embarking on, yet Niki couldn't deny the relief that came with no longer hating each other. It might even be possible to paper over some of the fissures of the past, close that broken circle by exchanging a few pleasantries now and again. It wouldn't hurt anyway.

Niki didn't write to Eva again or hear from her as the Toronto trip approached. She immersed herself in preparation for the two games—one against a university all-star team and the other against Team USA. She ran grueling practices, to the point where the team hated them and looked forward to getting on with the games.

She blew her whistle, its shrill squeal a skull piercer. It was the final practice before tomorrow's plane ride to Toronto and the last chance for her players to perfect the new breakout system they'd been working on for a week.

"Come here, you guys." She waited until they fell to their knees and formed a semicircle around her at the boards. On the glass behind her was a large whiteboard in the shape of a hockey rink. "I need the center circling deep, just to the side of our net. Here." With a red dry erase marker, she indicated where she wanted the center to pick up the pass from the defenseman. "Then I want that winger here, so it's a bang-bang play. One, two passes. Third pass is the far winger cutting over. Voilà, we're out of our zone. But there can't be any hesitation. It's gotta be hard, it's gotta be fast. Got it?" The players rose to their feet. "And remember everyone, this only works if at least two of their forwards are in our zone pressuring us. If there's only one pressuring us, then we carry it for a bit before we pass. Okay, let's try it again."

Niki watched her players go through the breakout drill another dozen times, until they had it down without flaws. Each time, the women executed it faster, to the point where the breakout was happening in two or three seconds and the players could pass and receive the puck without looking. She smiled and nodded at Lynn. Things couldn't be running more smoothly.

"Okay, hit the showers, ladies. Good job today!"

"Well," Lynn said, moving next to her as the players filed off the ice. "That should put the Americans on their heels."

"I sure as hell hope so. If they can't pin us in our end, we're halfway to victory."

"Guess we'll find out in a couple of days if it works there as good as it's working here." Lynn hitched her chin in a clear challenge. "Race you around the rink once. Loser buys coffee."

Niki threw her head back and laughed, letting let Lynn get a few strides on her. She'd always been able to leave Lynn in her dust.

* * *

The puck fell to the ice and Eva simultaneously angled her body into her opponent, which in this case was her teammate Dani, while drawing the puck away and to her side of the ice. The act of winning the faceoff happened in a split second, so fast were Eva's hands and body movement.

"For fuck's sake," Dani exploded. "Why can't I win a single fucking faceoff from you?"

Amanda Fox, the assistant coach who had already dropped the puck for them at least thirty times, grunted at Dani. "She's the best there is, kid. Give it time."

But Dani didn't have time to be patient, not if she was to take over as the team's number two center. Privately, Eva felt Dani was nowhere close to shouldering the burden and might never be good enough to play center, never mind on the top two lines. But Alison seemed to have her mind set, and Eva could either help or pout and watch her team lose the gold medal game.

"All right, let's do it in slow motion," Eva said. "You've got to be totally still right before the ref drops the puck. No wasted energy. Watch the ref's hand, and as soon as it even begins to twitch in that downward motion, move your body sideways into your opponent. Like this. Use your stick at the same time to neutralize her stick."

Eva was no coach; she didn't know if Dani was ever going to get it, but over and over it they went until Dani began winning one in every ten drops against Eva. Ten percent against Eva, who was one of the best faceoff women in the world, meant about thirty percent against anybody else. Still insufficient, but better.

"Good," she told Dani. "You're starting to get it now. Keep at it."

"Thanks," Dani replied as they skated toward the gate that would lead them down the chute to the locker room—the rest of the team having quit practice ten minutes ago. "And hey. I'm sorry Coach put you on my wing instead of the other way around."

"Don't worry about it," Eva mumbled. She would never admit to Dani that Alison was right.

She lingered in the shower, letting the hot needles of water pelt her back muscles. Her knee was coming along. She was up to full practices now, although still sporting a yellow jersey. She expected to be game ready in a couple more weeks, and it couldn't come soon enough. Hanging back and watching the kids on the team do all the heavy lifting was something she could never get used to. Having the weight of the team on her shoulders drove her, made her the beast on the ice that she was.

Twenty minutes later, Eva slung a small backpack over her shoulder and headed to the arena lobby, unsure if Niki had brought Rory to the practice as she had suggested. She hadn't spotted them in the stands.

"Are you Eva Caruso?"

The youthful voice belonged to a girl, about ten or eleven with long dark hair and eyelashes almost as long. She smiled shyly and held out a Team USA hockey puck.

"I am." She went to the girl and the middle-aged woman standing beside her. "Hello there. Would you like me to sign that puck for you?"

"Yes, please." From the back pocket of her jeans, the kid pulled out a silver Sharpie.

"Ah, I see you've come prepared." Eva scrawled her signature and her jersey number, seventeen, over the USA logo. She handed the puck back to the girl. "And what's your name?"

"Rory."

"Wait. Are you Rory Hartling?" It sure as hell wasn't Niki standing beside her, but Rory was an unusual name.

The girl nodded, her smile threatening to swallow her face. Eva shook her hand.

"It's very nice to meet you, Rory. I'm old friends with your mom."

"I know," she said, tucking the signed puck into the front pocket of her Team Canada hoodie. "I play center. Like you."

Eva appraised the girl more closely, shocked by what she saw. With her dark hair and eyes and her long deer-like legs, she looked more like Eva's own kid or at least a niece. The resemblance was uncanny and she wondered if Niki thought so too. "Is that so? I'll bet you're awesome at it."

The woman beside Rory stepped forward and offered her hand. "Hi. I'm Jenny King, Rory's aunt. It's nice to meet you, Eva."

"How do you do? Are you the aunt Rory's living with while Niki's in Calgary?"

"I am." She touched the back of Rory's head. "She's staying with Tim and me and our six-year-old son Steven for a few months."

"And what's your mom going to say about you having a signed puck from the enemy?" Eva teased.

Rory's smile never wavered. "She won't care. But she says she's going to whip you guys."

"Oh, she does, does she?"

"Yup, but I tell her that as long as you're in the lineup, it won't be easy."

"What won't be easy, sweetie?" Niki walked up to them, surprise flaring and vanishing quickly in her eyes.

"Our team beating Eva's team."

Niki glanced between the two, clearly sizing up this blossoming friendship and not liking it much if her fiercely pinched brows were any indication. But she kept her manners, which came as no surprise to Eva. Niki never lost her cool in public.

"Nothing good is ever easy, sweetheart." She cocked her head at Eva. "So it'll make it sweeter when we *do* beat you."

"We'll see about that," Eva replied, meaning it but without a trace of combativeness. She liked Rory. And she liked the family unit Rory and Niki made together—the way they shared their own shorthand language, the intimacy and protectiveness with which Niki placed her arm around Rory's shoulder. Eva had never wanted kids before. Had never wanted much of anything that didn't include hockey or her renovation business in Traverse City. But now she wondered what being a mom would be like, how putting herself second would work. She'd never done that, and she wondered if being a mom could ever fill the void that would come with life after hockey. Maybe she'd ask Niki more about it sometime.

"Honey," Niki said to Rory. "I have to go do some work to get ready for tonight's game. Why don't you and Aunt Jenny go back to the hotel, and I'll meet you guys later for dinner, okay?"

"Okay," Rory mumbled at her shoes. "Boring, stupid old hotel."

"Hey," Eva said. "Somebody gave me a couple of tickets this morning to the Hockey Hall of Fame. I don't suppose you'd want to go with me, do you?" She raised her eyebrows at Rory, then Niki.

"Oh, yes, please! Can I go with Eva, Mom? Is that okay?"

Niki hesitated, cut a sharp look at Eva that said she was overstepping and better watch it. When Jenny broke the silence by saying she'd welcome the time alone to do some shopping at the Eaton Center, it did nothing to diminish Niki's reluctance. And who could blame her? Eva *was* overstepping the boundaries with this little stunt. But the kid was bored and Eva had nothing better to do. And hell, she liked Rory.

"All right," Niki finally said. "But can you bring her back here by five o'clock? And I'll need your cell phone number in case I need to reach you."

"Of course." They exchanged numbers before Eva turned to Rory. "C'mon, Rory. We can walk from here."

Rory flocked to her side without a second glance back at her mother.

CHAPTER TEN

Bench Minor

Dinner was rushed because Niki needed to get back to the Air Canada Center for the game between her team and the university women all-stars. Her thoughts kept straying to her line combinations and the temptation to make further changes, but Rory's constant praise for the Hockey Hall of Fame—and for Eva—was like a persistent and very annoying alarm clock that wouldn't let her sleep.

"She's super cool, Mom. And some of the people there even recognized her! She had to sign autographs and everything."

"That's nice, sweetie."

Rory reached into her backpack under the table and pulled out a Team USA practice jersey. "Look what she gave me. And she autographed it too! I'm going to wear it at my next practice!"

Niki glanced at the yellow jersey with the big USA logo on the front. If Eva was giving it to Rory, it probably meant she was moving to a regular practice jersey, which meant she would be game ready very soon. "That was nice of her. But put it away, all right? We're eating dinner."

Rory squirmed in her seat. "And you know what else, Mom?"

Niki resisted a good eye-rolling. "What, sweetie?"

"Some of the other kids at the Hockey Hall of Fame thought Eva was my mom. Isn't that cool?"

Niki halted as she was about to stuff truffle-infused mashed potatoes into her mouth and set her fork down with a loud clank. She exchanged a look with Jenny, who didn't appear offended. But Niki certainly was. "Excuse me?" she said, her eyes laser beaming into her daughter's.

Rory's face flushed, and with those two words from her mother, she was crestfallen. "Sorry. Somebody said I look like her, that's all."

Niki cursed under her breath. She was making a big deal out of something that she shouldn't. This wasn't necessarily about Rory missing Shannon or about Rory feeling neglected lately. It could simply be that she liked Eva. That she liked the attention Eva was giving her. *I can't make her feel guilty over this.*

"It's all right, honey. I didn't mean to make you feel bad. I'm glad you like Eva."

Rory brightened. "You do?"

"Yes. I do." She smiled at Jenny, who nodded in agreement.

"Good, 'cuz she said I could sit with her in the stands tomorrow when you guys play her team."

Great, Niki thought.

"Mom? How come you and Eva broke up a long time ago?"

Niki signaled the waiter for the check. "That, my dear, is a conversation for another time. I have to get to work, okay?"

"Eva told me she's never forgotten you."

Niki's heart thundered in her ears like a low-flying jet plane. She'd never forgotten Eva either, but not forgetting someone didn't have to mean anything more than that. The hopeful glint in Rory's eyes was evidence that the girl wasn't mature enough to understand such things yet.

"Well," Niki said casually. "Friends shouldn't forget each other, right?"

What else, she wondered, had Eva said about her.

* * *

Eva lined up her pool cue and broke the triangular formation of balls. She loved the sound of the sharp crack as the balls careened into one another, followed by the soft snick when one slid into a pocket. She'd spent a lot of time around pool tables during the many months and years of rehabbing injuries. Playing pool had always provided a calming distraction.

A few of her teammates crowded around the table. They were at a bowling alley that featured as many pool tables as bowling lanes, and the team was making use of both activities as a way to unwind and relax before tomorrow's tilt against Team Canada. None of the women was drinking more than a single beer—Eva saw to that. She knew from experience that the body only performs according to how it's been treated, that if you disrespect it, it'll let you down every time.

While waiting for her next shot, she noticed two of her defensemen and her center, Dani, whispering furiously in a corner, huddled over a cell phone, twittering like grade schoolers.

Eva insinuated herself between them. "What's the big secret, ladies?"

Dani struggled to pocket the phone while the others shuffled from foot to foot, avoiding eye contact with Eva. "Nothing," she said flatly. "Just some rumors I heard about Canada trying out a new breakout strategy on us tomorrow."

Eva narrowed her eyes at Dani. "Really? And where did you hear that?"

Dani grinned, the secret ready to burst from her like a dam being breeched. "Word around the rink, that's all. Wanna know what it is?"

"No. If the information is important—and accurate—Coach will tell us before the game." She refused to get sucked into gossiping about her opponent or second-guessing them. It was a good way to get mind-fucked about a game before you even hit the ice. "How do you know somebody's not messing with you?"

"They aren't," Dani said, holding firm.

"Well, I'd be careful about believing that kind of information. If it's wrong, you'll look awfully foolish chasing ghosts around the ice. You'll be out of position and scrambling to catch up. Best to worry about yourself and your own play."

The trio nodded politely, but it was the kind of indulgent politeness you gave your crazy old aunt at a family dinner. As they shuffled off, they stole a look back at Eva, their expressions saying they didn't believe her. *Well, hell*, Eva thought. *Of course they think they know better. I did too when I was their age.*

Her cell phone chimed an incoming text. When she saw it was from Niki her stomach sprouted butterflies.

Thanks for taking Rory to the HOF. She had a great time and hasn't stopped talking about it!

Eva thumbed the keypad of her phone.

It was fun, I had a blast. She's a great kid!

It took a couple of minutes for Eva's phone to chime again.

My kid has a huge girl crush on you! ;)

Nice! Eva texted, insanely thrilled. How about her mom?

No response. Eva took her pool shot, then another because she was on a roll. When her turn finally expired she checked her phone again. Nothing. Her heart sank. *Dammit!* She'd gone too far with her last comment. What had she been thinking? She was only teasing, but it was obvious Niki wasn't amused.

If she were honest with herself, she was pushing Niki's buttons for a reason. She wanted—needed—for the two of them to talk about what happened all those years ago. And she needed Niki to tell her how she felt, not philosophize about what went wrong and why, like they were dissecting a new hockey drill. Had Niki ever been sorry, sad about their breakup? Did she feel *something, anything*, about Eva now that they were regularly bumping into one another? Not attraction, and certainly not love, but maybe some regret for how things had gone down? A shared feeling that they'd both been foolish and hasty? That they'd never given the proper closure to their relationship? Even an expression of anger that she'd wasted her youth on Eva would be better than this...this...we're-sort-of-friends-but-not-really attitude. On the other hand, maybe digging up the past was a mistake that could only lead to more arguments, more blame. Either way, it wouldn't change anything.

"Your turn, Cruzie."

Eva stepped back to the pool table, determined more than ever that she needed to let this thing with Niki go.

CHAPTER ELEVEN

Unsportsmanlike Conduct

Niki raised the glass of Chablis to her lips and took a bird-like sip. She always advised her players to never consume more than one drink the night before a game, and the rules applied to her too. She was not the kind of coach who preached one thing and practiced another.

Jenny poured herself a second glass from the bottle. The two sisters-in-law sat at the small table for two in Niki's room, while Rory slept in the adjoining room.

"It really is harmless, Nik."

"Sorry, what?" Niki was thinking ahead to tomorrow's game against Team USA, worrying at the details of her new breakout strategy. She hadn't let her team use the techniques all weekend because she wanted to spring it on the Americans tomorrow. If it worked, it would give her opponent one more thing to worry about.

"Rory's little crush on Eva Caruso."

"Oh. That." So Jenny had noticed too.

"I can tell it worries you, and it shouldn't." Jenny had a level head about her, and she'd been very close to Shannon.

"I don't want her getting attached to someone she's never going to see again after the Games are over, that's all."

"Really? That's all?"

Niki absently swirled the remaining wine in her glass. Of course her feelings on the matter were more complicated than that. "Rory has me. And you and Tim and Stevie. Isn't that enough?"

Jenny sat back in her chair and coolly appraised Niki with eyes eerily similar to Shannon's. "Sorry, but I'm going to be blunt here. You know what I really think this is about? I think Rory's feelings about Eva mirror your own. And that's the part that scares the hell out of you."

"Oh, please. Eva and I were finished a long time ago. We were oil and water. Still are, from what I can tell."

"It's been over three years, Niki. It's okay to be attracted to someone else. And it's okay to act on that attraction. Shannon wouldn't want you to be alone forever. We both know that. And I know for a fact Shannon told you as much."

The prick of tears behind Niki's eyes came as an unwelcome surprise. It wasn't that being around Eva made her feel guilty that she was in some way being unfaithful to Shannon. It was Eva, in fact, who had come first, Eva who had been her first and most intense love—something that Shannon had always been mildly jealous of, though she either suppressed it or made light of it. What bothered Niki was people's reluctance to respect her self-imposed aversion to thinking romantically about another woman. Why couldn't people understand that she wasn't ready yet? And why did they think they knew better? Truth was, she didn't need or want anyone's permission, but it wasn't worth doing battle with her sister-in-law.

"No, Jen. I don't want to fall in love with anyone again. It's too…hard."

"It doesn't have to be. It wasn't so hard with Shannon, was it?"

That part was true. She and Shannon had slid easily into one another's life, like a hand fitting into a glove. They were comfortable together, didn't fight or disagree very often. Theirs was a drama-free, peaceful equanimity, and it was exactly what Niki needed at the time, and it was especially needed because they were raising a daughter together. She swallowed another mouthful of wine for courage. "Do you think she loved me, Jen? I mean, really loved me?"

"Of course she did." Jenny grasped her hand on the table and squeezed it. "Why do you doubt that?"

"It was good with us, don't get me wrong. We both needed the tranquil life we made together. But there weren't a lot of fireworks, you know?"

"Like there were between you and Eva?"

"I guess." Niki hated that they were having this conversation and yet she was relieved too. "Look, there's nothing to talk about with Eva and me. We're barely friends, and that's all we'll ever be." She wished she could stop comparing Eva to Shannon, wished she could stop analyzing the way each woman made her feel, because the whole exercise was stupid and pointless. Neither woman was in her life anymore. What only mattered now was Rory and these damned Olympic Games; everything else was inconsequential. "How's Rory been doing in my absence? Are you sure she's okay?"

"She's more than okay. She's loving the change of scene at our place, and she loves the fact that you're in the news at least once a week and on the sports highlights on TV. She's proud of you. And I think she's really happy you're getting on and doing what you do best."

Maybe she hadn't given Rory—and herself—enough credit for their ability to finally adapt and grow beyond their grief. Because as much as she hated being apart from Rory, joining Team Canada had given her life purpose again. And had given her a sense of pride in herself and in her work. "Good. That's a huge relief to me. And I can't thank you and Tim enough."

Jenny stood and smiled. "You don't need to thank us, we're family. And we want you and Rory to be happy. I mean that."

"Thank you, Jenny." Niki hugged her sister-in-law goodnight. It wasn't terribly late, but she needed to be up early tomorrow to prepare for the afternoon game. And then it was a red-eye flight back to Calgary, while Jenny and Rory would catch a Monday morning flight to Windsor.

"Oh, about the game tomorrow," Jenny said, halfway to the door that separated Niki's room from the room Jenny shared with Rory. "You're okay with Rory having invited Eva to sit with us in the stands?"

Niki didn't have the energy to be upset. She threw up her hands in resignation and grinned. "Fine. Just don't let Eva give her anymore Team USA jerseys and pucks and crap. I don't want that kid getting her loyalties mixed up."

Jenny laughed. "I'll make sure of it."

* * *

Eva handed the bag of buttered popcorn to Rory before turning her full attention to the play on the ice fourteen rows below them. Both teams were locked in step, trading back-and-forth plays, matching one another's shots on net. As the first period ground on, Canada was being hemmed in its own end more and more, pinned there helplessly while Team USA leapt into the passing lanes and jumped on Canadian players to create turnovers. A quick glance across the ice at Niki told her how frustrated she was. She paced behind the bench, her jaw clenched. Something had clearly gone off the rails.

A minute before the buzzer signaled the first intermission, Eva excused herself and made her way down to her team's locker room. Scratched players watched games from the stands but were expected to spend the intermissions with their team, in case they could impart any helpful advice.

The smell of sweat hit her like a wall. Damp gloves and soggy shin pads were the worst. *Funny*, Eva thought, *how you never notice the smell when you are one of the offenders.*

"Good job on preventing those breakouts," Alison was saying to the players. The private look she flashed at Dani failed to escape Eva's attention. "Now that they don't have a clue how to get out of their own end, I want shots on their net. Lots of them. Got it? Put everything on the net and make sure someone's in place for the rebounds."

Alison nodded at Eva. "Cruzie, anything you're seeing out there?" It was a team bonding ritual to refer to one another by their goofy nicknames.

"Not really. We're doing a really good job at being first on the puck. And I've never seen us pin them in their end so badly. Good job, women."

Alison left the room to let the players talk among themselves. Loudly, they replayed all the things they'd done right in the period, reliving the glory moments. Eva slid onto the bench next to Dani.

"So," she said quietly so the others wouldn't hear, "did you really know ahead of time how Team Canada was going to get out of their end? Was it more than just innocent gossip around the rink? Huh?"

A tiny smirk curled Dani's lips, and Eva wanted to smack it off her. "You said yourself last night not to believe any of that kind of talk, so I didn't. It was obvious to me early on that they were trying to get the puck to their centers, who were coming in deep to help, instead of sending it up the boards to their wingers."

Dani wasn't the most perceptive—or the brightest—on the team. Figuring it out on her own just seconds into the game was highly unlikely. So where the hell had she gotten her information? Was she involved in something that wasn't aboveboard? Was she outright cheating? It was a disturbing thought, and it would be damned bad for the team if she was. Cheating could get them all expelled from the tournament. It was serious stuff, but an awfully big leap at this point. "Well, good on you, then."

Eva returned to the stands in time for the start of the second period. Team USA came out hard and potted a goal—the first of the game—within the first minute.

"Uh-oh," Rory complained. "Mom's not gonna be happy about that."

"No, I suppose she won't," Eva said distractedly, her eyes following every move on the ice. Canada was still having trouble breaking out, which meant their goalie and defensemen would be fatiguing. She thought about what advice she'd give her own team and what she'd tell Team Canada if she were their coach.

I'd tell my own team to keep their foot on the gas and to get another goal before the period ends. And if I were Niki I'd tell my defensemen to start skating the puck out, which would open things up. They just need to regroup, and having their defensemen skate the puck out instead of passing it would put my team on their heels.

Eva bled red, white and blue, but she almost felt sorry for Niki and her team. If they lost this game, it would seriously damage team morale. A pattern of losing was not a pretty thing, especially when you kept losing to the same team. It got in your head until you started thinking you couldn't beat your opponent. Everyone knew the gold medal game would be between Canada and USA. They were the elite of women's hockey, in a class all by themselves. If USA kept beating Canada in these pre-tournament games, it would be mentally devastating.

As the third period began, Eva noticed right away that Niki must have read her mind. Her defensemen were suddenly making the adjustment, skating the puck out of their end and surprising Team USA. It took only a few more minutes before they scored, knotting the game at a goal apiece. From there it was an evenly matched dogfight, and the game ended in a 1-1 tie. There would be no overtime or shootout, since it was only an exhibition game.

Eva threw her arm around Rory's shoulders. "Guess a draw is a good thing, right, kiddo? Because if your mom's team lost, she probably wouldn't let us hang out anymore."

"Yeah," Rory agreed. "And if your team lost, you wouldn't want to be friends with us anymore either."

Eva gave her a squeeze. "That's not true. I promise I'll be friends with you win or lose, okay?"

Fans began filtering away. Eva was about to usher Rory and Jenny down the stairs when she caught sight of Niki stomping her way toward them. It was not only unusual, but unheard of. Coaches always went immediately to the locker room for parting words to their team and a postgame debriefing.

"Mom!" Rory exclaimed. "What are you doing here?"

"Hi, honey. Jenny." She locked eyes with Eva. Eyes that were hot coals. "Eva, can I talk to you for a minute?"

"Of course." Eva excused herself and followed Niki to two empty seats a couple of rows up. Niki was breathing hard through her nose, and it wasn't from the exertion.

"Did I do something wrong, Nik?" She couldn't imagine what.

"I don't know, is that your guilty conscience speaking?"

"What are you talking about?"

"How did your team know exactly how we were going to break out from the minute we hit the ice?"

"I have no idea. But I did notice right away you guys were trying something new. And that it wasn't working."

The grinding of Niki's molars was as loud as a band saw. "We haven't used it in other games before today, nor in any practices open to the public. Nobody outside our team knew we were going to try this. What the hell, Eva? Is Alison planting spies among us now? Hacking into my computer? What?"

"C'mon, that's a little over the top, don't you think?" They both knew Alison hadn't met a scruple she liked. But spying? Hacking into computers? Alison was a win-at-all-costs jerk, but she wasn't the Kremlin.

"Are you forgetting what she did to me—to us—right before Nagano?"

Ah, yes, the floppy disks. About time they got around to this long overdue conversation. "Look, I tried to tell you a long time ago that I was sorry I didn't believe you when you said you had no idea how those stupid things got into your possession. But you didn't exactly try very hard to deny it either. Of course Alison did a stupid, unforgivable thing planting those disks in your bag, but we didn't handle it well. And that part's on us."

Niki looked away in an attempt to conceal the crack in her mulish determination. "Forget I brought it up. I don't want to talk about it, about us. All I'm trying to say is that I don't trust Alison."

"And you don't trust me either, it seems."

"I didn't say that." Niki met her gaze this time. Her voice cracked as she said, "What is it you want from me, Eva?"

They sat in silence, Eva unable to put into words what she wanted, how she felt. Niki stood finally, a flash of anguish on her face before it disappeared completely. "I don't know who to trust in this goddamned business anymore. It's fucking lonely sometimes, all right? It just, I don't know, it pisses me off that we tried so hard with this new strategy and it was all for nothing."

Eva touched Niki's wrist, knowing that in the mood she was in, it was a risky thing to do. "I know. But I'm not Alison, okay? You know I don't believe in that unethical shit." She wasn't about to share with Niki that she didn't trust Dani Compton either, because she had no hard evidence that Dani—or Alison—had done anything wrong.

Niki gave her a last look before brushing past her, leaving Eva to wonder whether they'd reached a new understanding or just widened the fissure between them.

CHAPTER TWELVE

Empty Net

Being back home, though it wouldn't be long enough, was a slice of heaven for Niki. The best part was sleeping in her own bed, but a close second was waking up to find Rory attempting to make them pancakes for breakfast. It was the Christmas break, and the two glorious weeks at home would give Niki some much-needed rest. She would put in a few hours of work too though, going through game and practice videos, mapping out new drills and new strategies, responding to emails, conducting a couple of telephone interviews with journalists. There wasn't much time left to fine-tune the team.

Niki poured herself a cup of coffee from the pot Rory had made. She took a sip and the bitterness nearly made her wince, but kudos to the kid for trying. "This looks great, honey. What do you want to do today, anything special?"

Rory used two hands on the spatula to try to flip a pancake. She pulled it off with only a splatter or two.

"Wow, you're getting good at that." What else was she missing living away from her daughter? It was a little thing, a stupid thing, but it was almost enough to make her cry.

"It's no big deal, Mom. It's just pancakes."

"Ah, pancakes today, gourmet meals tomorrow."

The scowl Rory gave Niki was an instant preview of her teenaged years, which were rushing at them with lightning speed, it seemed.

"Do you want to go to the pool at the university? Or maybe see a movie?" Niki asked.

"I want to work on my school project. I have to hand it in as soon as the holidays are over."

"But the holidays are just starting." Already, she could see that Rory was going to be an overachiever, much like she had been at her age. She hated seeing her daughter put stress on herself so early in life. Lord knew there was more than enough of it to go around in adulthood, but kids always wanted to grow up so fast. Enjoy being a kid for as long as you can, she had told Rory many times, but it usually fell on deaf ears. "What's your project about?"

"I have to pick a hero and write an essay about them."

A horrifying thought occurred to Niki. *Please don't tell me you're going to pick Eva.* She clutched her coffee mug in a death grip. "Do you know who you're going to pick?"

"I can't pick a family member or an athlete." She rolled her eyes, a mini teenager again. "Cuz my teacher says athletes aren't real heroes. So I was thinking I'd pick Roberta Bondar. You know, Canada's first woman astronaut?"

Niki blinked in relief. "That sounds perfect, honey. I remember when she went up in space. My high school class got to watch the launch on TV. Want some help with it?"

"Okay." Rory lifted the pancakes from the frying pan and carefully stacked them on a plate, which she carried to the kitchen island. Maple syrup and a can of whipped cream stood beside their plates and utensils. She'd thought of everything.

"Mmm, this looks wonderful. Thank you for making us breakfast."

Rory shrugged like it was no biggie and sat down beside her mother. "Mom. Can I ask you something?"

"Of course." Niki poured syrup on her pancake and forked a piece. Her waistline didn't need the whipped cream.

"How come you and Eva broke up?"

Niki barely managed to swallow the lump of pancake in her throat before she choked on it. "Why do you want to know about that? It was a long time ago. Before you were born."

"I know. But I like her. And you're my mom. So…"

Niki hedged. She wasn't ready for heart-to-heart talks about romantic relationships with her kid. Or maybe there was no such thing as being ready. Maybe you had to go with it when the opportunity presented itself and hope you didn't sound like an idiot. "It's sort of complicated."

"Mom." Rory scolded her with eyes that were shiny and black as oil, so much like Eva's that it stole Niki's breath for a moment. "I'm not a *baby*. You can tell me, and I want to know what happened."

"Fine." Niki took another bite to stall for time. She didn't know how much to say, what to leave out and what to leave in, how much Rory would understand. Yes she was still a kid, but she was growing up fast, and she was much more mature than the average ten-and-a-half-year-old. "We met in college. I was a year ahead of her. She was a rookie on our hockey team that year."

"Was it love at first sight?"

Would this kid ever stop surprising her? "How do you know about that kind of stuff?"

Rory shrugged. "I watch TV. I read books."

"I see. And have *you* ever felt, you know, love at first sight with somebody?"

"I thought I did with James, but he was too into himself. But now I think I might be, you know, with Margot. She moved to my school in the fall. She's, like, the bomb!"

More hurt than stunned, Niki clamped her mouth shut. If her daughter was in love with somebody, especially with another girl, then she needed to be here for her. She needed to support her. Jenny and Tim were good people, great people. But Rory was her daughter, her responsibility. It tore her in half to think that she hadn't known her own kid was in love with another girl.

"I see," she said carefully, hiding her pain from Rory. One thing she'd learned early on about parenting was to emphasize the positive, to try to be a good role model, even when it was hard. Especially when it was hard. "That's wonderful, honey. When can I meet Margot?"

"She and her family went to Florida for the holidays, so it'll have to wait. But you're changing the subject, Mom."

"Fine. How did you get so smart anyway?"

Rory shrugged. "I've always been smart."

"Of course you have. Okay. Yes. It was love at first sight. Eva and I were inseparable for four years. We did everything together, especially hockey."

"So how come you broke up?"

Niki explained about the top secret floppy disks that had been planted in her hockey bag for Eva to discover. She watched her daughter's eyes widen in shock, then in outrage.

"Eva blamed you?"

"At first, yes."

"But why would she do that? Didn't she love you? I mean, didn't she trust you?"

"I guess the answer isn't that easy. We were both under a lot of pressure. It was the first Olympic Games for women's hockey, so the stakes were huge. Eva's coach wanted us to hate each other. She thought that's what needed to happen if her team was going to win. We were both a bit, I don't know..." Niki paused, thinking back to how preoccupied she and Eva had been at the time, how insulated and narrow-minded they'd become in the cauldron of the Olympic Games. "We were immature. Too into ourselves. Neither of us seemed to want to fight very hard for our relationship."

"How come?"

Niki thought for a long moment. "We were young. So at the time, it seemed simpler to give up. You see, sometimes when you're young, and you have your whole future ahead of you, you think that you have time."

"Time for what?"

"To get it right. To find somebody else. To find that kind of love again. Or maybe to do the whole thing over again." She hadn't known how to fight for a relationship, and neither had Eva. They only knew how to fight for the puck, how to battle to win a hockey game, how to compete against others. Oh, yes. They were good at competing, but not so good at harmonizing, at putting the other above their own needs and desires, at seeing and appreciating the bigger picture. It was no wonder their relationship had self-destructed.

"Do you wish Eva and you never broke up?"

Testifying in court would be easier than this, but Rory had a right to know her. Which meant knowing and understanding her past, warts and all. "Yes and no, as confusing as that sounds. As much as we loved each other, I'm not sure we were meant to be together forever."

It took a moment for the panic to register on her daughter's face.

"But you were meant to be with my mother, right?"

Niki reached out and placed her arm around Rory's narrow shoulders. "Yes, honey, I was meant to be with your mother. We loved each other very much. You don't ever have to worry about that."

Rory leaned into her. "Good. So you won't forget about her, right?"

"Nope. Never."

* * *

Eva groaned in the direction of the massive departure board. Her flight from Minneapolis to Detroit was delayed for at least another hour because of a snowstorm that had planted itself over Chicago. She was used to the Midwest's volatile winter weather; she just didn't like it when it messed with her travel plans.

She pulled out her phone and texted Kath, who was also somewhere in the airport, waiting for a flight to Denver so she could spend Christmas with her parents. Eva texted her that her flight was delayed and asked if she had time for a drink in one of the airport bars. Kath said she did.

"You look royally pissed off. I didn't think you were that anxious to get to your brother's," Kathleen said to her.

"I'm not. Spending time with my brother's not exactly at the top of my Dear Santa list. But I am anxious to have some rest and to see my nephews."

Eva's brother Michael was four years younger and worked in the IT department at University of Michigan in Ann Arbor. As kids they'd been close, though it was mostly adoration on Michael's end as he attempted to emulate everything his big sister did. The problem was, he wasn't nearly as good in sports as she was and as he wanted to be. They grew apart as their athletic accomplishments became more disparate. Once Eva left for college, they only saw each other a couple of times a year. With both their parents out of the picture—their father had suffered a fatal heart attack nine years ago and their mother remarried a wealthy Greek national and lived in Crete—the siblings felt compelled to spend Christmas, or at least part of it, together.

"How long are you staying with him?"

Christmas was four days away. "Not long. I'm going to Traverse City on the twenty-fourth to spend a few days at home before I come back here. I'll probably have to think up an excuse to leave his place on Christmas Eve."

Kath sipped her beer. "If you need me to place a timely call, let me know."

"Hey, that's not a bad idea. I could always say the property managers of my house are calling to tell me my pipes are frozen or the roof's caved in from snow load or something." She grinned. "Thanks, Kath. I feel better already."

"Well, in any case, enjoy the change of scene."

They clinked glasses before Eva took a sip of beer. "I will. I can't wait to spend ten days thinking of everything *but* hockey. I'm not even going to pick up a hockey stick, unless it's to play some road hockey with my nephews."

Kathleen laughed. "Can you really do that? Take that kind of a mental break from hockey right now?"

"Probably not." She'd run every day and hit the gym every other. She'd probably watch hockey on television. And think about Niki and what she and Rory were doing over the holidays, particularly since they'd be so close geographically—Niki in Windsor and Eva right across the border.

The holidays always made Eva feel as though she were a scrap of paper being picked up and tossed in the air by every gust of wind, with only random places to land. She envied Niki for having Rory, for having a family, but the thought only made her feel guilty, because while Niki had gained a daughter, she'd also lost a wife in the process. Christmas was probably a sad time for them.

"You know," she said to her friend, consciously turning her thoughts elsewhere, "something's been bugging me about that game in Toronto against Canada."

"Me, too," Kath replied with a straight face. "We couldn't score more than one goal against them. What was up with that?"

"No, I'm serious. The fact that we deciphered from the very first shift how they were going to bust out of their end. It's like we knew what they were going to do before they did it. The whole first period, they couldn't get out of their own end."

"Lucky guess on our part?"

Eva shook her head. "No. It was Dani who jumped on it right away. Kath, Dani's not *that* good. She knew what they were going to do. And she knew it before the game even started."

"What do you mean?"

"The night before the game, at the bowling alley, she and a couple of others were whispering and giggling like little kids. When I asked them what was up, Dani said she'd heard talk around the rink about a new breakout strategy for Canada. I figured it was just bullshit. You know how rumors like that fly around all the time."

"And now you're thinking she actually did know."

Something hollow formed in Eva's stomach. "Niki told me afterward it was top secret, that nobody outside her team knew about it. I asked Dani about it after the game and she denied she knew anything for sure. But she knew, dammit. She knew exactly what Canada was doing before they even did it."

Kathleen closed her eyes and rubbed her temples. "Shit. It's kind of making sense now."

"What's making sense?"

"That same night, I didn't feel like dinner in the hotel or joining you guys at the bowling alley. I went for a long walk and stopped at this tiny bistro on Bay Street. I was about to walk in the door when I saw Alison and Lynn O'Reilly at a table for two, their heads together."

"What?" Eva's throat went dry. "Heads together how? Like lovebirds?"

Kathleen shook her head. "Definitely not that kind of thing going on. They didn't look particularly happy or cozy. But definitely like they were having some kind of serious discussion. Needless to say, I didn't want them to see me and hightailed it away from there."

"Jesus, Kath. Those two having dinner together, that's definitely not cool. It sounds downright dirty to me." The possibility of some kind of spying or collusion going on incensed Eva. It was looking more and more like a repeat of the Nagano Olympics, when Alison's disingenuous and morally corrupt antics led to her and Niki's ugly breakup. Couldn't people just damned well play hockey to the best of their abilities and let the chips fall where they may?

"Easy now," Kathleen said, reading her anger in her clenched fists.

"God, that's such bullshit. Isn't it enough to try to beat Canada on the ice? Do we really have to resort to dirty tactics to get the upper hand?" She scrubbed her cheeks in frustration. "I should have known Alison hadn't changed a bit."

"Of course Alison hasn't changed. It's who she is."

"That's not good enough. She ruins peoples' lives with this crap." She'd certainly ruined a future together for her and Niki. "I should walk out on this fucking team. Or report her ass."

Kathleen's hand locked onto Eva's wrist. "You're not going to do either one. The team needs you. And not just your skills, they need your leadership, your moral compass too. You're a role model, and if you leave, Alison's dirty ways win the day." She relaxed her grip on Eva. "And besides, we don't know that she and Lynn O'Reilly were up to anything unethical. There's no proof that it wasn't anything but a friendly dinner. And there's no proof that Dani wasn't acting on a hunch. A hunch informed by rumors that just happened to be accurate."

Eva stewed a few more minutes before reluctantly agreeing she wouldn't do anything rash or stupid. Which included alerting Niki that some sort of colluding might be going on. She checked her watch, saw it was time to head to her gate. She gave Kathleen a hug.

"Stay in touch," Kathleen said, hugging her back. "And stay out of trouble."

"You too. And Kath? Thanks for staying friends with me after…you know."

"It's okay. I always knew we made better friends than lovers."

CHAPTER THIRTEEN

One-timer

It was late in the evening and well past Niki's preferred bedtime when Team Canada's shuttle bus eased up in front of the Westin Resort in Whistler, B.C. Their flight had been delayed a couple of hours and traffic on Highway 99 from Vancouver to Whistler was so slow, Niki threatened she could have made it faster by walking. It was two days after New Year's. Perhaps, she thought with further irritation, everyone was stuck back in 2009 and in no hurry to get on with the present.

While a team staff member registered the group with the desk clerk, Niki, Lynn and the players hovered in the lobby awaiting their room assignments. The players would bunk two to a room, but rank allowed Niki and Lynn their own rooms.

The laughing and whooping of a group of players, all veterans, jolted Niki from her exhaustion.

"What's up?" she said, wandering over to their circle.

"Look!" Britney laughed, pointing at a hotel luggage trolley stacked with Team USA hockey bags.

Niki slammed her eyes shut. Could this evening get any worse? Now the Americans were staying here too? At the same time? What were the odds of that? She took a step closer to peek at a nametag on a piece of luggage. Yup, it was them all right.

"Did you know Team USA was going to be here?" she whispered to Lynn.

"I'd heard something about it." Her shrug was one of indifference. "Didn't you know?"

Niki seethed inside. "No, I didn't. So much for getting some R and R and some team bonding time."

It was supposed to be a fun week, a relaxing week before heading down the highway to Squamish for a couple of weeks of intense practices and workouts. Niki had been looking forward to Whistler—acclimating to the mountain air, shopping, sightseeing, snowshoeing with the team. It was to be the final breather before the hype and pressure of the Games ramped up, because one thing she knew from experience, it wouldn't be long before all of them would be able to do nothing *but* think about the Games. "Why didn't you tell me about this? I probably could have had us relocated to another hotel." It would be impossible now; Whistler was typically booked solid months ahead.

"It's not that big of a deal. Is it?"

"Yes. It is a big deal. I don't want us seeing the Americans or thinking about them right now. There'll be plenty of time later for them to fill our heads." She shouldn't have to spell it out for Lynn, and the fact that she did was one more example of how they weren't clicking much lately. When she took this job, she thought she and Lynn were on the same page. Now she wasn't even sure they were reading the same book.

"Sorry, boss," Lynn said flatly.

Niki studied her long-time friend. She looked tired, nerves strung a little tight, probably much the way Niki felt. The last few months had been exhausting—the twelve-hour days, the travel, the grind of practices and video analyses, the strategy sessions, the media interviews. With less than six weeks to go, it was time for a reboot between she and Lynn. Time to get back on that same page. And as head coach, she knew it was her job to get through to Lynn, to take the initiative in patching up their differences.

Towing her suitcase behind her, Niki followed Lynn up to the fourth floor and to her room, which was next to Lynn's. She closed the door and collapsed on the king bed for a moment, relishing the quiet. Her ears still rang from the loud bantering and singing on the bus—the players had sung songs Niki didn't know the lyrics to and didn't care to. It made her wonder if she'd acted that silly, that carefree, when she was in her early twenties. Probably. But in those days, she and Eva had mostly cocooned themselves, spending all their spare time together, happily shutting others out. They worked out at the gym together, read books out loud to one another, made tofu stir-fries and baked oatmeal cookies in their tiny apartment, sat side by side in the locker room when they played together in Wisconsin. They didn't have the time or need to participate in adolescent games like singing and pranking others. They didn't need anything or anybody else.

Niki sat up and swung her legs over the bed. The brochure said the hotel had a marvelous hot tub and heated pool on the second-story outside deck. She'd never swum outdoors in the winter, and the promise of cold air and hot water sounded like exactly the tonic to put her into a deep, restful sleep for the night. A coma, with any luck. She rifled in her bag for her swimsuit, threw it on and draped an oversized towel from the bathroom around her shoulders.

Outside on the pool deck, the cold mountain air produced small, sharp needles in her lungs. Steam rose in a misty cloud from the pool, shrouding it. Beyond it was the hot tub, and it too was crowned in a warm fog of air. Diffused lights of green and blue glowed from somewhere deep in the pool, shimmering brightly on the surface, like a large jewel, perhaps one that belonged on the pendant of a giant. Snowcapped mountains perched not more than a thousand yards away, visible in the soft glow of the moonlight. The tableau was beautiful and vaguely romantic, although romantic thoughts were well and truly wasted on her. Her grief had slammed the door shut on that, in spite of her sister-in-law's not-so-subtle suggestion that it was time she allowed herself be attracted to someone else.

She decided to do the hot tub first, get nice and hot and then dive into the pool, which would be a few degrees cooler. Following the little glowing lights along the stone pathway, she picked her way to the hot tub and tossed her towel onto an empty bench nearby. Halfway to climbing in, she halted when she noticed through the fog that the tub was occupied. It was a woman, a dark-haired woman, who had her back to her. Damn, she thought, wanting to be alone. But the need to submerge her body in warm, rushing water won out and she climbed the rest of the way in, slowly, one leg at a time to adjust to the temperature, and eased herself down to the seat. Warmer than a bathtub, the water was almost too hot.

"Good evening, Niki."

Niki's head snapped up. Her heart stopped. It was Eva, reclining in water up to her neck. In her smile there was not a trace of surprise that they should meet here, high up in the mountains in the darkest part of the night. If anything, Eva looked as though she fully expected Niki to show up. And that wasn't cool. Not in such an intimate setting as this. And not when she was striving to keep their friendship on a superficial level.

"How did you know I was going to be here?"

* * *

"I didn't." It was the truth, and Eva knew that her pleasure at having Niki to herself was infusing her voice, dropping it an octave. Running into one another privately was exactly as she had hoped, once she realized both teams were staying at the same resort. But this—Niki in a bathing suit, sharing her hot tub—was a gift. "I heard on the bus ride earlier today that your team was coming in tonight."

A smile had yet to approach Niki's face. "So much for our teams keeping their distance until the Games start."

Eva tried to bite back a laugh and failed. "Alison's having a fit. We're supposed to hate you guys, and in her playbook, it's easier to think of you all as monsters if we don't have to see you on a daily basis. You know, as in seeing that you do human things like eat breakfast and enjoy each other's company. The nerve of you all!"

Finally, a smile. "Please don't tell me your team is moving onto Squamish next, or I'm going to start thinking you're following us. Or we're following you."

"No such luck. We're going to Kamloops after this. We'll be back in Vancouver at least a week before the opening ceremony. That gives Alison lots of time to whip us into a hateful lather."

Niki closed her eyes and leaned back against the edge of the tub. "I guess we're all stuck with each other for a week. I'll try to stay out of your way."

"Please don't. Seeing you, I mean, being around you, makes me feel normal. Alison and some of the girls…" She didn't want to finish her thought because she didn't know how much, or if at all, she should share her suspicions that something nefarious was afoot between their teams. The wise choice was probably to keep her mouth shut.

"What?" Niki said gently. "What's wrong?"

"Nothing." Niki's attention was zeroed in on her like a gunsight. "Why do you say that?"

Niki could always read her, but it was more than that. Niki possessed the kind of face, the kind of self-possessed stillness that said she was a safe place to lay your pain or your worries. It was also her honest eyes, her mouth that broke into an easy, genuine smile, the faint lines around her eyes that evoked wisdom and patience, in spite of the pain she must have endured from her wife's illness and death and from single parenthood. It was hard to remember she'd once been so angry with Niki, so willing to walk away from her. And it was hard now to remember a reason why she shouldn't confide her suspicions in her.

"You've got that look you get when your opponent's cheating in the faceoff circle," Niki added. "That look that says oh-no-you-don't."

"I wish it was something that simple."

Niki tried for a joke. "Somebody's cheating at more than just faceoffs?"

Eva groaned. "Dammit, Niki."

"Eva, look. I know fairness in this game is as important to you as it is to me. What are you not saying? What's going on? Because clearly something has you rattled."

Rattled, yes. Tossing and turning at night, definitely. This thing with Dani anticipating Canada's breakout plays, the dinner meeting between Alison and Lynn, it was eating at her. Smaller things too like little indecipherable looks between Alison and Dani, and the fact that Dani had no business being rewarded with the kind of ice time she was getting. Something was off, and maybe Niki deserved to know about it. No, Niki *did* deserve to know, not only because Lynn O'Reilly might be involved, but because Niki had already once been screwed over by Alison's win-at-any-cost gamesmanship and didn't deserve to be her victim again. "Remember in Toronto, when you confronted me in the stands about spies and hacking into computers and—"

"I showed poor judgment, Eva. I was emotional and I was lashing out, talking nonsense."

"No, you weren't."

Eva quickly told her about her team's deciphering of Team Canada's breakout strategy and how she didn't believe it was a coincidence. She told her about Alison and Lynn being spotted having dinner together the night before the game. She left out the part that it was Kathleen who'd seen them; no need to drag her into things for now. And she told her that her gut said something was going on.

"Jesus, Eva. Are you kidding me with this?"

For Niki to be sympathetic, to be an ally, to be as concerned about the problem as she was, was a given. Or so she thought. "Unfortunately, no."

"Look, I believe you. I think." Niki put a hand up to halt Eva's protestations. "I'm sorry, but I'm being honest. I appreciate you telling me, but the thing is, I can't afford to jump to false conclusions, because if I do, it could hurt my team. And it could distract me into expending a lot of mental and emotional energy on something that might be nothing. As a coach, I can't let myself go down that road. Not right now. I've got more than enough to worry about on the ice without worrying about cloak-and-dagger stuff off the ice."

Eva watched the way Niki's eyes changed as she talked. They seemed as much a part of her communication as her words, amplifying each statement with fine yet uncertain shades of meaning.

"All right, I understand." She didn't entirely, but then she wasn't a head coach of a national team playing for Olympic gold in their home country. She couldn't really put herself in Niki's shoes. If Niki didn't want to hear about this stuff, then so be it. She wasn't about to force it down her throat.

She sank lower into the water, soothed by its heat and power, and closed her eyes, willing herself to relax. But relaxing had never been her strong suit. If Alison and Lynn were up to something, Dani too, she damned well wouldn't turn a blind eye. She'd get to the bottom of it, with or without Niki's help or permission. Because the bottom line was, she didn't want a gold medal—or any medal—if it wasn't won fairly.

"I'm sorry," Niki said softly beside her. "I don't want you to think I don't care, it's just that—"

"It's okay." Eva's hand found Niki's under the water. "You're right, you've got other things to worry about. Pretend I never said anything."

Niki squeezed her hand back. "I know I've been...a little standoffish with you. The timing of all this isn't great, is it?"

"No. It's not."

"On a number of levels," Niki said in a voice barely audible.

"Niki, I don't want us to hate each other ever again, okay? It's not worth it, and I won't let it happen. I know we have to keep a certain amount of distance right now. But..."

"Yes?"

What, exactly, did she want to say? So much and nothing at all. There was an emotional gulf between them far too wide and too difficult to bridge right now, not while the Games loomed closer. The physical chemistry that lay between them, however, was another matter. It thrummed and danced like electricity shooting the length of a wire, and it came without any effort, without any conscious thought whatsoever. Eva could feel it crackling in the hot mist rising over their heads, and most importantly, in the insistent pulse between her legs. She couldn't be around Niki and not be attracted to her. It was some kind of sick law of physics that endeavored to make her life miserable.

"How about this?" Eva finally ventured, her throat constricting with fear. It was only the relentless throbbing between her legs that made her brave. And foolish. "We could, you know, do things for each other while we're here this week. To help us relax. To relieve the…the stress we're under."

Niki's mouth curled into an amused smile. "You're not suggesting…"

Of course she was. Mind-blowing, no-holds-barred, no-strings, multiple-orgasm sex. But she couldn't find the guts to verbalize it.

Niki extracted her hand, still smiling. "Don't you already have a friend with benefits?"

Eva felt the blood rush to her face. "Kathleen? No, not for a while. It, she and I, weren't a good idea together."

She wished Niki would ask her why, but she didn't.

"I'm flattered. Really, I am. But I can't imagine that it would be a good idea. Under the circumstances."

"Right. Okay." Eva sat up straight, her humiliation complete. What a stupid, stupid mistake. And just when she and Niki had finally come to be civil toward one another.

"What I would like, I think," Niki said, "is if we could be friends. No benefits. And discreetly, of course."

Eva wanted to holler her relief. Instead, she said, "I'd like that very much."

Niki got to her feet and stepped out of the tub, Eva's eyes following every curve of her body, every flexing muscle, every drop of water that fell from her smooth, soaked skin. Not a single ounce of her sexiness had diminished in the last decade. She was a beautiful woman.

"How about tomorrow night?" Eva chanced.

That same streak of amusement flashed in Niki's eyes. "What?"

"Here, I mean. Meet as friends," Eva quickly amended. "Same time, same place?"

"All right. Same time, same place." Niki shook her head. "You don't give up, do you?"

CHAPTER FOURTEEN

Roughing

Niki followed Lynn onto the chairlift, a two-seater that would take them to the top of a ski run that didn't look too difficult. While neither woman resembled anything close to an expert skier, Niki had suggested taking a couple of easy runs together as an excuse for some private time so they could talk candidly. The players had been sent to the village to shop and hang out—skiing was forbidden to them because the risk of injury was too great.

"How'd you sleep last night?" Niki asked.

"Good, how about you?"

"Fine." More than fine, actually. The hot tub had soothed her, and Eva, well… Eva and her friends-with-benefits suggestion had fired Niki up in places that had too long been dormant. "Lynn, is everything…okay with you?"

Lynn looked at her like she'd grown two heads. "Of course. Why do you ask?"

"No reason. How about us, then? Everything okay between you and me?"

Lynn nodded coolly. "Sure. Far as I'm concerned, anyway."

There had been no open defiance from her, but Niki sometimes had the feeling that Lynn didn't always agree with her methods, her strategies, her way of doing things. There was often a moment of hesitation from her in carrying out Niki's instructions. A sigh or a tilting of the chin or a stiffening of her shoulders that struck Niki as contrary. Yet when she had attempted to recruit Niki to the coaching job, she'd had nothing but praise for her and her coaching style. Her attitude now didn't make sense, and yet there was so little Niki could put her finger on.

"You know that you can talk to me, right? If there's something I'm doing you don't agree with? Or about anything else, for that matter. Any problems we might have with each other, we can work them out, all right? I'm available to talk anytime."

"Of course, Nik. We go back a long way."

"We do." Which was why this growing chasm of emotional distance between the two of them was so mystifying. Over the span of fifteen years, there was a shared trust that went back to their time as teammates and, more recently, from coaching together.

The lift deposited them at the top of the hill. There was no more time to talk as Lynn dug her poles into the snow and pushed off. Niki skate-skied a few steps behind her, then headed down the hill. The snow was light, powdery, like sifted flour, and it took little effort to ski quickly and smoothly, her leg muscles remembering what to do. It had been at least five years since she'd skied, and as the tree line rushed past her and the cold air zapped her lungs, she couldn't think why she'd let it go so long.

Lynn was faster, more powerful in keeping ahead. Which was fine. They could talk again on the ride back up. Eva's warning last night about Lynn, that something might be going on between her and Alison, hadn't strayed far from her thoughts. She'd played it cool with Eva, meaning it when she said she couldn't afford to become emotionally embroiled in something that might very well be a nonstarter. But what if Alison was, in fact, up to her old tricks? What if she was snaring Lynn in something devious? And what kind of a leader would she be if she ignored the warning bells going off in her head? It'd be negligence. And she wasn't a negligent or irresponsible coach. As much as she dreaded it, if something underhanded was going on, she needed to ferret it out and deal with it.

"I need to ask you something," she said carefully to Lynn as the lift inched its way back up the hill. "Is there something going on between you and Alison?"

A hard stare from Lynn, then an instant recalibration of her gaze that was like a stage curtain being lifted to unveil a completely different set. "What do you mean?"

"Are you friends with her? Secretly meeting with her? Inadvertently sharing information? Anything like that? Anything that could compromise this team that I should know about?"

Lynn's face began to pink and not from the cool air. "If you're accusing me of something, then just come out with it."

"I'm not accusing you. I'm asking. There's a big difference."

Lynn's hesitation confirmed there was plenty for Niki to worry about, and with it went her trust for Lynn. *Dammit!* How could they have success on the ice if her assistant coach couldn't be trusted to have the team's best interests at heart? What the *fuck* was going on? Her stomach pitched, and for a moment, she wanted to lean over and throw up.

"There's nothing going on with Alison. You asked me to keep an eye on her, and I am. That's all."

There had to be more, much more. But there was no proof of anything, and little chance Lynn was going to make it easy and give her a big confession. At the top of the hill, knowing she had little other choice, she said, "If there's anything, *anything*, that could compromise our success on the ice in five weeks' time, you need to tell me. And you need to tell me now, because the Olympics is as big as it's going to get for us as coaches and for most of our girls. We can't have anything jeopardize that. We've got to be united in this."

Lynn's smile looked like it was chiseled on her face. "Don't worry, Nik. Everything's going to be fine. We're in the driver's seat, I promise."

As her friend disappeared down the hill, Niki stood on the precipice and wondered, not for the first time, what the hell had gone wrong between them the last few months. And where the hell things were going.

* * *

It was beyond laughable to Eva that both teams should end up at the same time in the hotel restaurant for dinner. Fate was fucking with them, though she knew Niki would be far less amused. Alison looked like a gasket or two was about to blow inside her head. But Eva could see little sense in fuming about something she couldn't control. Maybe there was even a reason they were being thrown together this week. And if there wasn't, hell, it was worth it to sit and watch Alison have an aneurysm.

She chanced a shrug and a smile in Niki's direction before turning her attention to her seatmates. With deadly accuracy, Alison's eyes lobbed darts at Team Canada, which made Eva want to laugh at her display of childishness. If only she spent all that energy coaching them on the ice, Eva thought, they'd be the favorites instead of the underdogs who hadn't won a gold medal since those first Olympics in 1998.

Three seats over, Dani madly texted on her cell phone. Each press of the tiny keypad grew more forceful, as though she might poke her finger right through the phone's metal sheath and into the guts of the thing. Her scowl too looked like it might crack her face. Whatever was going on, it was clear she was pissed about something. Her frenetic texting stopped, but she tapped her phone impatiently, cut a hard glare across the room. Eva followed it, watched it land on Lynn O'Reilly, who suddenly picked up her phone. She read something on it, then typed. It wasn't but a few seconds before Dani's phone chimed with an incoming text.

Holy shit, Eva thought, watching the two text each other, Dani stopping only to glare at Lynn. Lynn didn't return the look, but it couldn't be coincidence that every time Dani texted, Lynn picked up her phone and vice versa. *What the hell are those two up to*? First it was Alison and Lynn with their heads together in that restaurant in Toronto, and now Lynn and Dani were texting? And was Alison aware that she wasn't the only one on the team Lynn was communicating with? She turned her attention to Alison, who had suddenly become engrossed in her menu, either deliberately or coincidentally turning a blind eye to what was going on.

Eva tossed her own menu down, queasiness taking her stomach for a roller-coaster ride. She wanted to tell Niki about the new development, but Niki said last night she didn't want to hear about any of it. Niki wanted to put her head in the goddamned sand and pretend there was no off-ice bullshit, no politics at play, no diabolical manipulations by people who would do anything to gain the upper hand. And there were people on both teams who fit that description to a T.

She tried to capture Niki's attention but couldn't. They'd meet again in the hot tub tonight, and though Niki might want to ignore whatever was going on, Eva sure wasn't going to.

As Dani finally slid her phone back in her pocket, Eva crooked a finger at her to follow her.

In the ladies' washroom, Dani fixed her with a sly look that was meant to be funny but wasn't. "I'm not into washroom sex."

"Ha ha. Want to tell me what you were doing texting Lynn O'Reilly?"

Smugness came easily to the sophomore forward; admission of fault, not so much. "I don't know what you're talking about."

"I saw you doing it. But we can solve this little disagreement right now if you want to show me your phone."

"Like, what*ever*. I don't owe you an explanation about anything I do, especially not about who I text or don't text. You're not my mom, though you're probably old enough to be."

Anger hardened Eva's jaw, but she wouldn't give Dani the satisfaction. "You're right, you don't owe me an explanation, but I'd like one." She couldn't threaten Dani with going to Alison, because chances were Alison was involved in this little scheme too. Scheming and Alison were on a first name basis.

"Yeah, and I'd like a million dollars. Ain't gonna happen."

"You little bitch," Eva muttered under her breath, stepping closer to Dani, towering over her but not touching her. "I won't tolerate a team that has to cheat in order to win, if that's what you're doing. And I'll do everything in my power to stop your bullshit. And Alison's too."

Dani stared her down, not an ounce of respect for the older, more experienced player who would one day be named to the hall of fame. "You've got an inflated sense of self-importance around here, Cruzie. But if you want to tattle on me to your girlfriend, go right ahead. Won't do any good."

"I don't have a girlfriend," Eva seethed, her fists clenched at her sides.

"Whatever. I've seen you making moony eyes at Niki Hartling and I know you two used to get it on, like, a million years ago."

"You know what, Dani? Fuck you. And remember, shit like this has a way of coming around and biting you in the ass. It's called karma. And it's a bitch."

Eva stormed out without a look back. She had no idea what she would do next. It wasn't like her to sit back and play it cool, but maybe that was exactly what she needed to do for once. If Alison and Dani were up to something, it would become evident soon enough.

CHAPTER FIFTEEN

Body Checking

Niki eased herself into the hot tub, already fevered at the sight of Eva, whose arms were cockily spread along the edge of the tub as if she owned it. There was something dangerously alluring about these clandestine, nocturnal meetings in the hot, burbling water with a gorgeous woman who used to be her lover. She should probably feel guilty, but she didn't, because she needed to do something for herself, something a little on the edge, a little unscripted and totally away from the glaring spotlight of the approaching Olympic Games. In this little corner of the world, with Eva, she could be herself and she could let all her tension drain away.

"How was your day?" Eva asked, as though they'd done this a thousand other times. And they had, come to think of it, although it'd been a long time ago.

"Pretty tame, actually. Took the team to see an IMAX film and then we went for a snowshoe hike. How about you?"

"Not so fun. Alison had us hit the gym pretty hard, then forced us to watch that film *Miracle on Ice*. Which she shows the team every year." Eva rolled her eyes. "Next thing you know, we'll all be ordered to wear underwear with the stars and stripes on them."

Niki laughed. "Just don't give my kid any. She has enough stars and stripes stuff, thanks to you."

"Ah, yes, my evil plan to corrupt Rory first, then you."

"Good luck with that. The maple leaf is firmly stamped on my ass."

"Really?" Eva's smile was nervy. And sexy as hell. "I'd like to see that."

"I bet you would." She studied Eva's eyes, at the mischief lurking there, and, if she wasn't mistaken, the sexual desire too. Fleetingly she considered the wisdom of getting the hell out of here, fast, because something was happening between them. Something she couldn't quite name but wanted to. Was the flirting advancing to more serious territory? Was the volatile chemistry between them flaring to life again? All she knew for certain was that thoughts of Eva had filled her mind all week and filled her heart too. Seeing her like this—with her defenses down, her trusting nature exposed, her teasing nature on full display—made Niki long for the woman she'd fallen for when they were barely adults. The advice of a childhood friend's mom drifted back to her, hauntingly so: "Choose your first love wisely, because first loves leave an imprint on your soul that stays with you forever." She refused to believe it at the time, like any fourteen-year-old would. But now? Now the veracity of it was something she'd never question or doubt again.

"Niki…"

"Do we have to?" God, she did not want a deep, emotional discussion about their past, not now. She knew what Eva was going to say, what she wanted from her. But what good would rehashing the past do now? Besides, she wasn't in the mood. She wanted to relax, not have to think about anything at all.

"Yes. I want to talk about us. Because we never have, and because I can't quite reconcile the fact that we both walked away without a look back. I mean, haven't you thought about why we—"

"Seemed to let go so easily?" Of course she had thought about it. They were both competitive people who liked to win, so why *had* they given up so easily? "Eva, I don't know what good—"

"Please, Nik."

Niki sighed, understanding it made sense that if they were to be friends, they were going to have to clear this hurdle. "Fine. I don't know. It was easier to walk away than to fight our way through it, I guess. Look, it's not going to change anything after all these years, all right?"

Eva's face twisted in anguish, shocking Niki, who'd only ever seen Eva express such despair after the loss of a big game. "It might solve the mystery of why my heart can't seem to love anyone else the way I loved you."

"You mean all those women you had after me never managed to capture your heart?"

"I'm being serious."

"So am I." She'd heard plenty of gossip over the years about Eva's many girlfriends, a butterfly sampling the nectar from a multitude of flowers. She stopped herself from twisting the knife a little, because she knew doing so would help loosen the fury anchored at her core.

"I wasn't like you, Nik. I never found someone I wanted to *marry.*"

The sting in Eva's voice was like a slap, and Niki instinctively reeled back. "Look. I wanted stability. I wanted a life that didn't involve chasing a dream I knew was over. I wanted a real job and I wanted to come home to someone at the end of the day. Not…not…act like I was twenty years old forever." She knew her words were a condemnation of the life Eva had chosen, but it was a life she couldn't understand—playing hockey until her body gave out and being paid peanuts to do it, traveling from city to city, flitting from relationship to relationship, never putting down permanent roots. It was a transient, incomplete life. And it wasn't for her.

Eva's gaze settled on the distant mountains, dark shadows contrasted by stark white caps of snow that almost looked like smoke. "I was so stupid back then. I thought there'd be lots more Nikis in my life. I thought there'd be time to find someone else. That there would *be* someone else, someone like you. And I thought I could just go on playing hockey like this forever, I guess." Eva's eyes returned to her, and Niki could feel the weight of their soulfulness. For a moment she had to avert her gaze to keep from getting sucked into their depths.

"I think," Niki said quietly, "when you're young, starting over seems easier than mending what you have. And then at some point it becomes easier to wall off the damage and leave it there." It's what they'd both done.

"Did you love her more than me?"

The brutal bluntness of the question stole Niki's breath, and she tried hard to muffle the audible gasp that escaped her lips. "Of course I loved her. I wouldn't have married her if I hadn't." She knew she hadn't really answered the question, and it angered her that she should be expected to compare, like she was choosing between chocolate and vanilla ice cream.

"But, what I mean..." The glisten of unshed tears was bright in Eva's eyes.

"Eva, don't." It didn't feel right talking about Shannon. At least, not with the woman who'd come before her. And yet, she'd confessed to Shannon everything about Eva, and Shannon hadn't taken it well. Shannon forever after was insecure about Eva, flinched whenever her name came up, sulked openly at the thought, no, the worry, that Niki might have loved Eva more or deeper or better or something, and that she'd been more sexually hungry for Eva than she'd ever been for her. Why, Niki thought with rising frustration, did women become so emotionally preoccupied with third parties? With psychoanalyzing every relationship to death? It should have been enough for Shannon that she had chosen her to marry, and it should have been enough for Eva that she'd been her first love.

"Fine," Eva replied tonelessly. "I get it." She began to rise, but Niki clutched her wrist and held her back.

"I'm not trying to punish you or to be cruel to you."

Eva sat back down and gathered herself. "No. I'm sorry. I had no right."

For several minutes there was only the sound of the water rushing and swirling around their bodies. Niki couldn't still her thoughts, couldn't let herself relax into the kind of tranquility she craved and hadn't found much of since Eva had reappeared in her life.

"Eva, I won't lie to you. I loved you with everything I had. All right? *Everything*."

"But it wasn't enough, was it?"

Niki shook her head. "I think *we* weren't enough. We didn't know what the hell to do with that kind of love. We were kids. Kids who thought everything would continue to come easy to us. Kids who thought the things we had were expendable. Replaceable. Including our relationship. But we can't go back. And we've got to stop kicking ourselves in the ass."

"I'm not asking us to go back."

"Then what?"

Eva leaned close, in the dim light her eyes black and liquid and beguiling. "Kiss me."

* * *

The kiss was a struck match closing in on the tinderbox that was her heart, her sexual core, and Eva didn't, for the moment, care if she got burned. Astonishment that Niki would acquiesce so quickly, that she would so thoroughly return the kiss, quickened Eva's blood and the rush of arousal that threatened to swamp all of her senses. She thirsted for Niki and always had. It wasn't the time to think about what the kiss meant as her lips pressed against Niki's, softness melding with softness, noses and chins and cheeks adjusting and fitting together seamlessly, not having forgotten a thing. They'd always fit perfectly together, even in the early days when they were all awkward fingers and fumbling hands and inexperienced but eager tongues.

It was several breathless moments before Niki gently pulled away.

"I've been wanting to do that since the first time I saw you after our breakup," Eva confessed.

"You mean last fall?"

"No. Six years ago at that charity auction for women's hockey at the Hockey Hall of Fame."

Niki laughed. "You didn't exactly look like you wanted to kiss me, if I remember correctly. You looked like you wanted to duct tape me to a hockey net and take slap shots at me."

"No, I wanted to kiss you. But yeah, I was hurt and angry." Eva grinned. "Slap shots wouldn't have been a bad idea, though."

"Why were you angry with me?"

"I was pissed that you were married and that she was there with you. That she wasn't me. It was unreasonable, but at the time, I wanted to blame you." Eva's voice was barely a whisper now. "It was easier than blaming myself."

Niki's lips pursed together, maintaining her silence.

"I know you don't want to talk about her, Nik, but I want to apologize. I acted badly. I was jealous. Hurt. Maybe I still am, I don't know."

Niki's voice shook with reproach. "She was my wife. And she's dead. You can't possibly be jealous of a ghost."

Yes, I can, Eva thought. Any further discussion was dashed when Niki heaved herself out of the tub. "Wait, Nik, please." *Goddamn it!* She'd fucked things up again. She couldn't help but think Niki didn't want to hear her deepest thoughts, just as she hadn't wanted to hear her suspicions about Alison, Lynn and Dani. *Why do we always seem to misunderstand each other?*

"It's late. I need to get back."

Eva bit back her disappointment. "Tomorrow night. Instead of the hot tub, I rented the ice at the arena down the road for an hour. Just for the two of us. Bring your skates, your stick, your gloves. I'll bring pucks. What do you say?"

Niki quirked an eyebrow at her. "Are you suggesting a little one-on-one?"

Eva hitched her chin. "I am. If you're not scared, that is."

"Ha! I'm not scared. I could always beat you one-on-one."

"That's right. Past tense. But if you're so sure, bring some pocket change."

"Oh, I'll bring more than pocket change."

They laughed, Niki's eyes alight with mirth. It felt so damned good to laugh together again.

"All right. I'll see you there at ten o'clock. As long as we don't have an audience."

There was an unspoken agreement that neither wanted to provoke malicious gossip by being seen publicly together. There was nothing technically forbidden about it, but it could easily be misinterpreted and provide an unwelcome distraction.

Niki draped a large towel around her shoulders. "See you there."

CHAPTER SIXTEEN

One-on-one

There was nothing better than a shiny, glistening virgin sheet of ice. Niki loved how it was free of blemishes, free of blades having dug in and carved out previous journeys. She liked being the first one on the ice, the first to brand it, and tonight was no exception. Her skates snugly tied, she stepped onto the ice and took off at a running start, building up steam, leaning and tucking low into the first turn, the way a race car tightly hugs a curve. She hadn't lost much speed since her playing days, half a stride at most. Many had told her that she could and should still be playing at the highest level, but she responded to their flattery with ambivalence. Years ago, becoming a wife and a mother had fully occupied her heart, with the setting down of roots in one place too tempting and then too fulfilling to ignore. Coaching had challenged her, had filled any void left by hanging up her skates. She had no regrets.

Eva's blades dug into the ice behind her, gaining on Niki, but Niki wasn't worried; it would probably take half a lap for Eva to catch her at this point. Once Eva did catch her with her long strides, she'd leave her in her dust. Unless Eva's bum knees were giving her trouble tonight.

Three laps later, Niki and Eva glided to a stop at center ice, both equally spent.

"I see your knee is okay," Niki said, panting.

"You want the full scouting report on it and if I'll be playing at a hundred percent?" Eva smiled between gulps of air.

"Nope. No shoptalk tonight. I just wanted to know if I need to take it easy on you or not."

"In your dreams!"

Eva took off, stick in one hand, a canvas bag in the other. At the blue line, she dumped pucks from the bag into a disordered pile. Next, she skated to the net and duct-taped paper targets to each of its four corners.

"Oh, no you don't," Niki said, shaking her head. "You were always a more accurate shooter than me. What are the stakes?" She'd forgotten to bring cash.

The playfulness in Eva's eyes bordered on dangerous. "Why don't we let the winner decide what the loser forfeits?"

"Hmm. Not sure I care for my odds right now. What other little contests have you dreamed up for us?"

"Don't worry. Stuff that you'll kick my ass in, like puck handling and deking." Eva's voice dropped an octave. "And one-on-one, of course."

She thought about retorting that they'd both win at one-on-one but decided the double entendre was too much.

"You know something," Niki said after each had taken eight shots, Eva hitting all four targets with her first five shots, Niki taking eight shots to hit them. "I never thought we'd be friends like this again."

"Me either. But I'm glad. And relieved. Especially since I admitted my juvenile jealousy last night. You'd have every right to throw me into the nearest snowbank."

"Ha. As if I could." Eva had four inches on her and probably fifteen pounds of muscle.

"All right, since you can't, then I'll risk a question." Eva busied herself setting up a dozen small orange pylons she'd found on one of the benches. By the time she finished, Niki figured she'd forgotten the question. No such luck.

"Last fall," Eva said. "You were jealous of Kathleen. Why?"

"I wasn't, not really."

Eva's eyebrows rose slowly and cynically. It was a look that, in the past, more often than not elicited a quick confession from Niki. It still had, it seemed, the same annoying effect.

"All right, it wasn't jealousy so much as feeling annoyed. I know you've had a lot of girlfriends since we were together."

"I've had a few, yes. Why does that bother you?"

Oh for God's sake, Niki thought. Why must they play this little game of true confession about stuff that was ancient history? What did Eva want her to say? That lately she woke up wet dreaming of making love with her? That she'd never fully expunged her from her heart, even while she was married to somebody else? That many, many times, she'd quietly wondered what would have happened if they hadn't broken up twelve years ago? And yes, that it hurt like hell whenever she heard Eva was with someone.

Instead, she looked around and said, "What are we doing with *this* little contest?"

"Deke around the pylons. With speed. A point gets docked for every pylon you touch."

With her stick, Niki claimed a puck and weaved her way through the tightly placed pylons, barely nicking the last one. "Your turn."

Eva took off, the puck on the end of her stick as though it were on a string. Her hands moved in sync with her feet as she curled the puck around the pylons, but first her stick, and then the puck, hit the final two pylons. "All right, best out of three?"

"Fine. Go for it, but I'll still kick your ass."

Niki did.

"All right, one-on-one for the tiebreaker. Best of seven."

Eva started first, with Niki defending. She came at her with so much speed and aggression that it put Niki on her heels. It was a tiny hesitation, but enough to allow Eva to easily deke around her and shoot the puck into the net. When it was Niki's turn, she used her quick hands and feet to get the best of Eva, kicking the puck to her right skate, then back to her left and up to the blade of her stick for a quick shot.

"Nice job! You know, don't you," Eva said, preparing to take her turn, "that there's no need to be jealous."

Niki thought Eva was talking about their one-on-one contest. "I'm not. I'm extremely confident in my superior abilities."

Eva laughed. "And so you should be. But I'm not talking about hockey." Her eyes turned serious. "None of them made me forget about you."

Niki's mouth fell open as Eva stormed past her, planting the puck in the back of the net. "Dammit, that's not fair. You distracted me!"

Eva grinned with that brand of cockiness that was so familiar. "Your turn."

Niki took a puck and started around the pylons, her concentration shot. Did Eva mean it, that none of her transitory women could compare? And if so, why did the declaration matter so much? Was her own ego really in that much need of a boost? And most of all, why did it matter *now*? She didn't want to consider why her mouth had gone dry and her legs weak.

As she rounded on the final pylon, her back skate caught the one behind it and in the next instant she was sailing through the air, her only thought being that she hoped it didn't hurt too much when she hit the ice, which felt like cold cement. She tried to cushion the blow with her gloved hands, since she didn't have the comforting protection of elbow pads, chest protector or the padded hockey pants. As she hit the ice she became a curling stone skidding out of control, the smooth nylon of her wind pants every bit as slippery as the ice surface. She spun as she slid, stopping only when she hit something hard and stationary. She gasped as Eva dropped like a tree felled partway up, tumbling ungracefully onto Niki. They spun to a stop together, Eva on top of her.

"Oh my God," Niki said, afraid for Eva because of the frailty her knees. "I'm so sorry. Shit. Are you okay?"

Eva, collecting herself, hadn't moved much. She placed her hands on the ice on either side of Niki, her face inches away, her body touching Niki's along the length of it. *Oh Jesus*, Niki thought, sucking in her breath, not wanting to release it. Not wanting to release Eva either. What was it about wanting, no, needing, Eva's touch lately? Was she really that starved for another woman's touch? For her body to take a trip down memory lane?

She thought of Shannon, gone for almost three-and-a-half years now, sick for months before that, and a sob collected in her throat. She burned with fury, again, at being left alone. When she married Shannon, it was supposed to be for life. A long life. She never signed on for being lonely, for having to figure out the rest of her life alone, for starting all over again. She'd been cheated. Shannon, of course, had been cheated most of all, and so had Rory. None of it was fair, dammit.

She hadn't noticed Eva's finger reaching up until it brushed a tear from her cheek.

"I'm okay," Eva whispered. "But you're not, are you?"

Niki cleared her throat. She didn't want to expose herself this way to Eva. "I'm fine."

* * *

Eva's chest hurt, so badly did she want to kiss Niki. All it would take was closing the inch or two of space between their mouths. And the way Niki was looking up at her, with the glisten of tears shimmering in her eyes, with her lips parted in anticipation, it would be so easy to kiss away her sadness. She burned with the thought of it, with the memory of their languid, sensual kiss in the hot tub last night. She'd thought of little else since.

Something in Niki's expression made her stop cold. Fear maybe? Too much raw need? Eva had the feeling that if she kissed Niki now it would be all wrong, that one or both of them would regret it and that it would *never* happen again.

Eva pulled back an inch. There was so much to say, and yet her mind drew a blank. "I'm sorry, Niki. But I'm your friend and I'm here for you, okay?"

"No, you can't be," Niki said, swiping at a stray tear on her chin and forcing Eva to ease herself off. "Both our teams hit the road the day after tomorrow. We won't see each other until the Games start in five weeks. And even then, we'll only see each other on the ice."

"I know." *Shit.* Eva sat up, and so did Niki. "But we can email, text, talk on the phone."

"No. I don't want a paper trail. After Alison's stunt twelve years ago, I don't want any emails or texts getting intercepted or hacked or leaked or whatever. We can't chance that kind of communication."

"All right, you're right. We can talk on the phone, then. Please. Nik, I meant what I said about being your friend. About being here for you. You're not the only one who gets lonely, you know." She wasn't being entirely truthful, because she wanted more than a distant friendship with Niki, much more. But now wasn't the time or place to press.

Niki stood up and skated to the gate that led to the change room, leaving Eva no choice but to follow.

"Wait," Eva implored. "Promise me I'm not losing you just when I found you again."

Niki looked one minute like she wanted to collapse into Eva's arms, the next like she wanted to run away as fast and as far as she could. There had to be a tug of war going on in her mind.

"Tomorrow," Eva said, unwilling to accept that this might be the last time they see one another until the final game of the Olympics. "It's our last day here. Can you sneak away at five o'clock?"

"My girls are meeting with a sports psychologist all afternoon in a seminar, and the dinner's being catered. Why?"

"How about meeting me at the Whistler Brewing Company for a drink and dinner. My team's busy too, so there'll be no chance of us running into others there. It's a quiet place off the beaten path, I promise." She rolled her eyes. "Alison's having us all meet with a nutritionist, who's going to put us to work cooking dinner. I've done it a million times before. I'll say I'm not feeling well. Can you get away?"

"Yes, I can get away, though I'm not sure meeting in public's a good idea."

Eva lowered her voice. "How about my hotel room, then?"

"Absolutely not!" Niki smiled, and although it was a weak smile, it was enough to make Eva's heart cartwheel. At least they'd have one more evening together. "All right, against my better judgment, I'll meet you at the restaurant."

"Hey." She stepped closer until she could feel the heat from Niki's body, but she was careful not to touch her again. "I had fun tonight."

"So did I. Thank you, Eva. I needed it. And I'm sorry about—"

"Forget it. Is it okay if I hug you?"

Niki stepped into her arms and they held the embrace for a few seconds. It wasn't long enough, but it was just as well, because any longer and Eva might not be able to stop herself from doing something stupid.

"Goodbye, Eva."

"See you tomorrow night, Nik. Sleep well."

* * *

Eva spent the next day fidgeting and counting down the hours until five o'clock rolled around. She arrived at the restaurant early so she could grab a table in a dimly lit corner from which they could see the door. It didn't hurt to be too careful.

"I feel like we're having a torrid love affair," she said after Niki strolled in wearing a heavy coat pulled up to her ears and sat down across from her. There was no trace of the pain that had been etched so clearly on her face at the arena last night.

"We practically are." Niki laughed. "Minus the sex."

We can easily change that, Eva wanted to say but didn't dare. "I ordered you a beer. Dark, as I recall." She'd ordered a honey lager for herself.

"Thanks. Good memory."

A waitress set two sweating glasses down in front of them along with a couple of menus. She recommended the corned beef on rye, which was a good enough sell for both of them.

"I know I'm going out on a limb here," Eva said after a sip of beer. "But I think you feel guilty around me sometimes. Because of Shannon, right?"

"Eva—"

"No, Nik." This time she was ready to throw all her cards on the table, because it would be weeks before they saw each other again. Leaning across the table, she whispered urgently, "We need to talk about this. It's important for me to figure out how we feel about one another. Do you know how much I want to take you in my arms? How much I want to kiss you again? How badly I want to make love to you? God, don't you know I've never fallen out of love with you?"

Niki slammed her eyes shut. "I can't. We can't. It's—"

"What? Wrong? Is that what you were going to say?"

Niki opened her eyes only to lose herself in her glass of beer. Why did she try so damned hard to always be in control? She had to be the moral one, the rule minder, always doing the right thing. For once, Eva wished she'd find the courage to go with her gut, her heart.

Unwilling to wait any longer for Niki to reply, Eva said, "Well, it's not wrong. We're both single. We both have feelings for one another."

"You think we're supposed to pick up where we left off all those years ago?"

"Yes. I do." Well, not exactly, but it was close enough to the truth.

"In case you haven't noticed, we're on two rival teams embarking on our biggest battle in four years. On the biggest stage in the world. We'd be a sideshow, and I won't have that."

"I know that, but I wasn't talking about this minute. I can wait another six or seven weeks. Mostly." She winked to lighten the mood, even as sweat broke out on her hairline and under her arms. "Or we could just keep sneaking around."

The last part was meant as a joke, but Niki thumped her glass down hard, some of the beer sloshing over. Her eyes were ablaze. "A lot has changed in twelve years. I have responsibilities now. A lot of them, in case you haven't noticed. I'm not…I can't just sleep with you or have a fling with you."

Calmly, Eva said, "That's not what I'm asking."

"Then the answer is an even bigger no."

Eva felt the blood drain from her face. "Why?"

Their sandwiches and sweet potato fries arrived, the timing providing Niki a convenient escape route. They both chewed their food for a few moments before Eva attempted to resume the conversation. She couldn't let it end without at least some answers.

"Why won't you give me, us, another chance?"

"Eva, like I said, my life is complicated now. I have a job. I have a kid. And right now, the past is exactly that, the past."

Anger rose in Eva like a geyser. Her Italian blood was set to boil, and it took all her willpower to keep from exploding. "The past is where, I think, you spend a lot of your time. Too much. That and stewing in guilt and self-punishment."

Niki's face darkened predictably. Eva had hit the nail on the head, that at the root of Niki's stubborn resistance was her guilt. And her refusal to allow herself some happiness. "I'm not going to talk about this with you anymore."

"Fine," Eva said tonelessly, taking a big bite of her sandwich, confident that Niki couldn't evade her questions forever. She was deep enough, smart enough, to give the proper consideration to the matter. But in her own due time. "We can talk about how my team's going to kick your ass in Vancouver in a few weeks."

There was a long, tense moment before Niki broke into a slow grin that was as welcome as a cool breeze on a sweltering day. They raised their glasses and clinked them in the communal embrace of this strange and unique situation—former lovers, somewhat friends, who in a few weeks' time, would do all they could to destroy one another's gold medal dream.

Eva's desire to kiss Niki was never stronger.

CHAPTER SEVENTEEN

Penalty Shot

The altitude and the cold January air made for a frigid walk back to the hotel, but at least it was a dry cold, Niki convinced herself, and not at all like the humid cold off the Great Lakes back in Windsor that made it feel much colder than it was. Nevertheless, she wrapped her scarf a little tighter around her throat and gave a little shudder.

"Cold?" Eva, walking beside her, moved close enough for their shoulders to touch.

"I'm fine." She didn't want Eva wrapping her arm around her, disguised as a warming gesture. Eva had made her intentions clear back at the restaurant, and while Niki didn't want to talk about it, she couldn't stop thinking about it. How could Eva possibly suggest they get back together? Had that one kiss made her lose her mind? So much time had elapsed, so many things had happened in the interim. Especially to Niki. She'd married Shannon and then lost her, become a single parent to Rory, hung up her skates as a player, joined the coaching ranks, left the coaching ranks to teach at the university, joined the coaching ranks again.

She wasn't the same person anymore. Grief and the responsibilities of parenthood had tamed once and for all any adventurous streak she might have had. So had coaching a group of women who, for the most part, were a decade or more younger than she was. Spontaneous, she was not. Carefree, no way. She was mature, methodical, a leader. She didn't take risks or do stupid things like have a fling with her ex-girlfriend. The fact that Eva was anxious to get involved again, well, what did that say about Eva? That she was still a rolling stone with nothing to lose. That she remained somehow stuck in the past, blinded by something that no longer existed. Or by something that could never last. Yeah, that was Eva, looking for the next thrill, this time at Niki's expense. Well, hell. It wasn't going to happen. Not this time.

Eva guided her into a narrow cobblestoned alleyway, a shortcut back to the hotel, she explained.

"Eva, look. I was thinking, back at the brewery, I didn't explain myself ver—"

In one swift move that Niki never saw coming, Eva pushed her up against the brick wall, crushing her body against her. She pressed her mouth to Niki's, cutting off any further conversation, and kissed her hard, unequivocally, possessively, thoroughly. Niki inserted her hands between them to create space, but Eva was having none of it. She pushed herself harder into Niki, kissed her more deeply, until a warmth, thick as honey, began to roll through Niki's insides. She shivered again, but not from the cold this time.

The kiss went on, ungluing her from all sense and rational thought. *Oh fuck*, she thought, silently acknowledging that all the road signs pointed to danger ahead and yet all she could do was press harder on the gas pedal. It'd been so long since she'd felt this kind of animal attraction for someone, been so swamped with desire. The feeling was foreign, like a memory she couldn't quite bring to the front of her mind, and yet it was the most familiar thing in the world. It was wrong and yet it couldn't be more right. It was Eva, the first woman she'd ever made love to. Her first love. Her only sexual addiction. When they were young, they couldn't get enough of one another. Sex in the shower, sex before (and after) breakfast, sex before (and after) dinner, sex at bedtime, sometimes sex in the middle of the night too. One had only to lift an eyebrow in the other's direction before they were peeling off clothes, grinding into one another or sliding hands, mouths, tongues, between legs, sending one another to the moon and back on wave after wave of orgasm.

Her hands found Eva's thick hair now, her fingers clutching and tangling themselves there. She pressed her mouth and her body against Eva's, matching her power, reveling in the familiarity of Eva's body—the feel of her hard muscles that at the same time easily yielded and molded to her, the smell of her skin and hair (cedarwood and jasmine), the softness of her lips. How, after all these years, could her hunger for Eva ignite so effortlessly? So quickly? So completely? And what did it say about her love for her wife? Was it gone, buried six feet under along with Shannon's cancer-riddled body? Or had her marriage been a sham to begin with? Why else, it occurred to her, would she be so demolished, so trashed, by her desire for Eva.

The thoughts raced around in her mind like a carnival ride, fighting what her body demanded. Hands, warmer than they should be, reached under her coat and crept up to her breasts, making her gasp and clench her teeth as Eva's mouth dropped to her throat. Her nipples, goddamn them, tightened painfully, and she reared her head back against the brick wall. She had to take control of this before it was too late.

"No, Eva." She put her hand to Eva's chest and pushed her away. "We can't do this."

"We don't have to talk about the future right now. I get that." Eva's voice cracked with unspent desire. "We can take it a step at a time. One slow step at a time. I can wait for this, Niki, I promise you I can."

Still catching her breath, Niki said, "That's not the message your body is sending. It seems to me like you want it all right now."

Eva's grin brought a rush of warmth to Niki's face. "Of course I want you in my bed. I've never stopped wanting you in my bed. And you know I want more, but I also understand why we can't. At least right now."

"So what was all…this about?" Niki spread her hands out. "For old time's sake or something?"

"Dammit, Niki!" Eva ran her hands through her hair. "I wasn't thinking, okay? I just…I don't know." She sagged against the opposite wall, the tension visibly leaking from her body like air from a balloon. "I've never stopped loving you. Never stopped wanting you. All those other women…I meant what I said at the rink last night. They weren't you. And I guess I thought eventually one of them would be like you, but they weren't. Not even close. You ruined me for anyone else."

Niki stepped closer. There was a tear on Eva's cheek, illuminated silver by the soft glow of a streetlamp a dozen yards away. Eva never cried, and seeing that she was doing exactly that knocked the air from Niki's chest.

"I'm so sorry, Eva."

Roughly, Eva said, "I just want a chance, Nik. Even if we can't, if we don't ever…I need something that gives me a sliver of hope, all right? I want to somehow make things right with you again."

Niki swallowed. There were too many confusing things tangled up in her mind, in her heart, right now, to even consider having an honest conversation with Eva about where they stood. She needed time. And some distance, because when they were together, her brain went as mushy as the snow beneath her boots.

"Look," Niki said. "I promise you, you're not the only one who suffered from our breakup. And I'm not saying never to us, okay? But I *am* saying not right now."

Eva straightened, wiped the tear from her cheek. "Well, I guess that's something, isn't it?" Her tone had a bite to it, which Niki chose to ignore.

"Walk me back to the hotel?"

"Of course," Eva said, but she remained silent during the five-minute journey.

"I'll go in first," Niki said. "Maybe you could wait a couple more minutes."

"Fine."

"Eva, I know you want more, but you've got to give me space. Time. I have some things to work out before I move on with anybody. Including you. I'm not there yet, and right now I need to focus all my energy on these damned Games, all right? That part, I know you get."

Eva nodded soberly. "I guess I'll see you in Vancouver in a few weeks."

"You will."

"Is Rory going to be there?"

Niki's heart stuttered a beat at the mention of her daughter's name. She hadn't forgotten how well Eva and Rory had hit it off in Toronto. On the phone, Rory still asked about Eva. "She's flying in for the two weeks."

Eva smiled, and the sadness it failed to veil cracked Niki's heart. "Good. I'll see her there too, then."

Niki took the stairs to her fourth-floor room, glad for the time alone in the echoing, cinder block stairwell so she could clear her mind. She was taking the easy way out with Eva, telling her she needed to concentrate on hockey right now, on getting her shit together, which was true. They both had their priorities, and becoming lovers, or something more, wasn't— couldn't—get in the way of those priorities. As for beyond the Games, well, she simply didn't have the mental or emotional energy to think about that right now.

In the corridor, the sound of loud voices made her stop in front of Lynn's door. There was shouting, two women going at it, but their words were muffled, impossible to decipher. She hesitated only a moment before rapping sharply on the door. If Lynn was in some kind of trouble, perhaps she could help, or at least break up the yelling match. But as she knocked, the yelling halted. *Goddammit, Lynn, open the door.* She knocked again, faintly making out some rustling noises in the room, before Lynn finally opened the door.

"Are you okay?" Niki asked. "What's going on?"

"Nothing, why?"

"What do you mean, nothing? I heard yelling, two people arguing, a minute ago." She tried to look past Lynn, but her assistant coach was a big woman.

"I'm the only one here," Lynn said with a look of bewilderment. "I had the TV on, maybe you heard that?"

It damn well wasn't a television she heard; it was Lynn arguing with someone. But she couldn't exactly force her way into the room. "You're sure you're okay?"

"Yes, absolutely. Thanks for checking, though. Goodnight."

Niki stepped back, more convinced than ever that Lynn was up to her ears in something. But if it was personal, it wasn't any of her business, just as her own private relationships—her renewed friendship with Eva, for instance—wasn't any of Lynn's business. "All right. Goodnight."

* * *

Eva watched her tape-to-tape pass to Dani bounce off her stick and sail wide into the corner. In frustration she smacked her own stick against the ice and shot a look at Alison, who quickly looked away. Dani was about as focused as a five-year-old kid on a sugar high. It was the third consecutive pass she'd outright missed. Passes that should have been easy to corral.

On the next drill, Dani's lack of concentration sent the entire line in offside. Once again Alison, who would have had a stroke if it'd been anyone but her precious Dani screwing up, didn't seem to notice.

Eva skated to Dani and tried to cool her temper before she spoke. The team was supposed to be getting tighter, cleaner at this point, not sloppier. The Olympic Games started in a little less than two weeks, and if her line didn't get its shit together, the three of them were going to be busted down to the fourth line. "What's up, Comps? You seem distracted today."

"I'm fine," Dani hissed and peeled away.

Great, Eva thought, *she won't even listen to me*. Alison was being of absolutely no support. She was so sick of all the drama and bullshit. She didn't remember it being this emotionally exhausting twelve years ago in Nagano or eight years ago in Salt Lake. Well, okay, maybe it was this bad, but she knew one thing: her patience, her ability to let things roll off her back, had diminished over the years.

She leaned against the boards, watching the next line of forwards execute the power play drill perfectly—the way her own line should have done. A curtain was slowly lifting in her mind, because for the first time she could remember, she could envision a future that didn't include ever playing competitive hockey again. The picture was a bit gauzy, very much unfocused, but it was there. And it wasn't entirely because her body was breaking down from all the wear and tear, nor because of all the drama and stress. Mostly it was because her needs, her desires, had begun to shift and change, taking on new shapes. Niki's reappearance in her life made her see that there was much more to life outside the hockey rink. She'd been stubborn, selfish, too immature to realize it the first time around with Niki. A glory seeker, an adrenaline junkie, that's what she'd been those years ago. More recently too. But the sun didn't—couldn't—stay at high noon all day. And she no longer wanted it to.

Her thoughts drifted to what it would be like coming home to someone at the end of the day, sharing her life with that person—the big things and the little things, the highs and lows and everything in between. Where she didn't before, she was beginning to understand the appeal of building a life with someone, of becoming something that was bigger than herself. A vision of Rory floated through her mind, and she smiled. What would being a stepmom be like? Especially to a young girl who seemed to click with her, a kindred spirit in a four-foot-nine frame. She could easily imagine herself and Niki teaching hockey skills to Rory, cheering her on at her games. Maybe the two of them even coaching her team. Now that would be a hoot! Rory was—

"Psst! Eva!" Kath waved frantically to her from the gate that led to the locker room.

Eva skated over to her. "What's up?"

"There's something you need to see." From behind her back, she pulled out a copy of the *Vancouver Province* and held it up for Eva to see.

"Yeah, so?"

Kathleen flipped to the sports pages, pointing to a headline above the fold that read: "Coach Caught in Compromising Position with Rival Player."

Eva's face, her whole body, went numb. "Oh, fuck."

CHAPTER EIGHTEEN

Checking from Behind

Niki's BlackBerry buzzed with an incoming call. "Hello?"

"Coach Hartling, this is Jason Danko from The Sports Network. Do you care to comment about the photo in today's *Vancouver Province*?"

"Excuse me? What photo?"

The reporter hesitated, cleared his throat like he didn't want to have to spell things out. "Uh, the picture of you in a hot tub, kissing Eva Caruso."

"What?" She was walking to her rented car in the rink's parking lot and couldn't be sure she'd heard correctly. She adjusted the volume on her phone. "Can you repeat that please?"

He did. Niki's knees wobbled and she leaned against her car to steady herself. Everything she'd put into her job since early September—the long hours on and off the ice, the punishing travel, the endless meetings, the agonizing over strategies—was quicksand moving and shifting and sinking beneath her feet. Because she knew what this meant. "No, I have nothing to say right now."

As soon as she ended the call the phone rang again. "Hartling here."

It was a radio reporter this time, asking the same thing. "No. I have nothing to say at this time."

She got into her car and started it. She'd been planning to get a bite to eat, but now all she wanted was the sanctuary of her hotel room. A complimentary copy of the paper was stuffed under her door every morning, and earlier today, like every other morning lately, she'd been in a hurry and stepped over it.

Her phone buzzed again. "What?" she barked into it.

"Niki, it's Dan Smolenski."

Shit. There went her final shred of doubt that a compromising photo did, in fact, exist. "Guess we need to talk. Are you in town?"

He'd flown in last night, he told her. With the opening of the Games eleven days away, the executives of all the leagues were beginning to arrive in Vancouver. The women's team had been ensconced in the city for a few days now, getting acclimated to the city and to the rink at GM Place, where they would play their games.

"I'll book us a conference room at your hotel," he said, his tone divulging nothing of the shitstorm that was surely coming. "I'll be there in an hour. Make sure you and Coach O'Reilly are both there."

Niki's heart leapt to her throat. How stupid, stupid, *stupid* of her to have kissed Eva. And in public, no less. A minute, two tops, of reckless, selfish, irresponsible behavior in that damned hot tub. And for that, she, and by extension her team, were going to pay for it with something worse than their blood— their dreams.

She stopped at the nearest convenience store for a newspaper, unwilling to wait for the one sitting in her hotel room. With trembling fingers, she opened the paper to the sports section.

The headline screamed out at her like a wagging finger of condemnation: "Coach Caught in Compromising Position with Rival Player" and the subhead, "Hartling Kisses Up to Team USA—Literally." Below was a photo, the size of at least a third of the page, showing two women kissing in a hot tub, the caption suggesting it was Niki and Eva getting cozy in a resort hot tub last month in Whistler. The photo was dark, grainy, but the two figures did vaguely—okay, a little more than vaguely—resemble her and Eva. The story, mercifully, was short and little more than speculation from unnamed sources. The only named source was a so-called friend of a player on one of the teams, who said Niki and Eva had once lived together—that wasn't news—and that rumors suggested they'd rekindled their romance. Another source, an anonymous "insider" with Team USA, squarely fixed the blame on Niki, saying an affair with Eva meant she'd intentionally compromised her team and that her credibility as a coach was damaged beyond repair. The source practically dared Hockey Canada to keep her on the bench.

The shadow of a migraine began to throb as Niki drove back to the hotel, her foot pressing harder on the gas pedal than was wise. The story and photo had to be Alison's doing. Her record spoke for itself—that she'd stop at nothing to drive a wedge between her and Eva, that she'd do anything to give her team an edge, that she'd be only too happy to destroy and humiliate Niki in the process. And even if Smolenksi didn't blow things up, she knew that a distraction like this so close to the Games could be catastrophic for her team.

Lynn was already aware of the situation by the time Niki collected her at the hotel. In the elevator to the floor that housed the conference rooms, her assistant coach could hardly look at her.

"I suppose you knew nothing about this until today?" Niki asked carefully.

Lynn concentrated on the ceiling. "Of course not."

"Are you going to tell me I was reckless? That I was courting danger having anything to do with Eva in Whistler?"

Lynn continued to stare at the ceiling. "Nope." Her tone implied that she couldn't be more disinterested.

"It never went beyond what happened in that photo, you know. I'd never put myself, or my team, at greater risk than a stupid, ill-timed kiss." Niki was more fucking sorry than Lynn or anyone else could ever try to make her feel. And yes, there'd been that dark alley too, but she couldn't even think about that right now.

Lynn shifted from foot to foot, pressed the elevator button again as if by doing so, it would speed up and she could escape Niki faster. Niki wondered why Lynn hated her so much, what she could have possibly done to offend her so much. And why couldn't she have her back like a good teammate? She would never expect Lynn to lie for her or cover for her, but couldn't she show at least a little support?

Dan Smolenski and a woman he introduced as Megan Reed, a lawyer for Team Canada, greeted Niki and Lynn in the conference room, their postures erect, their faces funereal.

Niki took the offensive and explained, in a matter-of-fact tone, what happened in Whistler. She was not going to act like a victim, like she'd been set up. The blame was entirely hers, but she wasn't going down without a fight. She looked at Megan. "I suppose it's pointless to file a libel suit against the newspaper."

"Yes, it's pointless, because they're not saying anything that isn't true."

"But I haven't rekindled my relationship with Eva Caruso nor am I having an affair with her, so that part is untrue. We're friends. We had a moment in the hot tub. But that's all it was, a moment and a regrettable one at that. I would never do anything that would hurt my team or risk my credibility as head coach of that team." Thank God, she thought, that things hadn't gone any further with Eva, that she'd come to her senses in time.

"Still," Megan said, "that's splitting hairs, and I think the last thing you want to do is go into great detail about what did and didn't happen between you and Eva. It'll only give the story legs."

"Right," Dan added. "Don't breathe any more life into it than what's already there."

"Well, I'm not going to lie about it," Niki said. "I'm not going to write a tell-all book about Eva and me, but I can't deny that something happened."

"No, you're right about that," Dan said, steepling his fingers on the table in front of him. "We'll just say it was a one-off, that you two were talking about old times or something, that you both got carried away for a few seconds."

"That's basically what it was," Niki said. "Except I don't want people thinking I regularly go around kissing women in hot tubs."

Dan waved his hand impatiently. "Nobody cares about that. They only—"

"I care," Niki cut in, her voice rising. "I don't want my players thinking I'm—"

"Whoa, wait," Dan cautioned. "That's a conversation between you and your players. A private conversation. I'm talking about the media. We keep it short, sweet, to the point, and as truthful as possible." He glanced at Megan, who nodded her agreement. "Then we hope like hell the reporters have somebody else to talk about tomorrow."

That wasn't good enough for Niki. "What about finding out who's behind this? Aren't we going to address that?" She glanced at Lynn, willing her to lend some verbal support to the idea, but Lynn was a stone.

"Absolutely not," Dan said. "Whoever it was, we don't want to give them any more power over this than they already have. We own it, we take responsibility for it, we move on. End of story."

Niki could feel the room spinning, and for a moment she had to shut her eyes against it. Maybe it didn't matter to the rest of them, but it mattered to her who was trying to undermine her. It was obviously someone who had a great deal to gain. And who was to say they'd stop at a photo?

"I've called a press conference in the lobby thirty minutes from now," Dan continued. "We're going to draw up a statement, which I'll read, although I want you both there." He looked from Niki to Lynn. "And I'll be the only one taking questions. Understood?"

Both women nodded.

"One other thing," he said, the ropey muscles of his jaw working. "Niki, it's too close to the Games to remove you from the coaching staff. It would cause pandemonium at this point, both within the team and in the public sphere." His gaze swung to Lynn. "Lynn, from now until the Games are over, you'll take over head coaching duties with Niki as your assistant. Basically, you'll be swapping roles."

A gate crashed down in Niki's mind. "What?" she managed to croak.

Dan shrugged, snapped shut his briefcase. It was a *fait accompli*. She looked next at Lynn, who hadn't moved, hadn't said a thing, but there was a sense of satisfaction in her eyes that irked Niki. If Niki wasn't mistaken, Lynn looked happy about the turn of events.

"I'm sorry, Niki," Dan said, "but we have to do something in response. This will send a message that your behavior in Whistler is not acceptable, that we take very seriously any insinuation that the team's interests have been compromised. This assures the team, our sponsors and our fans that the team is bigger than any one person. But keeping you on the bench means we still have faith in your abilities, that the team will have some continuity. In other words, your actions were careless but not criminal."

"Gee, thanks for the vote of confidence." Niki rose from her seat in a daze, tears prickling the backs of her eyes. "I need some air."

* * *

Listening to Hockey Canada's press conference live on the radio, Eva paced her hotel room like an automaton, needing to keep her body in motion. A sports station was carrying the presser, which was just as well, because Eva was this close to crashing the event.

The news that someone had deliberately set out to hurt her and Niki was a stunner and a painful reminder of how far people would go in the world of sports to hurt an opponent. It was clear that Niki was the target, which only roused Eva's protective instinct. She imagined holding Niki, saying soothing things, promising things that would make it all better. In truth there was little she could do to make any of it better except to see how Niki was doing, and even that was ill-advised. Besides, Niki was probably pissed as hell at her. And understandably so.

"Dammit," she said to Kathleen, who sat on the opposite bed watching her. "I was such an *idiot*, kissing her like that. A stupid, egotistic jerk. She warned me there could be trouble if we let things get out of hand, that it wasn't the right time. But did I listen?"

"You couldn't have known you guys were going to get found out like that."

She balled her hands into fists. "If—no, *when*—I find out who did this, I'm going to kick their ass all the way to the other coast."

What they'd done in Whistler, simply expressing their attraction to one another, an attraction that had never really stopped simmering below the boiling point, wasn't wrong on its own. But in the greater context, she could see how the kiss could be interpreted as disloyalty, a betrayal to their teams and to the fans of their teams. Niki was the one with the most to lose, and Eva was so fucking sorry, it hurt.

"Stop beating yourself up about this," Kathleen said, reading her mind. "Niki's a big girl. She can take care of herself."

"I know, I know. It's so unfair. I swear we didn't cross any ethical lines. It's not like we swapped playbooks from our teams or something. Niki bleeds red and white for Christ's sake. As if a kiss could make her break ranks, for God's sake."

She could hear Hockey Canada's president on the radio apologizing for what had happened and giving assurances that the integrity of the team had not been compromised in any way, that it was simply a friendship between two people that had suffered a brief lapse in judgment, nothing more.

Asshole, Eva thought. *What does he know about it? About us?*

"Nevertheless," Dan Smolenski was saying, "I felt it was appropriate and necessary to make a not-insignificant change with respect to Coach Hartling's duties."

Oh shit, now what?

"Coach Hartling will remain behind the bench for the duration of the Games, but as the assistant coach. Lynn O'Reilly will take on the head coaching duties from now until the conclusion of the Games."

Reporters began lobbing questions all at once, loudly, and Eva switched off the radio. "Good God," she said to Kathleen. "It's worse than I thought." She sat heavily on the bed. "She must be going through hell right now."

Kathleen caught her glancing at her cell phone on the nightstand. "It's not the worse thing that could have happened."

"Like hell it isn't."

"No, the worse thing would have been if she'd been fired outright."

"I don't know about that," Eva grumbled, knowing the demotion was a kick in the balls that would break Niki's heart.

"And don't even think about it," Kathleen warned in a low voice, nodding at the phone.

"Look, I just want to leave her a message, that's all, saying I'm sorry and that I hope she's okay."

"You can't, Eva. If anyone were to discover you two are still in contact, the conspiracy theorists would go nuts and you'd both be thrown off your teams. If you want me to pass a note under her hotel room door or something, fine. But if you want to help her, you need to be reasonable and figure out how to handle this, not go acting impulsive."

Eva didn't know if she could be reasonable about Niki, not when her heart was about to explode. Being unreasonable and impulsive looked pretty damned appealing right now. "After practice tomorrow, I'm going to corner Alison. Her fingerprints are all over this thing."

"Are you crazy? You can't go after Alison or anyone else until you have some kind of evidence or at least something more than a hunch. Do you want Alison to go after you next?"

Eva resumed her pacing. "Yeah, well, I dare Alison to throw me off the team. Cuz if I go down, she's going down with me. I'll air every single piece of dirty laundry on her I have. And then some. She's dirty, Kath. Dirty as the underside of my boot.

And so is Dani, as far as I can tell. They can think again about fucking with me."

Kathleen flashed her a warning smile. "That Italian temper of yours is taking over the steering wheel."

"Fine, then tell me what to do, since you're so *reasonable*."

"Hey. I'm trying to help."

In frustration, Eva ran her hand through her thick mane. "I know. Sorry."

"Okay, how about this? At practice tomorrow, while you guys are all on the ice, I'll grab Dani's phone and check it out. See if there's anything incriminating on it about that hot tub photo."

Whenever the players practiced or had a game, they put their cell phones in a bin inside the locker room, on a shelf beside the door. There was a no-phone policy, a blackout essentially, that took effect one hour before every game and practice and continued for an hour afterward.

"All right, that's better than anything I can suggest. What about Alison's phone?"

"No, she keeps it under lock and key."

Eva paused to look out the window. The mountains, hazy from low-hanging fog, hovered in the distance, their presence felt more than seen. The cold from the shadows they cast stretched all the way to her heart.

"What'll we do," she said, "if we find something incriminating?"

"I don't know yet. Let's take it a step at a time, okay?"

"All right." The more frightening thought was what they'd do if they didn't find anything incriminating. Because the photo, and the fallout from it, was only the beginning, Eva feared.

CHAPTER NINETEEN

Double Minor

"Is it true, Mom? You're not the coach anymore?"

Niki clutched her phone until her fingers cramped. The pain and confusion in her daughter's voice was a lance to her heart. *I caused this*, she thought. Someone once told her that parents disappoint their kids as often as kids disappoint their parents. Maybe more. Now she knew it was true. "That's right, honey. I'm sorry you had to hear about it before I could tell you myself."

A small part of her, but only a small part, wanted to lie or sugarcoat things because her instinct was to protect Rory from the kind of politics and backstabbing and gossip that too often pervaded elite sports. It was a bitter lesson for a ten-year-old, that merit alone wasn't always enough to succeed and that others sometimes wanted something so badly that they would use any means to get it, even if other people got hurt.

"But people are saying things about you, Mom. Mean things that can't be true. I got into a fight about it with another girl at school today."

Niki pinched her eyes shut so she wouldn't cry. "I'm sorry about that, honey. And thank you for coming to my defense, but I promise, your old mom can take care of herself, okay?" It took effort not to give into her emotions, because doing so wouldn't help Rory. "People sometimes say mean things when somebody's having a tough time," she said. "I don't know why and it's not right. I guess it makes them feel like they're a better person or something, or it makes them feel not so bad about their own mistakes. But it's important to remember that not all people are like that."

"But it's not fair!"

"No, it's not, but it's human nature sometimes. What's important is that you know the truth."

"Is it true you're with Eva now, Mom? And that's why you can't be the coach anymore, because Eva's on the wrong team?"

"No, I'm not with Eva, but some people think I am, and so that's why my bosses don't want me to be the coach anymore. At least not right now."

"But if it's not true, then you have to tell them!"

A tiny laugh escaped from Niki. If only things were as simple as an almost-eleven-year-old's view, the world would be a much better place. "I did tell them, sweetie, but for now they want me to be the assistant coach instead of the head coach, at least until things cool down. I'll still be behind the bench. And I'm still going to do my best to make sure Team Canada wins the gold medal. Nothing's going to stop me from trying my best, okay?"

It was a long while before Rory finally mumbled a reply.

"Rory, are you okay?"

A dramatic sigh. "Yes."

"Are you disappointed in me?"

"No. Well, maybe about one thing."

"What's that?"

"That Eva's not your girlfriend."

Niki smiled through the tears forming in her eyes. "You think Eva should be my girlfriend?"

"I think she already is, in your heart, anyway."

Niki held the phone to her chest, tried to gulp air through her tightening throat. "No, honey," she finally said. "Eva and I are friends, that's all."

"But the newspaper said you kissed her."

"It's true, I did kiss her." And more than once, but the second time, up against the brick wall in the alley, was something she was trying hard to forget. It seemed the jerk who secretly snapped the hot tub photo hadn't followed them the rest of the week, thank goodness. Because there had been nothing innocent, no simple explanation of why Eva had pressed against her, her thigh between Niki's legs, her hands under Niki's coat, her mouth mashing against Niki's. Nor about Niki wanting all of it. "But that doesn't mean—"

"I kiss Margot sometimes, and she's my girlfriend."

Niki laughed, glad for the subject change. "Do we need to have a talk about the birds and the bees?"

"I already know about all that stuff. Besides, Margot and I are too young to do anything but kiss. And not even with our mouths open."

"Well, then. See that it stays that way for at least eight more years."

Rory shrieked. "You mean I have to wait until I'm eighteen to do tongue kissing with her?"

"Yes!" Niki laughed again, and so did Rory.

"Mom," Rory said, her voice stern. Niki could picture her waving her finger in the air for emphasis, the way she did when she was lecturing their cat, Hector, for leaving his toys strewn around the house. "It's okay, you know."

"What's okay?"

"If Eva becomes your girlfriend. I like her. She's nice. And she's pretty hot too."

Niki gasped. Where had her little girl gone? "You're not supposed to think about people being hot, young lady. Especially not people old enough to be my friends."

"Whatever. But you and Eva should be together. That's all I'm saying, Mom. Everybody can see it."

Maybe that was the problem, she thought, that everyone could see the chemistry, the bond between them. She and Eva were the elephant in the room, kiss or no kiss.

"Did I ever tell you that you're growing up way too fast?" It was conversations like these that reminded her how smart and precocious Rory was. Kids had a way of distilling things to the core, to getting at the truth in the most direct way. And while reuniting with Eva might seem simple in Rory's young mind, it wasn't. The Games aside, there were so many other things to consider, not the least of which was Shannon's place in her and Rory's hearts and in their memories. Her heart, she feared, wasn't big enough or strong enough to let anyone else in.

"We'll talk about it another time, all right? You need to get to bed and I need to get back to work."

"Will I see Eva when I get there?"

Rory and her Aunt Jen would be arriving in Vancouver in little more than a week, right in time for the opening ceremonies and the start of the round robin games.

"I don't know, sweetie. It's going to be hectic around here, and the teams are pretty much sequestered once the Games start."

Rory was not to be derailed. "She'll see me. I know she will."

Niki shook her head. Her daughter's crush on Eva showed no signs of abating.

* * *

Eva snuck a glance at Kath, who gave her a nearly imperceptible nod before disappearing to the locker room.

On the ice, she readied herself to receive a puck. Once it was on her stick, she took off at full speed, looped around a faceoff circle, passed the puck to a teammate at the red line, received it back again and tracked straight toward the net, only veering at the last second to slide the puck off her backhand and into the net.

She did the same drill heading in the other direction, but this time flubbed a pass and had to start over again. She scolded herself by slapping her stick across her shin pads. From her eyes, she shot darts at Alison and Dani, believing with every fiber that the two of them were responsible for Niki's very public and unfair fall from grace. They looked like they deserved one another—beady-eyed and small-mouthed, the smirking faces of first-class bitches. Somehow, she was going to prove they were behind it all before these Olympics were done.

Doubt gnawed her. If Kathleen failed to come up with something from Dani's phone, what then? In her fantasies, she confronted Alison and Dani, threatened them and did whatever it took to elicit a confession. But her calmer self said that kind of thuggery would get her nowhere and might prematurely tip her hand that she was onto them. Kathleen was right about taking things one step at a time, about playing it smart. Hockey too was very much about having a plan and executing it, not running around the ice without rhyme or reason.

She leaned against the boards, grabbed a water bottle and sprayed her face. She was stupid to have come back to the team, to have thought that Alison had risen above cheating, unprincipled manipulations, connivery. To have thought that a team presided over by Alison Hiller could win the gold medal fair and square. Or maybe she did know deep down that things would degrade to this, but thought she could look the other way for the sake of a shot at gold. Well, maybe she could have if it hadn't been for Niki getting caught in the middle. Niki was her Kryptonite, her conscience, her soul, the better part of her that made her want to do things by the rules. It hadn't always been that way, but it was now, and the realization that she was no longer the person she'd been the last time she played for Team USA or the last time she'd been a part of Niki's life hit her like a blind body check smashing her into the unforgiving boards and glass, dizzying her for a moment.

She rejoined the drill, took a pass and went in on the goalie, scored again. Today, she seemed to be able to score at will. Some days were like that in sports, where everything came easy. Tomorrow, who knew? Tomorrow the stick might feel like a foreign object in her hands.

Kendall, a young defensemen who'd won the NCAA's top award last year, skated up to her, a grin splitting her freckled face. "You keep scoring like that, Cruzie, and there's no way we're gonna lose."

Eva shook her head. "It won't be up to me. Or you. Or any one player. It's all of us, kid. And then it's something else entirely out of our control."

"What do you mean?"

"We can and do work our asses off, try to be our very best—"or cheat and manipulate—"and there's still a force out there that has nothing to do with any of that stuff and yet has everything to do with who wins and who loses."

Kendall's eyebrows pinched in confusion. "You lost me, Cruzie."

"Luck. Karma. The hockey gods. Don't ever discount that stuff. And right now, I've got a bad feeling those three things aren't working in our favor."

Kendall skated off, shaking her head, the stubbornness of youth making her believe that she and her teammates were the only architects of their future. Eva once thought she knew it all too.

After the last whistle, Eva sprinted to the showers. If she hurried, she would have Kathleen to herself for a few minutes in the therapy room. She'd let Kathleen rub down her hams and quads with an anti-inflammatory cream because it would give them the excuse to have their heads together if anyone walked in.

"Find anything?" Eva said to her.

"A little, but not as much as I would have liked. Her Hotmail account on her phone is password protected, so I couldn't get into that."

"Did you try to guess her password?"

"No, no time." Kathleen chuckled quietly. "But knowing the half-wit she is, it's probably her jersey number and her nickname."

Comps34. Or 34Comps. "I'll try it later if I can borrow your laptop."

"Be my guest. The good news is, I was able to check out her text messages from the last few days."

"Jackpot?"

"Not exactly, but better than nothing."

"All I want to know is if she was the one who took that damned hot tub picture."

"Can't prove it. I quickly scanned the photos on her phone and it's not there. Which doesn't mean she didn't erase it or move it somewhere else." A triumphant smile tugged at the corners of Kathleen's mouth. "I checked the texts she hasn't gotten around to deleting yet. Stuff from the past week or so."

"Please tell me you found something."

"I did. Not hard evidence that she's directly involved, but a few texts gloating to friends about Niki's demotion and the scandal the whole thing caused."

Eva's spirits dropped. "I wouldn't expect anything else from her. There's got to be something else, Kath. I know she had something to do with not only that damned photo, but all the other weird shit, like knowing Niki's team plays and stuff like that."

"Well, there was a curious exchange between her and Alison. I don't know if some of the texts were deleted or what, but there was one from Dani saying she just wants to play hockey now and to please don't ask her to do anything else."

"And what was Alison's response?"

"Something about the luck of the Irish on their side and how the leprechaun was coming through in spades."

"That's weird."

"Of course it is, but it *is* Alison we're talking about. And then she said she expects Dani to do whatever she asks of her until the Games are over. That's it, that's all I got."

"What do you think it means?" The information hadn't done anything to change Eva's mind about Dani and Alison's guilt, but it was a riddle that was nowhere close to being solved.

Kathleen lowered her voice as clanging doors in the distance signaled the approach of others. "I think your gut instinct is right about them, but it's not enough to confront them. Yet."

"Hell, I'm thinking of going over their heads with what I've got."

"Don't, Eva. You don't have anything concrete. Not even close."

Eva sighed in exasperation and swung her legs over the side of the massage table. "Will you put a note under Niki's door asking her to meet me? Tell her it's important."

CHAPTER TWENTY

Penalty Kill

She'd been crazy to agree to meet Eva, but here she was skulking around Stanley Park, near the gigantic totem poles that stretched forty, fifty feet in the air, where she'd been instructed to wait. It was dusk and she'd thrown on an oversized Canada Goose parka and matching aviator hat, the fur trim of it flopping over her face and, she hoped, disguising her.

With the opening ceremonies only two days away, the city buzzed with Olympic fever. People of all nationalities and ages swarmed the streets and the shops like ants on honey. Roads were blocked off, traffic rerouted, cops patrolled in an ever-growing army. Signs welcoming visitors sprouted like weeds, urging them to shop here, buy this, visit that. Languages, most of which Niki didn't recognize, floated on the air like smoke.

Concentrating on her team and on her duties was more and more difficult when there was so much to see and hear and smell. Even the street food vendors were going international, the aroma of sauerkraut, curry, fish, cabbage, lime juice, garlic infusing every breeze.

"There you are."

Eva's voice, deep and warm like a cup of hot chocolate on a bone-chilling day, heated her insides, and Niki jumped at the sheer, sudden closeness of her.

"Sorry," Eva said. "I didn't mean to scare you. You're actually the second person I did that to. It was your boots that finally gave you away."

Her Columbia lace-ups were practical, if a little on the butch side. "If I'd worn Uggs, you'd never have found me, right?"

"You're right about that. I've never seen so many Uggs! I might be scarred for life." She pointed to her own feet, clad in Sperry topsiders. "We're probably the only two women in this city wearing practical boots that you could actually hike with in the mountains."

"We never were much for fashion, were we?"

Eva steered her behind a massive red cedar, its girth as big as a compact car. The sudden movement and the illicitness of it shot a bolt of excitement through Niki. A forbidden excitement that reminded her of the hot kiss in the alley.

"I'm sorry for making you meet me out here," Eva said. "But I think we need to talk about what happened and what we're going to do about it. What they did to you…"

A shadow fell over Niki's heart, Eva's words a stark reminder of why they were here. Seconds ago she'd wanted Eva to kiss her and to hell with everything else. Kissing had always defined their relationship, had always been the marquee to their attraction. They'd never skipped it and gone straight to sex, all the years they were together. Kissing was an adhesive, sometimes a salve on bad days. Always, it was the low-burning flame that sustained and nourished them and aroused them. Now, kissing had put Niki into one hell of a mess.

"Wait a minute," Niki said, putting her lusty thoughts out of her head. "*They* didn't do anything to me. We did this, Eva. We kissed in that hot tub, out where anyone could have seen us. And apparently somebody did. We were reckless, and now I'm paying the price."

In the day's fading light, Eva's eyes darkened to the pitch of night. "No, Nik. We didn't do anything wrong. Somebody's been gunning for us all along. Even before the hot tub. Look at how my team miraculously figured out your team's strategy ahead of that game, and Lynn and Alison having dinner together. And then at the hotel in Whistler, I saw Dani Compton and Lynn O'Reilly texting one another."

"Wait. You never told me about that."

Eva shook her head. "No, I didn't, because you didn't want to go there." Her voice thickened with worry. "I want to know how you're doing, Nik. How you're feeling. About what happened."

Niki closed her eyes, leaned against the sturdiness of the tree. It had been there for hundreds of years, and the thought of its longevity, momentarily at least, reduced her worries into fleeting annoyances. "It sucks. And it totally blindsided me. But there's nothing I can do about it. For the sake of my players, I'm going to see this through. They're the reason I haven't walked away from this whole thing, because that would be worse for them right now."

"Aw shit, Niki." Eva kicked lightly at the base of the tree. "I'm so fucking sorry. It's not fair, what's happening. And I know we can't undo what we did, but I want to find out who's behind this."

"Don't." Niki employed her harshest tone. "You need to concentrate on hockey right now, not run around playing Sherlock Holmes. Besides, the damage has been done. It's over."

"Don't you want justice against whoever did this? They don't deserve to get away with it. Jesus, Niki! For once in your life, fight, goddammit!"

Niki's throat tightened with the words jumbled there. Eva was wrong; she *was* a fighter. She'd successfully beat back her grief and despair and loneliness enough to raise a daughter by herself. Was that nothing? Well, Eva wouldn't know about that. Eva had only ever lived for herself, doing whatever she wanted, erupting into temper tantrums, disregarding consequences, letting her emotions rule her. Well, not Niki. Emotions slowed you down, clogged the road, diverted you until you got lost in one hell of a hurry. It was why, in Shannon's final weeks, she shoved her emotions aside so she could be strong, stoic, a wall that wouldn't crumble. She couldn't imagine what it would have been like for both of them, for Rory too, if she'd lashed out or crumpled into a quivering heap of raw emotion.

In a trembling voice, she started to say, "You have no right," when Eva's mouth suddenly found hers, snuffing out the rest of her words, scrambling her brain until no other words or thoughts could form. The kiss was a trip wire beneath her running feet. And oh, was it sweet.

Eva pressed lightly against her, her body firm, familiar, reassuring. Niki grasped her shoulders, held them like she was clutching onto the sides of a lifeboat. She kissed Eva back, drawing strength from her steadiness, her mere presence, and from her fierce sense of right and wrong. Eva was no less a rule enforcer than Niki, even if she went about it in a way that was loud and raw.

Eva's lips brushed her jaw, her ear. "We can't let this happen again," she whispered urgently. "We can't lose each other again over this...*this nonsense*. Please. Help me find out who did this."

Eva was right. They couldn't undo what had happened, but they might be able to stop any further injustices. "How?"

* * *

Eva told her about Kathleen checking Dani's cellphone and about the strange text exchange with Alison. "This luck of the Irish stuff and the leprechaun, it bothers me," Eva said. "Like it's a code for something."

"Shit." Niki's face paled. "It could be nothing, but Lynn O'Reilly is Irish. And very proud of it. On game days, she always wears either a tiny leprechaun brooch or shamrock earrings."

Relief swept through Eva, but not for long. They were onto something, but solving it wasn't going to be easy. "That's got to be it, then. We have to find evidence that Lynn's involved in this. Can you get into her phone? Or her laptop or something?"

"I suppose. I don't know. I'm not good at this clandestine stuff."

"You can do this, Nik. You have to. We can't let them get away with this."

Niki looked shaken, but not scared, not weak. She was trusting Eva. "She has her phone with her all the time, but I can get into her laptop. I know her password, since it's team property."

"When can you get into it?"

Niki thought for a moment. "The best time would be during the opening ceremonies. We'll both be there, but in the chaos, I could easily sneak off. Especially if I use Rory as an excuse, that she's tired and has to go back to the hotel or something."

"Won't she be pissed at having to miss part of the ceremonies?" Knowing what little she did of Rory, the kid wouldn't want to miss any of the action.

"She will, but not if I promise to make up for it somehow."

"And how are you going to do that?"

"She'll want to see you. She talks about you all the time. What if I promise her she can have a lunch date with you? Maybe you could give her a tour of the athletes' village or something?"

Before Eva could do anything to stop it, tears pressed against the backs of her eyes. "Niki, I…" She cleared her throat roughly. "Of course. I'd love to." Spending time with Rory was an honor, and it was all she could do not to get ahead of herself, not to picture the three of them as a family. Rory was a great kid, easy to get to know, fun to be around. She felt like she already knew her so well, like they had a bond and a shared sense of familiarity that transcended the small amount of time they'd spent together.

"All right. It's settled. I'll see what I can find on Lynn's laptop. And I'll have a quick look around her room. But if I don't come up with anything, then what?"

Eva didn't have another plan, and she told Niki as much. She'd managed to hack into Dani's email account last night, but it had been wiped clean. For all she knew, Dani had several email accounts. "We should meet again after you do it. Here at our tree. I'll text you from Kathleen's phone, okay?"

"No. I don't want anything on my phone tracing back to anybody with Team USA. Text my sister-in-law's phone. And use the code word Stanley and the time. I'll know you want to meet here at our tree."

Our tree. Eva asked for Jenny's number and committed it to memory. She'd enter it later on Kathleen's phone.

"Promise me you'll consider dropping this little game of detective if I don't find anything, all right?"

Eva set her jaw. "You'll find something."

Niki began to step away, but with a tug on her coat, Eva pulled her back. She wanted to talk about after the Games. Wanted to wring out every last drop of what might happen to them as a couple or as a not-couple, when all this was over. She remembered with the same lump of dread in her stomach that day almost thirteen years ago, when they both discovered they'd made their respective national teams and that they'd be playing against one another in the first Olympic Games for women's hockey. It was what they both dreamed of and worked so hard for. It was the top, the very pinnacle by which their success on the ice could be measured. They celebrated by treating themselves to dinner out, a bottle of wine, but they'd stared watchfully at each other across the little flickering candle, afraid to rejoice too deeply because they knew that one's success at the Games would mark the other's failure.

"What?" Niki implored.

"When this is all over…"

"One thing at a time, okay?"

"All right. And Nik?"

"Yes?"

"As long as Lynn's the head coach, I'm going to be especially happy to kick your team's ass."

Niki's laughter cut the tension like the sun breaking through the storm clouds. "I don't blame you one bit."

CHAPTER TWENTY-ONE

Cross-checking

Niki held tight to Rory's hand as they sat in the stadium watching the opening ceremonies unfold. It wasn't that she was afraid Rory might wander off or trip and fall—she wasn't a baby anymore, as she was only too happy to remind Niki. The contact was because Niki had missed her these last few months. Had missed her more than she had accounted for. Her work had kept her supremely occupied, but she'd mistakenly thought that being back in the arenas and around the players and on the ice would happily transport her back to the days when she was a player and had no encumbrances. The opposite had happened. Being away from Rory reminded her of how much she wanted the responsibility of raising a child, of how far her life had drifted from being a player who lived, slept, ate and breathed hockey, with nobody else to answer to, with nothing else to do but work out in the gym and perfect her on-ice skills. She didn't want that self-indulgent lifestyle ever again. Nor could she wait until these Games were over in two weeks and she could resume her life again.

"What's wrong, Mom?" Rory's uncanny ability to read her mind was as strong as ever.

"Nothing, sweetie. Just thinking about how glad I am that you're here."

"When will Eva be coming out?"

"The athletes will come out in a few minutes. And since Eva's with the United States, she'll be near the end."

Rory was as fixated on Eva as ever, and Niki didn't know what to make of it.

"Look," Niki said, pointing to the eight Royal Canadian Mounted Police in their bright red uniforms and Stetsons, parading a large Canadian flag onto the floor.

"That's what I want to be when I grow up."

"I thought you wanted to be a hockey player?"

"I do, but you can't be a hockey player forever, Mom."

Niki wasn't thrilled with the idea of her daughter being a cop or a hockey player, but she squeezed her arm with encouragement anyway. She was proud of her for having ambitions.

They watched the athletes enter through a tunnel and onto the perimeter of the main floor, garbed in the colors of their countries. They waved and smiled, as though simply by being there they'd already won the biggest prize. Sharp-eyed Rory picked Eva out of the crowd of athletes right away, in her white pants and blue bomber-style jacket, and she waved frantically at her, even though there was zero chance Eva could see her. When the Canadians, as host team, came out last, Rory immediately proclaimed that their outfits of black pants and red parkas with their fur-trimmed hoods were much cooler than anybody else's. She was awed, however, by the aboriginal dancers clad in white and the giant air-filled polar bears that glimmered and stretched toward the ceiling.

By the time k.d. lang took the stage in her white suit to sing "Hallelujah," Niki could put it off no longer. She broke the news to Rory that they needed to go back to the hotel right away, that there was important work she needed to do back in their room. Rory pleaded to stay with her Aunt Jen to watch the rest of the ceremonies, but Niki needed Rory for cover in case anyone questioned her absence. "They're almost done, honey.

After k.d., there's just some boring old speeches, and that's it, I promise." By the time she dangled the bait of Rory hanging out with Eva for an afternoon, the negotiations were all but over.

It didn't take much convincing of the hotel night manager to let her into Lynn's room with a pass key—a flash of her identification and a vague muttering of a work emergency was enough to do the trick. She looked around the room, not wanting to disturb anything in too obvious a way and not wanting to take too long in case Lynn returned to her room early. Plus Rory was alone in Niki's room three doors down, watching the rest of the ceremonies on television.

Everything seemed in its place. Clothing neatly in drawers and in the closet. A single glass and a coffee mug, both clean, on the dresser. An unopened bag of nuts. The bar fridge contained bottles of water, a six-pack of beer. There was nothing personal, like books or photographs or little mementoes. Lynn's was an antiseptic life that could easily be transported from hotel room to hotel room. She'd never known her to have long-term relationships, though Niki had met a couple of her short-term girlfriends a long time ago. It was a mystery as to whose company Lynn kept nowadays.

Lynn's laptop sat closed on the desk. Niki opened it, booted it up, typed in the password. She clicked on the email icon, but it was password protected. She tried a couple of guesses but none of them worked. Next she clicked on the finder window, scanned over the documents there. There were notes about the team, on-ice drills, articles saved about things like nutrition, leadership, scouting reports on their opponents. Then Niki saw a folder with the initials N.H. *Her* initials, she realized with a start. Her heart fluttered like there was a moth in her chest as she clicked it open. And then her heart stopped altogether. The picture of her and Eva in the hot tub, kissing, stared out at her. The exact same picture that had spread like wildfire through the media. She clicked on a file called Whistler 01/2010. It contained a list of dates and places Eva and Niki were known to have been together during the week in Whistler, as though somebody had been keeping track of their every movement.

She sat down heavily on the chair, her mind as blank as a white sheet of paper, disappointment so palpable that she thought she might faint. So Lynn had betrayed her. But why? So she could become head coach? Had Lynn been setting her up all along, convincing her to take the job in the first place only so she could later lead her like a lamb to slaughter? Had she thrown Eva into her path to lay down the trap Niki had so neatly and hopelessly fallen into? It would have been easier if Lynn had simply competed for the job to begin with, instead of dragging others into it, but her cynical side said Lynn didn't have what it took and probably never would have earned the job on her own.

She tried to clear her head, put aside her emotions—she'd grown good at that part over the years. Eva would tell her that what she'd found wouldn't amount to more than her word against Lynn's if she didn't walk out of the room with some hard evidence. She withdrew her BlackBerry from her pocket and snapped several shots of Lynn's computer screen, showing the files and the hot tub photo. She couldn't exactly take a screen shot and email it to herself from Lynn's computer, so this would have to do. She remembered to clear the computer's cache so Lynn wouldn't see that someone had been snooping, logged out and shut it down.

She was breathing hard by the time she returned to her room. Adrenaline pounded through her body with no means of escape. *What the hell do I do now?* she thought. If she confronted Lynn and Lynn denied it or blamed someone else, then what? Without a confession that she was actually involved, it wasn't really enough to go to Dan Smolenski. And even then, would he be prepared to do anything about it, now that the Games had begun? It'd be a terrible scandal for Hockey Canada and for the Games itself if it was revealed that Lynn was involved in some sort of conspiracy against her. Several people could kiss their careers goodbye if this blew up publicly.

It was an impossible situation. She wished Eva had never convinced her to go down this road. Life was so much easier if you stuck your head in the sand, if you gave people the benefit of the doubt, even when they didn't deserve it. But there was no going back now. If she let this slide, then Lynn and whoever else was in this with her would win. Cheating would win. Hurting other people would win. And Niki would lose, same way she and Eva had lost when a lie got between them twelve years ago. She wouldn't let that happen again, and neither, she knew, would Eva.

* * *

Her first shift on the ice, a blindside hit in the corner from one of Team China's brawny players gave Eva notice that the exhibition season was over; the Games had begun. And it was going to be painful. Full body checks weren't allowed in women's hockey, but it didn't mean you didn't regularly get knocked around. There was contact along the boards and in front of the net every single shift. And if a player felt like giving you an extra shove or slammed you into the boards, they didn't mind taking a penalty. For teams that knew they were in a losing contest, sometimes laying on a big hit was the only satisfaction there was; they were more than willing to trade two minutes in the box for it.

On her second shift, Eva niftily kicked the puck from her skates to her stick and snapped a wrist shot into the top corner and past the goalie's shoulder for a goal. The Americans were having their way with the Chinese, dominating puck possession and pace. Eva only needed to exert about fifty percent of her energy, which was fine with her. After this, there were two more round robin games, then the semifinals, followed by the finals. If all went according to plan, her team would steamroll its way to the gold medal final. Each game would get tougher, more challenging, so she'd need to conserve as much energy as she could.

Her conservative approach was sneered at by Alison, who kept giving her the stink eye from the bench. Canada had beaten Slovakia 18-0 earlier this afternoon, and while Team USA handing China its ass was a foregone conclusion, Alison wanted an equally lopsided score to keep up with the Joneses. She ordered her team not to hold back, but Eva had other ideas. She would be thirty-seven in a few weeks, and she'd be damned if she was going to put her body through the wringer before the playoff portion of the tournament. She had nothing to prove. A little more swagger in her step at the expense of a knee or a shoulder wasn't worth it.

By the second period, the score was six to one, and Eva took her foot off the gas a little more. Her shifts got shorter and she avoided the corners. She passed the puck more than she shot. By the third, Alison dropped her to the third line, which failed to rattle Eva. Less ice time meant more rest, as long as she made it back up to the first or second line by the time the semis rolled around. She told her teammates to stop celebrating goals after their eighth, because it wasn't classy and only served to rub the other team's nose in it. There's honor in winning, she said, but not in humiliating your opponent.

As the final buzzer sounded, Alison leaned over from behind the bench and gave Eva shit for not scoring a couple more goals. The twelve goals the team did score weren't enough, she said. They needed to show the world, especially the Canadians, that they could score a barrel of goals whenever and wherever they damned well felt like it. *Whatever.* Eva bit her tongue to keep silent. If Alison couldn't figure out by now that none of this meant a damned thing until the semis and the finals, then screw her. Like any good veteran player, Eva knew when and how much to turn it on.

She stepped out of a scalding shower, then lowered herself an inch at a time into an ice bath. Pain, razor-sharp from the frigid water, sliced into her, raising her heart rate and making her lungs clench. She cursed out loud, devising new phrases with the word fuck in it. She dreaded these damned ice baths, but they helped her sore muscles, and they'd help her stay off pain pills. The pills were a crutch, a crutch she'd been using a little too frequently since she'd rejoined the team last summer, and she was through with them. They made her dopey, but worse, she feared growing dependent on them. The pain, she reasoned, wasn't a bad thing, because it was a tangible reminder that her playing days deserved to be in her past and not in her future. She'd pushed her body to its limits lately, and if she pushed much more, she risked suffering permanent damage. Like, for instance, a full knee replacement before she was forty-five.

"Hey." It was Kathleen, setting a pile of warm towels on a table near the tub. "Nice and hot and fluffy."

"You're an angel, Kath." She started to rise.

"Oh no you don't. How long have you been in there?"

Eva gritted her teeth. "Come on, I've been in here at least four minutes, I swear."

"Good. Four more and you can get out."

Eva's teeth chattered, but she was still able to call Kathleen an evil, sadistic witch.

Kathleen laughed. "I love it when you talk dirty." She lowered her voice to a whisper. "Listen. Niki texted me a few minutes ago from her sister-in-law's phone. She wants you to see Stanley tonight, whoever that is."

Eva's blood warmed at the invitation. And at the idea of kissing Niki again up against that old tree and holding her in her arms. But it wouldn't be a social call. Niki was supposed to have searched Lynn's room and her laptop last night during the opening ceremonies. She either had something, or she had nothing and was going to suggest stopping their little investigation.

"When?" she asked Kathleen.

"Eleven o'clock. Do I tell her yes?"

"Yes. Now let me out of this torture chamber."

"Wait, one more thing. Since you don't have a game tomorrow, she wondered if you can do lunch with Rory. Is that her daughter?"

Eva smiled. Rory did that to her. "Yup. And tell her absolutely yes. Now let me out of this damned thing or I'm going to give you a taste of your own medicine."

CHAPTER TWENTY-TWO

Charging

Niki glanced nervously at her watch. Nineteen minutes after nine. She'd have to leave the hotel in an hour to make it to the rendezvous point with Eva in Stanley Park, but Lynn was taking her sweet time. They'd agreed to meet in the hotel's lounge at nine for a quiet beer together. Now as she watched the beads of sweat slide down her glass, Niki berated herself for not ambushing Lynn in her room instead of trying to be civilized about it. A drink in public signaled that they could work things out, that they could talk things over, that things were less serious, less confrontational, less final, than having it out in private, where it could get ugly.

Lynn finally waltzed in, her shoulders squared for a fight and haughtiness stamped on her face. She sat down across from Niki and ordered a beer, failing to apologize for being late. I'm doing you a big favor by being here, her attitude suggested.

"What's on your mind?" Lynn said directly, then failed to wait for an answer. "Because if you're going to dump all over me for trashing your attack-first approach, forget it. It's better to sit back the first period, lull our opponents to sleep, let them think they've got a chance against us, and only then let them have it. It's the approach we're taking from now on."

Niki hated the approach because it flirted with danger, especially once they faced the better teams, like Finland and Sweden. And of course, the Americans. The problem with sitting back is that you couldn't always switch it on again. Sometimes you simply lulled yourself to sleep too. No. It was far more effective to attack right out of the gate, to keep your opponent on the mat without a glimmer of hope of getting into the game. But Lynn was the boss now, a fact she liked to throw in Niki's face at every opportunity.

"I'm not here to argue about your game philosophy, Lynn."

"Good." Lynn's smile was sickly sweet and only underscored her autocracy. "Because everyone's watching to make sure you're falling in line. If our opponents—hell, our own players too—see any sort of crack in our unified front, that's it, we're finished."

Niki held back an urge to be sarcastic, to verbally hit back at Lynn and knock the smugness from her. If Lynn was innocent in the coaching swap, she wouldn't be acting as if she'd not only won the lottery, but that it was some kind of divine justice. The charitableness toward Lynn, not that Niki had much of it to begin with, began to disappear as fast as the beer from Lynn's glass.

"But there is something we need to discuss. Something very serious." Niki tried to keep her voice steady, but her temples throbbed, and her hands, which she stuffed under the table, had begun to shake. "It was that picture of me and Eva in the hot tub that led to all of this, and I want to know who was behind it."

"Who cares who was behind it, Nik. It's done. Over. You can't change any of it now, and even if you tried, it would only lead to more distraction, more digging up of dirt. Dan would have your head."

She was right, of course she was, but so what. Right didn't make Niki feel better. "I don't care. I'm tired of being the fall guy here. I didn't do anything wrong, save for a fleeting, misguided kiss that I thought was in private. And I think it's time the truth came out that somebody's railroaded me."

Lynn's nostrils flared, the only indication that she might be unnerved. "It's all about perception. You know the game. If people think you're trading secrets with the enemy, then it's as good as true. That photograph doesn't leave room for explanations."

Niki's blood pounded in her ears, and any chance of her remaining diplomatic, of taking the high road, flew out the window. "Well, you would know all about that, wouldn't you?"

"Excuse me?"

Niki pushed away her half glass of beer, her thirst gone. "You took that picture, didn't you? Or at least, you know who did. Why else would it be on your laptop?"

Lynn's mouth gulped for air like a fish out of water. Then she clamped it shut with a loud crunch of her teeth. Her eyes were flinty, unforgiving. "You had no right to look at my laptop."

"Technically, no, but tell me what right you had to follow me around, hoping to entrap me, and then taking a picture for all the world to see. And…and misconstruing what you saw."

"I didn't take any damned picture."

"Then tell me who did. And why it's on your computer."

They were two bulls in a ring, staring each other down.

"I tried to protect you, Nik. That's why the picture is on my computer."

"Oh, really? The same way you jumped to my defense with Dan? With the media? The way you defended me when you happily took the head coaching job?"

Lynn remained silent, and it was all Niki needed for confirmation. "What happened to you, Lynn? Did the desire to be head coach of Team Canada give you the license to screw people? To screw your friends? To trample on every rule in the book?"

"I didn't need to screw anybody." Lynn's voice was like a hammer. "You screwed yourself because you couldn't resist Eva. And you put this entire team at risk. I hope she was worth it."

Niki grabbed her coat and stalked out, unable to sit across from her former friend any longer. She shouldn't have expected

Lynn to take responsibility for her actions, to confess a damned thing. Lynn had proven once again that she was only out for number one.

* * *

One look at Niki's stricken face and Eva threw her arms around her. "It was Lynn, wasn't it?" she whispered thickly, her voice quaking with anger.

"I don't know." Niki burrowed further into Eva's coat.

Trying to protect Niki wasn't necessary and never had been, because she could certainly take care of herself. But the urge, especially now, was too powerful for Eva to deny. Guilty or not, she'd love to give Lynn a piece of her mind. And more. "What do you mean?"

Niki took a step back, cleared her throat. "The picture of us in the hot tub was on her laptop. I met with her, told her I saw it, but she didn't offer an explanation. She said it was on there because she was trying to protect me."

"*Protect* you?" Eva spat out the word. "I suppose she didn't explain that either."

"No, she didn't. But it's obvious she knows who's behind it. Whether she actively helped or just turned a blind eye, I don't know."

"Either way, she's betrayed you big-time, Nik. And she was the one with everything to gain. Think about that."

"I know. I accused her of screwing me to get my job, but she turned it around and said I screwed myself. Because I couldn't *resist* you."

Eva hoped that last part was true. Inside she felt it was, and yet Niki always managed to hold something back, to keep her deepest thoughts and desires private. One minute she might return Eva's kiss her as though her very soul was trying to fuse with Eva's, and the next…Well, the next she was being cautious. Or she was running away again. The pushing and pulling routine was enough to drive her nuts if she let it.

Slowly, Eva said, "What do you want to do next?"

Niki leaned against the tree. "I don't know. I need time. Not only to think, but to keep my eye on Lynn."

"I don't know that there's much to see anymore. Her little game's over because she got what she wanted."

"Then what's the link between her and Alison and Dani?"

That was easy. "They all have reasons for wanting you off the bench I guess. Lynn probably enlisted their help, and they were only too eager to give it."

"But why would they give a shit whether it was me or Lynn coaching the team? What difference does it make to them?"

"Sweetheart, you're the best at what you do, that's why. They probably feel that with Lynn at the helm, they've got a shot. Or at least, a better shot. You know Lynn's not half the coach you are." Only after she said the words did it occur to her that she had referred to her own team as *they*. Had she felt this disconnected to her team, this much an outsider, all along? Or was it since she'd learned Alison was up to her old tricks again? More than that, was her heart aligning itself to Niki in every way possible?

"Eva, will you keep an eye on Alison and Dani?"

"Of course, you know I will. But we've got nothing on them, and getting a confession would be like getting Russia to confess its athletes are the biggest dopers on the planet. Let's hope this whole thing is over."

"What if Dani and Alison are still trying to find out my team's strategies and things like who's injured?"

"That was all probably part of their plan to get you off the bench. To make it look like you were trading information for sex with me or something. I don't know. Come here, baby."

Niki stepped into Eva's arms, buried her face against her heavy winter coat. "It's so unfair, everything that's happened."

"I know it is." She kissed Niki's temple. "But the Games will be over soon. You'll have your life back and all this will be in your rearview mirror. The people who love you and believe in you, that won't change because of this. And you never did care what the general public thought anyway. This whole thing is a blip, a footnote in your life. Don't let it define you."

"Huh. How'd you get so wise?"

"I had a good teacher. You. And maybe I finally grew up a little."

Niki looked up at her, the darkness failing to conceal the bright blue of her eyes. "You surprise me sometimes."

"Good. I like keeping you off-balance. But there's one thing that shouldn't come as a surprise to you."

"What's that?"

Eva gently captured Niki's mouth with her own and kissed her with all the feelings that simmered below the surface, with all the things that made her crazy for this woman she never should have let go in the first place. She deepened the kiss, and before she lost her courage, whispered into Niki's ear, "Let's go get a hotel room. I want to make love to you, Nik. All night long."

Niki paused, her body trembling against Eva's. "Eva, we can't. I've got Rory and—"

"Isn't she staying in your sister-in-law's room?"

"Yes, but—"

"You could be back by daybreak."

"But you have a curfew. You're staying in the athletes' village. Breaking curfew could earn you a suspension for a game or two."

"I don't care, I'll take that chance. Please. I need to hold you. At least for one night, I need to forget that we lost twelve years together."

"There's more to think about than tonight. I can't go off with you when everything's hanging in the balance the way it is. Our teams could be playing against each other in a week, we could—"

Eva raised a finger to Niki's lips to shush her. "None of that matters to me right now. *You* matter to me. Only you. Always you. Everything else is just noise that won't amount to a hill of beans after that final game. Besides, what else have we got to lose?"

"If the media were to find out about this, it'd look like I'm guilty as charged. That I deserve what I got and more."

"They're not going to find out. And besides, there's no need for anyone to continue with their witch-hunt. They got what they wanted. But we'll be careful, I promise."

Niki kissed the two fingers at her lips, one at a time, heating Eva from the inside. She could see from Niki's eyes that she wanted this night together every bit as badly.

"Tonight has to be the only time," Niki warned. "For now."

"I know."

Niki was right. They couldn't repeat the risk. She dropped her hand, waited for Niki to clasp it. "Now let's go find that room."

CHAPTER TWENTY-THREE

Holding

It had taken what seemed to Niki a Herculean effort by Eva—with a little help from her friend Kathleen—to find them a room. The city was booked up solid—every hotel and motel, bed-and-breakfast, inn, campus residence, lodge and cottage. A half hour of back and forth phone calls finally got them a room at a downtown hotel, booked under Kathleen's name. The only reason it was available was because a Swedish team doctor was having a secret affair with a skier on the French team, and they no longer needed two rooms. Sex was the biggest of all the sports at the Olympics. If you weren't here having sex, you were angling to have sex, and nothing was off limits. Certainly not your marital status and definitely not your citizenship.

Eva was sweet the way she kept asking her if she was okay, if she was sure. There was a noticeable skittishness in her eyes, like she didn't believe Niki would really go through with it. And there were good reasons for Niki's hesitation, not the least of which was that they'd be doing exactly the thing they'd been accused of doing once the hot tub photo surfaced. Niki's inner child said that if she was going to be judged as guilty, she might as well *be* guilty. But that wasn't why she was in this hotel room with Eva. She was here because every time she looked at Eva, every time she was touched by Eva, she couldn't, in that instant, remember why she'd ever given her up. Why she'd ever thought she could make a life without her. Why she'd ever been so stupid and so arrogant, like her head knew better than her heart. But then, the way a dream vanishes with morning's first light, she'd realize that in letting Eva go, she'd gained Shannon. And Rory. She'd made a life without Eva that was a good life, a satisfying life, for a time at least. They had to let each other go to find what each needed to complete herself, because they hadn't, back then, completed each other. Eva had been so restless, so full of adventure and the pursuit of her own happiness. Niki had been the introspective one, the cautious one, wanting to plant roots, wanting to build a life where she stood. Their passion for each other and their sport had intersected for a time, but it had never been enough to build a life around. Not then.

"What are you thinking about?" Eva asked.

Niki sat down on the king bed, having only removed her shoes. Eva had slipped off her jeans, but no more, and stood patiently nearby.

"Is this just sex? Is that what we're doing? Because I don't think I want to be another one of your conquests."

Eva's jaw tightened. "Is that really what you think of me?"

It wasn't, not anymore, but Niki was confused. "No. I did once, but...I guess I don't know what the hell we're doing. And I need to know what we're doing, Eva. I have a daughter. A career. Or at least, I used to have a career. I don't do this kind of thing lightly."

"What is it you want to do? Because we don't have to have sex." Eva's lips curled playfully. "We can sit around and analyze the weather reports. Find a hockey game to watch on TV."

"I'm serious." She sighed and patted the bed beside her. Eva didn't waste any time accepting the invitation.

"Sorry. I am too. Look, I don't want to push you into anything you're not ready for, Nik. Hell, I don't even know if

I'm ready for this, now that we're actually alone together in this room."

"What do you mean?" Had Eva changed her mind? Niki tried to gauge her eyes, her face, for a clue.

"What I mean is…Have you been with anyone since Shannon?"

Eva, Niki noticed, never referred to Shannon as her *wife*. "No, I haven't." So that was it. Eva was put off by being Niki's first lover since Shannon, because with it would come a certain depth of seriousness, perhaps commitment, that Eva wouldn't be able to shrug off tomorrow morning, the way she might a hangover. Or a one-night stand. You don't sleep with a grieving widow and then dump her the next day. Niki shook her head lightly. *This is a mistake*, she thought.

Eva's fingers crawled into Niki's and clasped them. "Hey. I want us to be especially sure about this, that's all. It's a big moment for you. For me too."

"Are you going to run away screaming because I haven't been with anyone since Shannon?"

"Honey, I'm running *to* you because you haven't been with anybody else. Don't you know how much I admire you? How much I respect you? You make me want to be a better person, Nik. You always have. I've just been too stupid until now to realize it."

Love for Eva filled her heart, made her dizzy. She'd never stopped loving this woman, but she'd become so accustomed to shutting that part of her heart off over the years, it was hard to crack it open again. When she could finally speak, she said, "I'm flattered. I really am. And since we're being honest, I'm so damned tired of stumbling around on this, this, treadmill of grief. I want to move on, I really do. Even Rory wants me to move on."

"But?"

"I don't want to make a mistake. I don't want to get hurt." There. That was the nub of it. She'd suffered enough hurt when Shannon died, didn't want to travel another road that came to a sudden and painful end.

Eva's smile spread out slow and warm and with the power to melt her heart. "You always were a perfectionist."

"Eva—"

"I'm not going to hurt you." Eva's fingers moved to the underside of Niki's jaw and gently guided her face toward hers. "I won't. I promise."

When Eva's lips brushed hers, arousal flamed to life in her belly and a curl of heat slowly unfurled there. Instantly she grew hard. And wet. She wanted to fight this crazy attraction a bit longer to make sure Eva understood that they had solved practically nothing between them, that their relationship or status or whatever the hell it was remained extremely fragile. But…oh, God, it felt good! She tilted her head back to present her throat to Eva as her eyes slammed shut and her breath…was she even breathing? She moaned as Eva suckled the soft, fleshy part of her throat. She was tired of saying no to Eva. Tired of the sexual dormancy that made her forget she was a woman with needs.

She lay back on the bed, buzzing inside from the slow trail of kisses that meandered along her throat, her neck, her chest as Eva lazily, agonizingly, released the buttons of her denim shirt. She decided to trust that Eva wouldn't hurt her and to trust that she wasn't making a mistake, because she needed this almost as much as she needed to breathe.

After her bra was unclasped and her shirt pushed free of her shoulders, Eva's tongue began to explore the delicate flesh on the undersides of her breasts. It flicked, it tasted, its wetness not at all cold, but warm on her skin. Inside, Niki turned to liquid as Eva's mouth claimed her nipples. She clutched at the cotton sheets to keep herself from levitating off the bed as Eva sucked her, her mouth every bit as adept as she remembered. "Oh, God, Eva, I can't last much longer."

Eva raised her head to look her in the eye. "Don't worry. We have the entire night, and I plan to make use of every last minute of it."

Niki snapped her eyes open and stared down at Eva, wondering how it was possible that the passion between them was every bit as raw and white-hot as it'd been all those years ago. They weren't the same people, not at all, and yet their bodies remembered every breath, every twitch, every urging, every touch, as though nothing at all had changed. She shivered from the heat of Eva's kisses slithering down her abdomen, marveled at how familiar and yet how new Eva's touch felt on her goose-pimpled skin. All that was old was new again as, clamping her eyes shut, strands of light danced behind her eyelids.

* * *

Eva hovered over Niki's belly button and stole another glance at the woman she'd never stopped loving. Her neck was fully exposed, her mouth slightly open in anticipation, her eyes tightly closed and braced for pleasure. Her face was wonderfully kind in a way Eva knew infuriated her, especially anywhere near a hockey rink, where she tried to put on her stern game face. She was beautiful in a genuine, down-to-earth way that didn't scream out "Look at me," yet generated the same result. Eva could look at her all day, but there were other things she wanted, needed, to do at the moment.

She crawled lower, nestled her body between Niki's legs and breathed her in. She wanted to ravage Niki, plunder her with her mouth, her fingers. But her head told her to go slow, to make the moment last as long as possible. The years they were together—how short they seemed now—they'd made love almost recklessly, too fast sometimes, like they needed to hurry up and spend every last drop of passion for one another as if it might expire. But this...this was different. She'd never again take a single minute with Niki for granted. Would never again count on there being a next time. With anything.

Her first taste of Niki was celestial. It sent her passion soaring until it blotted out the rest of the world. She closed her eyes to let the taste and feel of Niki flood her senses. The velvety moist flesh, the hardening pearl nestled within were like a gift to Eva's needy mouth. Her tongue moved in sure, rhythmic strokes, building the tempo slowly in time to Niki's quickened breathing. They both moaned, Eva's low and gratified, Niki's pitched with arousal. With two fingers Eva entered her, not for a second disengaging her mouth as she continued to pleasure her. Niki cried out, breathlessly urging her to keep going, and Eva sucked and licked and pumped ever faster, ever deeper, not slowing as the trembling in Niki's legs intensified and rippled the length of her body.

"Oh, Eva," Niki exploded in a low, tremulous voice. "Oh, I'm coming. I'm coming."

Niki's body stiffened beneath her and around her fingers, Eva's own desire mounting as Niki's orgasm unfurled and unfolded in a violent shudder. She pushed one final time against Eva and cried out from deep in her throat. Slowly and only reluctantly did Eva remove her mouth and her fingers, crawling up Niki to hold her tightly, showering her with little kisses on her neck, below her ear.

There were so many things she wanted to say, but she needed Niki to say things too. She nestled into her, inhaled the salty moist sheen of her sweat. Her chest ached with love. Her heart floated in a current that pulled her, swept her away in its fathoms. All her life she'd always felt on the outside of happiness, a fingertip beyond its reach. Which quite possibly was, she thought, the reason she'd pushed herself higher and faster and harder with her hockey career and with her pursuit of women. It was probably why she'd let Niki go in the first place, because part of her didn't believe she actually deserved to be happy.

Well. Not anymore.

She swallowed against the lump in her throat and tried not to sound too eager, too nervous. "Do you love me, Nik?" *Oh, God, how I need you to.*

Niki looked at her with eyes the same hue of a cloudless sky at the height of summer—wide and warm and full of possibilities. "Yes. But I always have."

Eva moved on top of her so she could pin her with her eyes. "But can you love me *and* be with me?" That was the issue. They'd loved each all this time without being together.

"I don't know yet. Look, I'm being honest, all right? A lot has happened the last few weeks, the last few months. And a lot will be happening over the next ten days. After that, I need to sort some things out. I need time to do that."

The words fell like a guillotine on Eva's heart. And yet what Niki was saying was completely reasonable, sensible. Niki was giving her what she could, and it was enough. It would have to be.

"All right," Eva replied. "I love you, and you need to know that I'm not going to stop loving you, no matter what. And I'm not going to stop doing everything in my power for us to be together."

"Noted." Niki smiled. "Are you finished talking? Because I have things I need to be doing to you. Things that don't require any talking."

Eva laughed and rolled onto her back. "You always did know how to change the subject."

Niki crawled on top of her. "I do believe I'll make it worth your while."

"I do believe you'd better."

"Oh, I plan to."

Niki's hands found her breasts, and so did her mouth, which alternated between her nipples, suckling them gently, then harder, coaxing them into rock hard pebbles. Eva arched her body, anticipation leaving her hard and wet and ready for Niki to take her. Her mind jettisoned every thought but to come and to come at the hands of the woman she loved.

"Nik," she moaned. "I need you inside me. Please."

"But I want to taste you first. I want to suck you."

"No." Desire blinded her. "I need you now. I can't hold on much longer."

Niki danced inside her, hard and fast, exactly the way Eva needed her. She took her with a sense of furious possession, rocking her, eliciting yet more wetness and sending her to a new depth of desire she didn't know she could reach. Niki's mouth continued to pleasure her breasts until she could no longer hold back the tide that would momentarily annihilate her. *Yes, I want to be destroyed*, she thought. *And I don't ever want to come back from feeling this way.*

Her orgasm tore through her, shredding her, reminding her that it was in control at this moment, not her. She rode every last ripple for as long as she could, then pulled Niki up and kissed her long and hard and with every ounce of love that was inside her. To be sure, it was always about sex with this woman, but it was about so, so very much more.

CHAPTER TWENTY-FOUR

Odd Man Rush

From high in the stands, Niki watched Team USA and Russia battle it out. It was a one-sided battle of course, with the US potting three quick goals before the Russians even knew what hit them. Ostensibly she was there to scout the Americans, to see whether they were making subtle or overt changes to their strategies, their line combinations and so on. But she was also there because she wanted to sit in a far corner of the arena alone, to bask in the glow of her secret night with Eva. A night that hadn't ended until they'd both dropped into a deep sleep shortly after two in the morning. They awoke around five, said a lingering goodbye that culminated in hasty shower sex, before rushing off to their respective quarters. She needed the time alone today to macerate in the tingling sensations that coursed through her body, turning her insides to hot molten lava. Eva had, as always, managed to tap into her bottomless well of desire. The fact that it had been neglected and ignored for years hadn't at all diminished its power and depth. Last night she'd wanted, needed, Eva with every fiber of her being. Her body had needed sex with Eva like an addict needed another hit.

Now, desire and love for Eva mashed together indistinguishably, so much so that she couldn't tell where one began and the other ended. She couldn't be sure how much her love for Eva was lust too. But if she truly loved Eva, was in love with her, did it mean she hadn't loved her wife enough? Because if she had, surely there wouldn't be room in her heart for Eva this way, this much, this quickly. Had she betrayed Shannon by falling into bed with Eva last night? Or worse, had she betrayed Shannon from the start by never really abandoning her love for Eva? Had she been fair to her wife all those years, harboring feelings for Eva that she'd tried to convince herself weren't real?

Panic pulsed through her. What if last night was a mistake? Oh, she'd made mistakes all right, a ton of them. But was it in letting Eva go in the first place? Or was it in papering over her feelings for Eva and marrying Shannon? And now…Had she gone and made things worse? Thinking she could go back and have a do-over with Eva? Christ, she'd been married, widowed. She had a kid. She couldn't go back and pretend her post-Eva years had never happened, that they were chalk on a chalkboard that could be conveniently erased after a night with Eva. What a mess she'd made of things.

She wanted to bolt, but she forced herself to stay in her seat and watch the game. Eva was on the ice, striding up the wing (Alison still wasn't letting her play center, it seemed), having to hold up at the blue line for Dani, who, though much younger, was nevertheless a step slower than Eva. Niki shook her head. Why in hell Alison wasn't playing Eva at center, she couldn't guess. Yes, it was mostly a meaningless game, but to stay sharp on center, Eva needed to play the position. And she needed to stay engaged in the game. Eva was a thoroughbred, a champ, and the minute you shortened her leash or didn't let her go at full tilt, she mentally disengaged. And that was a huge mistake, not only for Eva, but most importantly for the team. You didn't want your best player tuning out and not giving a crap.

Niki scratched a note about it in her notebook, her coaching priorities inserting themselves. And then Shannon's face floated in front of her mind's eye. Shannon on her deathbed, looking beseechingly at Niki, making her promise she'd try to find love again. Tears stung her eyes now as her throat tightened. How could she have doubted her love for Shannon? She spoon-fed her in the hospital when she was too weak from the ravages of cancer to feed herself. Read lesbian novels to her, washed her hair with careful tenderness, made a playlist of all her favorite music to play on an endless loop during the hours she was alone, legally adopted her daughter. No. She'd loved Shannon, of course she'd loved Shannon, and that love wasn't—couldn't be—dispatched by the resurfacing of her feelings for Eva. A heart was capable of loving more than one woman. It had to be.

The US was up five to nothing now. Eva chased the puck into the corner, zigging one way, zagging the other to shake off her Russian shadow. She was almost free of her opponent when the Russian pinned her against the boards, knee on knee. From this distance she could see the wince on Eva's face, could feel the stab of sympathetic pain in her own knee. The Russian skated off with the puck and Eva dropped to her knees, doubled over in pain.

Niki stood for a better view, watched Kathleen slip and slide out onto the ice to tend to Eva. Jesus, how was she ever going to make it through these final games in one piece? Niki knew how badly Eva wanted this, but maybe she should pack it in for the sake of her body. Her future. Screw it, it was only a piece of precious metal to sit in a box on the shelf of a closet one day. That's where Niki's own Olympic medals were right now. But she knew Eva, and she knew Eva would pack it in when she was good and ready to pack it in. She would push herself on pure adrenaline and determination, even if that's all she had left in her tank.

Eva hobbled off but she stayed on the bench, which was a good sign. She played sparingly the rest of the game, a handful of shifts, but at least she played, which meant her knee couldn't be too bad. The Americans went on to thrash Russia 13-0, with only one game left—against the Finns—before the semis.

After the game, Niki kept pulling her phone out of her pocket, itching to text or call Eva, to find out how she was, but they'd agreed for propriety's sake that until the Games were over, they would only risk being seen together if others were present. Tomorrow was Rory and Eva's lunch date, she'd see Eva then, but only for a few moments as she handed Rory over to her. If she were smart, she'd stay completely away from Eva, because as soon as she set eyes on her again, she'd want to kiss her, she'd want to run her fingers through that mass of dark curls, would want to press her body into Eva's, would want to inhale the scent of her skin and her soap and her shampoo. *Yeah, but nobody said I was smart.*

She ran a hand through her own hair and sighed. The gold medal game couldn't come soon enough. Not only could she and Eva then begin to navigate their next steps, but she could finally put all the chaos and turbulence of the last few weeks behind her.

* * *

Eva waged an internal battle to keep her face from advertising her secret joy—and lust—as she acknowledged Niki before greeting Jenny and finally Rory. She wasn't worried about what Jenny thought; Jenny always seemed friendly, open toward her and definitely not judgmental. But Rory was a different story. The kid was as smart as a whip, observant as a watchdog. But she was at a vulnerable age, approaching eleven, and at a vulnerable time in her life, almost four years from having lost her birth mother. The last thing Eva wanted was for Rory to think she was trying to take her birth mother's place. And even if Rory didn't see it that way, was she ready for Niki to have a girlfriend? She'd need to tread carefully.

"How's the knee?" Niki asked carefully.

"Which one?" Eva deadpanned.

"Does it matter?"

"Not really. It's okay. Been worse."

"Mom, can I have ice cream for dessert?"

"You want ice cream in the middle of winter?" Niki asked.

"That's the best time, because it won't melt that way." Rory rolled her eyes as if the answer was self-evident.

"I'll have her back at your hotel in a couple of hours," Eva said.

"Take your time," Niki teased. "I'll have to figure out what to do with all that peace and quiet."

"Mom!"

"Only kidding, Rudolph."

Rory's face flushed and her dark eyes turned to granite. "I'm too old for that stupid name. Stop calling me that."

"Rudolph?" Eva said. "As in the red-nosed reindeer?"

Jenny laughed, ruffling her niece's hair. "When she was little, her nose used to turn red whenever she got excited. We all started calling her Rory Rudolph."

"Well then," Eva said, taking Rory's arm and steering her away. "It's always a good time to leave when family members start trotting out the embarrassing childhood stories."

That earned her a grateful smile, and they hurried off to the Tap & Barrel in the Olympic Village. It was a massive restaurant that overlooked the arena grounds, with a menu that featured everything from Pacific salmon to pad Thai. Rory ordered a burger. Eva couldn't resist the pulled bacon craft beer mac 'n' cheese with gouda.

She took a long sip of water to quell her nervousness. The only kids she'd spent much time with were her nephews, and while Rory seemed easy to talk to, it was a strain. With her nephews all she had to do was plunk a hockey stick in their hands, and there was no need to talk for hours. But Rory was bright. And curious about everything.

"Are you and my mom sleeping together?"

The water Eva had just sucked in from the straw shot straight up the back of her throat and into her nose. She reached for the cloth napkin beside her plate, grateful for the diversion of choking, because it let her stall for time.

"Sorry," she rasped, taking another sip. "Wrong tube."

"You are, aren't you?"

"What's that, kiddo?"

"Sleeping with my mom."

Okay, so playing dumb wasn't going to work. "I think maybe you should ask your mom that question." Yeah, that was it. Mothers were the ones who were supposed to answer the difficult questions, not friends of moms. And certainly not lovers.

"But I'm asking *you*." Her big dark eyes were probing, but something in them said her curiosity was academic rather than judgmental.

"All right," Eva said, deciding to be honest. It wasn't as if Rory was a little kid. She was in grade, what, five? Six? "Yes. I am. I mean, we are." Or were. She didn't exactly know how to describe things.

Rory looked at her for a long moment, during which Eva held her breath. Then the girl smiled so wide, it nearly split her face. "Okay. Good. I'm glad you are."

"You are?"

Rory nodded. "Yup. I thought Mom would never get off her butt and sleep with you."

"Okay, wait. Just to be clear. Um, you've had your sex talk, right?" God, did they really have to talk about this?

"Yes. I know everything that happens when two people sleep together."

"Well, I hope not *everything*." Eva felt the heat in her face. "Jeez. Why do kids always have to be in such a hurry to grow up?" she mumbled around another sip of water.

"Mom really likes you. I mean, like, *really* likes you."

"She does, does she? And what about you?"

Her heart raced as she realized how important Rory's answer was to her. But it would have to wait because it was at that moment the server delivered their food. Rory tucked into her burger as though she hadn't eaten in days, Eva figuring the question was long forgotten. Which was fine; she wouldn't press.

"I like you a lot," Rory finally said between bites. "You're cool."

Eva laughed her relief. "Well then, I'm super glad to hear it. What could be better than being cool?"

"Are you and my mom going to get married?"

Married? Panic swept aside Eva's relief, taking with it her appetite. "It's way too early for that. It's a big step. Like, a *huge* step, and there are a lot of things to consider. A lot of grownup things to consider."

"But you love each other, right?"

"Yes, we do. Or at least, I know I love your mom. But it's not that simple, kiddo. Your mom has a lot to think about because she has some awfully big responsibilities. And what about you? How would you feel about me being with your mom? About me being in your life like that?"

Rory looked skyward while she chewed, deep in thought. "I get lonely sometimes. And so does my mom. She's so sad a lot, and that makes me sad. When you're around, we aren't sad anymore."

Eva marveled at the simplicity with which children's minds worked. They knew how to get to the point, maybe because their minds weren't yet clogged up with worry and complications and insecurities. She wished Rory could stay this way forever.

"Well, thank you for saying that, Rory. I get sad and lonely sometimes too. It's always better when you're with people you care for, isn't it?"

"I guess so."

The girl's eyes dropped to her lap, her mouth firming into a hard line.

"What's wrong, Ror?"

A shrug. She hadn't realized how quickly kids' moods could change, like a weather vane hit by a strong, sudden gust of wind.

"Margot."

"Margot? Who's that?" With the subject change, Eva's appetite returned with a vengeance and she dug into her mac and cheese, which contained huge chunks of smoked bacon and globs of melted gouda that added to its smoky flavor.

"My girlfriend."

Eva smiled, liking, no, loving, this kid more and more every minute. "You have a girlfriend? That's awesome."

"Except we got into a fight right before I left. She's mad at me for telling all our friends that we kissed. She thinks people won't like us anymore if they know we're going out."

Ah yes, the homophobic crap that accompanies coming out. Apparently not a lot had changed over the years since she'd come out in high school, earning a few bullying sessions from some of the school's jocks and from a few of the girls too. She'd hoped things were different now, and they probably were, overall, but it didn't mean kids weren't still getting hurt and rejected and humiliated.

"It sounds to me like she's not as brave as you or at least not yet. Maybe she needs a bit more time, because sometimes people need to accept something as big as this at their own pace. But if she doesn't come around, then maybe she's not the girl for you. Right?"

It seemed an eternity before Rory looked up at her and nodded. "Mom told me I should break up with her if she's going to be embarrassed about being with me. But I like your answer better."

"Well, I don't want to go against your mom. But remember this, Ror: nobody should ever be embarrassed to be with you. Got that? You're perfect the way you are, and if other people don't see that, then it's their loss."

Rory beamed at her with newfound confidence. "See, I knew you were cool."

Eva laughed. She had a lot to learn about kids, but so far, it wasn't half bad.

CHAPTER TWENTY-FIVE

Tripping

The Swedes were giving Canada all it could handle in the first period. Niki could see fear and disquiet in Lynn's eyes, could hear the tension in the biting off of her words as she yelled at her charges to skate harder and faster, to start scoring some damned goals. She was coming unglued behind the bench, and already Niki could see the players absorbing Lynn's negative energy. They were getting sloppy, making bad decisions, gripping their sticks too tight. Each player was trying to do too much in a game in which they could only be successful if they played as a team.

Niki tapped her captain's shoulder, leaned down and quietly instructed her to relax and to play the game the way she knew how. Then she told the next player, and the one after that and the one after that, to take a deep breath, to play the game they'd been playing since they were five, six years old. "It's hockey. You skate, you pass the puck, you shoot it, you stop the other team from scoring. It's the same game whether you're playing at the peewee level or the Olympics. Okay?"

She was careful never to undermine or contradict Lynn in front of others. Not because she didn't want to, but because it was the kind of thing that fractured a team, shot morale all to hell. But when the second period began and Lynn unceremoniously trashed the strategies they'd worked on for weeks, Niki felt like losing it. In all three zones, Lynn now wanted the team doing things differently. Their breakouts, their neutral zone puck carrying, their offensive zone puck possession game. Her big idea was for the defensemen to overcommit and pinch almost every time. Yes, it gave them more scoring opportunities, but it was leaving them vulnerable to odd-man rushes and left the goalie hanging out to dry. Lynn also wanted the forwards to skate the puck into the offensive end and shoot before a teammate had time to screen the goalie or to get into place for a rebound. It contravened everything Niki had pounded into the team for months. It also contravened common hockey sense. And now, to change everything on the fly, one game away from the semifinals, was hockey suicide.

With considerable effort, she kept her mouth shut. Even when the players looked at her beseechingly, she gave them a simple thumbs-up or a brief word of encouragement. But she seethed inside, even as her team began to run away with the score. Canada won 13-1, but the score could have been much closer. More concerning was that the players were at loose ends—playing as individuals and scrambling in all three zones. After the final buzzer, Niki stormed off and marched into the coaches' office.

"What was that all about?" she said when Lynn joined her.

"All what? Winning the game?"

"No, not winning the game. The chaotic play out there. You've got those girls not knowing which end is up. Now they're going to be second-guessing themselves at every turn, playing as individuals. They'll stop relying on each other and they'll stop relying on us for guidance."

Her voice shook with rage and indignant accusation. In one single game, Lynn was imploding the team. And yet all she could offer Niki was a smug reminder that they'd won the game by a dozen goals. Being the head coach meant thinking much farther down the road than the game at hand.

"You don't get it," Niki thundered, and she saw Lynn's eyes widen in surprise at her insubordination. People frequently underestimated the heat and passion she was capable of, because it was often buried beneath her cool, reasonable demeanor. She rarely lost her head at the rink, but when she did, the walls shook. "Our team won in spite of the mess you created out there. We won because our players have a solid foundation of skill and confidence. But you keep on this track, and by next game, those girls will absolutely come apart. They'll forget everything we've been working on, their confidence will shatter, they'll be running around out there like a bunch of novice players. And they won't trust you worth a goddamned. I mean, Jesus, Lynn, have you lost your fucking mind?"

Lynn took a seat in the metal chair behind the austere desk that looked like it came out of a thrift store. Her face tightened and shadows crept beneath her eyes, edging out the cockiness she'd exhibited moments ago. "It's character building. Sometimes blowing up the same old mundane tricks motivates them to get out of their comfort zone a bit. That's what I'm doing!"

"But not the game before the semis! This is not the time to experiment with something you read in a bargain-bin *Hockey for Dummies* book."

Lynn's face turned to granite and so did her voice. "*I'm* the coach, in case you've forgotten. And I won't tolerate this kind of attitude from you."

"Oh blow me. You're stuck with me until this is over and you know it." Niki leaned against the cinder block wall, refusing to give Lynn the satisfaction of sitting across the desk from her like the subordinate she kept reminding her she was. "Something's going on around here. I can smell it." Niki made a face like the scent of garbage or shit had wafted in.

"Since you seem to have gone all Nancy Drew on me lately, why don't you tell me what's going on?"

"If I knew, trust me, I'd have you hauled up on Smolenski's carpet so fast, your head would spin. But I swear you're in bed somehow with the Americans. Because what I saw out there... Even for you, it's strange behavior." It felt good to let Lynn have it, to come out swinging.

Venom ate up Lynn's smile. "Oh, I think we know which one of us is in bed with the Americans."

Niki mentally recoiled. Had Lynn somehow found out about her night with Eva? Or was she bluffing? No matter. It was a nice try at deflecting the conversation. She relaxed her shoulders, settled her voice. "If you're in some kind of trouble, Lynn, I swear to you I can help."

"Trouble?" Lynn laughed, but her eyes shone with something else. Fear maybe. "You must be reading too many spy novels lately. There's no trouble here. And I am nothing but positive that the gold medal will be around our necks in five days."

Niki took a step closer, then another step, until she was in front of Lynn, leaning over as her arms straddled the desk. "I won't let you or anyone do anything to mess with this team and what we've worked toward for months."

A visible swallow, an almost imperceptible shake of the head from Lynn. "Whatever. But I'm not the enemy here."

"Then tell me who is."

"Nobody. You're imagining things, Nik."

My ass, Niki thought, but it was obvious Lynn wasn't going to budge.

"I don't think I am, sadly." Niki straightened and took a step back. "In spite of all the crap that's happened the last few weeks, I'm still your friend, Lynn. And I only want what's best for this team. I wish you felt the same."

* * *

Eva winced as Kathleen applied the last bit of tape to her poor excuse for a knee, which was killing her. Both knees were, and Kathleen's taping job left her trussed up like a mummy. But it would, Kathleen promised, hold her together for tonight's game against Finland.

"Can I even fit my gear over this mess?"

Kathleen rolled her eyes. "Yes, you'll be able to fit your gear over it. Think of the upside. You'll look like your muscles have expanded."

"You mean I'll look like the Michelin Man."

The door to the trainer's room barged open, spitting Alison into their midst. She was still clothed in the signature blue and red tracksuit specially designed for the Americans, not yet having changed into her dress slacks and sport coat for tonight's game. She held a clipboard in her hands. Clearly she meant business.

"Will you excuse us, Kathleen?"

"Of course," Kathleen said, already halfway out the door.

Eva hopped off the training table. She didn't want to be at a height disadvantage.

"You're not dressing for the game."

"What? Why not? My knees are no worse than ever. I'm good to go."

"It's not your decision."

If Alison was getting off on her I'm-the-coach act, she could go screw herself. Eva was too old to play this game. "The hell it isn't. I didn't come all this way and put in all this work to sit in the stands. Like I said, I'm good to go tonight."

"And like I said, you're not good to go."

"Look, I get why you want to rest me when we're a game away from the semis. But you know as well as I do that it's better if I play tonight, even if it's only a few shifts." Rust gathered quickly on Eva's knees if she didn't play. And she wanted—needed—to play. Being in the thick of every game was what fed her. It was what made her want to get out of bed every morning and put her body through the meat grinder. If she wanted to sit in the stands and knit, she would have skipped the entire past six months and enjoyed watching the Olympics on a nice big flat-screen television in some swanky bar with a frosty, overpriced beer in front of her.

"Frankly, Cruzie, you've become a liability. You've got the knees of a sixty-year-old. And your hands aren't as good as they used to be either. I'm going with youth. And not just tonight." Alison had the decency to look away. "You're a healthy scratch for the remainder of the Games."

It took a moment for the words to sink in, to realize it was no joke. Eva swayed a little from the dizziness rolling over her in tiny, relentless waves. Thankfully, she hadn't eaten anything but a banana in the last hour, but even it threatened to end up on her shoes now.

"You're shitting me," she finally said in a voice weak with disbelief, with hurt. No semifinal game? No *final* game? It was true her knees were severely compromised without Kathleen's magic, just as it was true she was a good step slower than she'd been a decade ago. But her hands were still sharp no matter what Alison said. Her shooting and passing were second-to-none, and she could see the game unfold in front of her as though it were happening in slow motion. She knew what her teammates and her opponents were going to do before they did it. She could *see* everything unfold about two seconds before it did. She *knew* this game better than anyone, save, perhaps, for Niki.

"You've served your purpose here. You've helped mentor and teach our younger players. Now it's time to get out of the way and let them carry all the weight."

Anger pounded in Eva's heart, each ferocious beat a sledgehammer she wanted to use to hit Alison. "I earned this spot on the team because of my skill and experience. I'm a top six forward on this team, on any team, and you *know* it. I'm the third highest scorer of all the teams in these Games so far. Now why don't you tell me the real reason you don't want me playing?"

Alison started to speak, stopped to regard Eva for a long moment with her beady, deceitful eyes. "You think there's another reason? If that's the case, why don't *you* tell *me*."

Eva debated how much to say, then decided to go for it. She had nothing to lose now, after all. She was off the team and Niki was only hanging on to her position with her own team by a thread. "I think you're scared of me, that's why."

"Scared of you?" Alison laughed. "Why would I be scared of you?"

"I think you're scared I'm going to find out exactly what the hell you and Dani and Lynn O'Reilly have been up to."

Alison visibly flinched, but her eyes didn't waver. "If you're referring to that hot tub photo, you're barking up the wrong tree. I have no idea who took that photo or who leaked it. But it's your own damned fault. If you'd kept your hands off Hartling, none of that shit would have happened."

"That hot tub photo did you a big favor, so don't tell me you had nothing to do with it. Niki was going to kick our ass in these Games if she remained the coach. With Lynn, we've suddenly got a chance. Don't tell me you hadn't figured all that out."

"Of course it works in my favor. I'm not going to look a gift horse in the mouth. But you're giving me far too much credit here."

Eva took a step closer, watched with satisfaction as Alison took a small step back. "Oh, I think you're capable of much more than that. And I'm going to find out exactly what you've done. And when I do, the world's going to know about it. You can count on it."

Alison held out her hand, palm up. "I want your key card and your credentials. Now."

Eva grinned, but not because she was happy. Although she did feel an odd sense of relief. She was free now. Free of the evil witch Alison and her merry band of cheaters. Free to be with Niki. Free to start the rest of her life. But not until she saw that Alison got what she finally deserved.

CHAPTER TWENTY-SIX

High Sticking

The knock on her door gave Niki a start. She glanced at her bedside clock and saw that it was ten minutes to midnight. She hadn't been asleep long, but as her head cleared and the thought that Rory might need her sharpened in her mind, she sat bolt upright and scrambled out of bed. She threw on her robe and yanked open the door.

"Oh, Nik." Eva rushed at her, threw her arms tightly around her, pressed her cheek against her neck. "I'm sorry, I know I'm not supposed to be here," she said haltingly. "I needed to see you."

The smell of beer, stale and a little sour, shrouded Eva like a halo. She was holding Niki so tight, she almost couldn't breathe. "Honey, what's wrong?"

She kept squeezing Niki, breathing rapidly, not speaking. They stood suspended in tense silence until Niki asked her again, gently, what had happened.

"It's over for me." Her voice sounded like gravel crunching under tires.

"What's over?"

"The Olympics. Everything."

Niki extracted herself, sat down on the edge of the bed and invited Eva to sit beside her. She flipped on the bedside lamp, but Eva told her to shut it off. Niki did, then reached for Eva's hand.

"Is it your knees? Did the doctor—"

"No. It was Alison. She kicked me off the team."

"Because of your knees?"

"No, no." Eva huffed impatiently. "She told me I was going to be a healthy scratch for the final three games. We argued. I told her I know she and Lynn and Dani have been up to something, and I threatened to go after them. That's when she revoked my credentials. Jesus. I don't even technically have a right to be in the athletes' village anymore. I don't even have a place to stay tonight."

"Nonsense. You're staying with me." Niki spoke before she considered the ramifications, the optics, of having Eva spend the night in her room. Consorting with the enemy, trading state secrets, blah blah blah. Well, it was too late for all that. She'd already consorted with Eva in the most intimate way possible, and if they were inclined to trade secrets about their respective teams, they'd have done so already. Hell, Eva wasn't even a member of Team USA anymore by the sounds of things. A technicality, but still…

"Baby, you don't have to do that. I can find a room somewhere."

"There aren't any rooms available in this entire city. Besides, I want you here tonight. I need you here tonight."

They fell into a hug that quickly turned into more. They began kissing—long, slow kisses that shimmered with the promise of so much more. "Oh, God, Nik, I can't keep my hands off you," Eva mumbled.

"I don't want you to." Niki's voice was tight with desire. She could hardly breathe as she ran her hands through Eva's thick hair, clutching great gobs of it before pushing Eva's head down to the V of her robe. When they were together like this, alone and in the vicinity of a bed, Niki couldn't think straight. Her mind emptied of everything but one desire, one goal, and that was to come. And to come hard. Afterward, maybe then she could think again, because there was a mountain of things they had to talk about, to figure out. But not now.

Eva eased her onto her back, parted the terry cloth robe to reveal her nakedness beneath. Her mouth, warm, wet, firm but soft, licked and kissed and suckled her hardening flesh. Niki arched, pushing herself into Eva's mouth, pushing the rest of her body into her too, like she might disappear inside of her if she only pushed hard enough.

She could come like this, simply from Eva's skillful mouth on her breasts, but she didn't want to be cheated out of the rest. She pressed her hips into Eva, moved them in undulations that beckoned Eva's hands, her mouth. "Take me, plunder me, possess me," her body screamed out. With Eva, she could never get enough.

The first stroke of Eva's tongue on her wet, moist flesh sent a spasm of desire rocketing through her. She trembled inside, clutched Eva's hair again, pushed against that expert mouth of hers and rode it faster and harder until she lost track of all sense of time and space. Immersed only in her own pleasure, everything else faded to black—every worry, every complication, even her grief for a wife who was never coming back. Only Eva and these crazy, magnetic feelings for her mattered now.

When Eva's fingers entered her, Niki's cries filled the room.

* * *

Eva snuggled against Niki, happy for the first time in a long, long time. An hour ago she'd been miserable. Distraught. And in denial that Alison had booted her from the team. She'd drowned her sorrows in a couple of beers and considered how she could get back at the woman who'd been a thorn in her side for years. And then all she could see, all she could think about, was going to Niki. Niki would make her feel better—safe, loved—and together they'd be able to figure out what to do next. It was Niki, she realized, who had always been the person she thought of first, the person she needed most, in the big moments of her life.

"Can you appeal Alison's decision?" Niki asked. "Go over her head?"

"No. With only the semifinal and the final left, there isn't time to go through an appeal. And let's face it, the powers that be wouldn't want the bad publicity from that kind of thing right now anyway. They'd bury it."

"What about *you* going public with what Alison did to you? That would put the pressure squarely on her to explain why she dumped you. And it might pressure her, or USA Hockey, enough to put you back on the team."

Eva had already thought about going to the media, but she risked forever burning all her bridges with USA Hockey. She also risked appearing petulant, disloyal, attention-seeking, selfish. And it would distract the team at a crucial time. "No. I don't want to do that. Worst-case scenario, it changes nothing and I come out of it looking like a sore loser."

"You don't deserve to be sitting in the stands, sweetheart. I'd have you on my team in a minute."

Eva brushed a strand of hair from Niki's forehead and kissed the spot where it had been. "Thank you, my love, but I'm afraid there's not enough time for you to marry me and make me a Canadian citizen."

She glanced nervously at Niki to gauge her reaction. Niki only smiled.

"If I go after Alison," Eva cautioned, "it can't have anything to do with me getting kicked off the team. It has to be about the lines she crossed with you, with Lynn. And whatever she roped Dani into."

"Then we need proof. And fast." Niki cut her eyes at Eva. "It's all in or else you walk away and forget about it."

"I think you know me better than that."

Niki hoisted herself onto her elbow. "Then let's go after Alison and whoever else she recruited to help her cheat."

"It might have some pretty big implications for you and your team too."

"I know, and I don't care. The chips will have to fall where they may, because what Alison, and by extension Lynn, did to our teams is unacceptable. And might still be doing to our teams." Niki chewed on a fingernail. "Something's going on with Lynn."

"What?"

Niki told her how Lynn had thrown the playbook out the window against Sweden. "It was weird and totally unnecessary. I can't figure out why she did it, but it makes absolutely no sense. It's been driving me crazy. It's like she's trying to destroy the team from the inside out."

"So what do you want to do?"

"There's nothing we can do that will guarantee results, but I can't sit around anymore doing nothing. I'm going to follow Lynn first thing in the morning. She always takes off on foot around seven, supposedly to get coffee."

"Okay, good. I'll follow Dani."

"Why Dani and not Alison?"

"Because I think Dani's up to her eyeballs in this. And I think I'll have better luck getting something out of her than I will Alison. Alison's a veteran at this game. She's slippery."

"Won't it be hard to follow Dani without credentials allowing you into the village?"

"I'll get Kath to help me. And I'll have to hope that Dani goes outside the village."

Niki's forehead crinkled as she thought for a minute. "There's got to be a better way than following people around like we're in a 1920s detective movie. You said back in Whistler you thought you saw Dani texting Lynn. Can't you just get Kathleen to have another look at her phone or something?"

"No chance. Now that we're into the playoff round, Alison's confiscated everyone's phones until after the final game. So Dani won't be texting anyone right now."

"All right. Then it's back to looking for a needle in a haystack."

"Not really. If Dani and Lynn are still communicating with each other, it has to be in person. Or they're using a go-between. In any case, we might be able to catch them at it."

"And what do we do if we see them together?" Niki giggled. "Tie them up? Place them under house arrest? Pretend we're Wonder Woman and Batgirl?"

"As long as I'm Wonder Woman, then yes."

Niki smacked her lightly on the arm.

"All right, no, but we can take photos and then confront them with it. If they won't cooperate, I'm sure the media would be as interested in them spending time together as they were with us and that damned hot tub. Even more so this close to the finals. USA Hockey would be forced to do something."

"Ooh, blackmail. I didn't know you had it in you."

"Desperate times, my love."

Niki leaned in and kissed her on the mouth. "I'm a little desperate myself right now."

"Me too, come to think of it."

Niki gently rolled on top of her, already eating her with her eyes. "Or you could just come and not think about any of it."

Laughter, deep and joyful, burbled up from Eva's throat. "Why, that's an excellent idea."

CHAPTER TWENTY-SEVEN

Shootout

Niki pulled her toque tighter over her ears. She was wearing sunglasses and a heavy winter coat too, but the streets were so packed with people that it wasn't difficult blending in. She'd hid behind a large planter in the hotel lobby a few minutes before seven, waiting for Lynn to emerge from the bank of elevators, feeling like a cuckolded wife hoping to catch the mistress on the premises. But enough was enough. She couldn't let Lynn destroy this team, *her* team. Nor could she stand by and watch Eva get shafted by her coach. It was a gamble, because the whole exercise could easily backfire, but she and Eva had little to lose anyway. Whatever the outcome, it would be worth it.

She followed Lynn down West Waterfront Road and toward Gastown, staying half a block behind, zipping in and out of pedestrian traffic in case Lynn suddenly decided to take a look around. So far she hadn't. So far, she'd trundled along, head down, like a woman on a mission and not a particularly happy mission. Her shoulders slouched, her legs moved heavily but with efficient determination. She looked like a kid on the way to the principal's office.

Niki wanted to feel sorry for her friend and former teammate. Or feel something that didn't involve anger and a sense of betrayal. They'd been close for a time, even rooming together at the Nagano Olympics and at three world championships. Naturally, they'd drifted apart as Niki pursued academia while Lynn continued to play professionally. As coaches, they'd crossed paths again, become friendly again. There'd been nothing back in August, no hint, to suggest that Lynn had a secret agenda or that she'd intended to hurt Niki, that she was a snake willing to sacrifice anything or anyone to get ahead.

There might very well be a reason for the way she was behaving, Niki supposed. She'd meant it when she told Lynn that if she was in some kind of trouble, she could help her. Perhaps something, or someone, had gotten to her. Was she being blackmailed? And if so, why? What could she have possibly done to invite blackmail? Hockey Canada was known to do their due diligence in vetting employees. Niki knew this because they'd done it with her. A criminal records check, credit checks, a medical check, interviews with family, interviews with colleagues, both past and present. If you had a drinking problem or a problem with your credit cards, Hockey Canada knew about it. If you were active on Match.com or on a gambling website, they knew that too.

Which all meant she was back to square one in wondering why Lynn was, by reasonable deduction, feeding information to the Americans and leaking that racy hot tub photo to the press. And then there was her sudden and inexplicable altering of team strategies that had been in place for weeks and months. There had to be a reason she was willing to risk losing her job and any future coaching jobs. A reason too why she was willing to risk a gold medal.

Ahead, Lynn ducked into a coffee shop. Niki stopped a couple of stores ahead and pretended to window-shop. Designer leather couches that she imagined were as soft as butter, rugs that were probably worth the price of a compact car. She snuck another glance down the street in time to see Dani Compton hustling into the same coffee shop.

Shit, Niki thought. Eva was right. Sweat began to collect beneath her heavy coat. As much as she'd suspected there was some kind of conspiracy going on, *knew* in her gut Lynn had become corrupt, part of her didn't want to believe it. She looked around and saw Eva sprinting across the street. They nodded at one another before Eva took up a post on the other side of the café.

Now what? Niki wondered. They hadn't planned anything beyond following Lynn and Dani, other than perhaps taking an incriminating photo. But the two weren't exactly skipping down the street hand in hand. They'd entered the café separately, so there was nothing to say it wasn't a coincidence. There was no evidence they were, right this minute, trading information or cooking up a scheme.

Eva peeked into the café's window before joining Niki.

"See anything?" Niki asked.

"They're sitting together at a table. It didn't look like a happy occasion. Dani's talking with her hands, which she does when she's emotional. Lynn's looking away. But that's it, I couldn't chance staying any longer."

"Crap. Do we go in and confront them?" Niki didn't relish the idea of a public scene but couldn't think what else to do.

Eva thought for a minute, her expression darkening. "No. I'm going to intercept Dani on the way back to the village. It's time she and I had a little chat."

"What about me? What do you want me to do?"

"Nothing. Go back to the hotel or the rink or whatever you need to do." Eva tilted her head forward and gave Niki a quick peck on the lips. "Can you get away later for lunch? We can go over whatever I might learn from Dani, plus figure out our next move."

"Dammit." Niki rubbed a hand across her tired eyes. "We're running out of time. Our semifinal against Finland is tonight."

"And the final is in two days. Believe me, I know."

Niki clasped Eva's hand. "I'm so sorry, sweetheart. But there's still a chance you'll be in that game. Playing my team for gold." There was nothing Niki wanted more, and though it was a long shot, there remained a chance Alison would change her mind or would be forced to change her mind.

"So…" Eva's eyes—steady, sure—pinned her. "Meet me for lunch?"

"Yes. I can get away. We have a light practice at two, so let's meet at half past twelve. How about Matchstick in Chinatown? That should be far off the beaten path."

"Okay, my love, let's do it." Already, she was backing away.

"And, honey? Please be careful."

Eva gave her a shrug that said what-could-possibly-go-wrong. Then she was gone, darting behind a tall stranger before dashing across the street again.

* * *

It wasn't difficult to follow Dani, who was either too stupid or too cocky to worry that she was doing anything wrong. She bounced along like she hadn't a care in the world. Or rather, like she was privy to a secret, to something glorious, that nobody else knew. Eva followed at a safe distance, waiting until Dani approached the opening of a narrow alleyway.

As Dani was about to step past the alley entrance, Eva took off at a sprint and shoved her around the corner and down the damp, dark alley that was no wider than if Eva stood in the middle and extended her arms.

"Jesus Christ, Cruzie!" Dani's face drained of color. "What the fuck? You scared me half to death. I thought you were some mugger."

"I'm not a mugger, but I am here to get something out of you." Eva stepped closer to prevent Dani from making a run for it.

"What the fuck are you talking about?" Dani's affected bravado was already beginning to crumble. Her eyes scanned a little too eagerly for the exit points, and she shifted her weight from foot to foot.

"I'm talking about you and Alison and Lynn O'Reilly. And you're going to tell me exactly what the three of you are up to."

Dani laughed. "Fuck you, Eva."

In a blur from Dani's blind side, Eva's left fist was suddenly at the younger player's throat, clutching her hoodie in a choking knot. She shoved her face into Dani's until she could smell the strawberry bubblegum on her breath. "You're going to tell me *right* now what the three of you have been cooking up. And don't bullshit me, cuz I'm not buying a single ounce of it."

There was a flash of panic in Dani's visible swallow, but her smile remained cool, unflappable. "It's too bad you're off the team. Won't be able to enjoy that gold medal around your neck in a couple of days. Like the rest of us. I've already bought a special glass case for mine."

"You're awfully confident of something that hasn't happened yet. Tell me why."

"Isn't every member of the team confident of a win? Isn't that what you told us once yourself? That winning starts in the mind. That there's no winning without believing you're going to win."

"Bullshit." She tightened her grip, knew she was going to leave a bruise. "How about we start with that hot tub picture. Whose idea was that, yours? Lynn's? Alison's?"

"Maybe it wasn't anybody's idea," Dani ground out. "Maybe it just fell into one of our laps or something."

She'd made a tactical mistake, Eva realized. Dani knew she'd never choke her, not for real. She released the knot she'd made of her hoodie, grabbed her by the right wrist and pinned it against the chipped brick wall and its faded mural advertising Kokanee beer.

"It didn't fall into anybody's lap. Tell me."

Another smile, a challenging one this time. She was daring Eva to make good on her threats. "None of that crap matters after tonight anyway. The gold is ours and we're gonna win it fair and square, you watch."

Eva had had enough of Dani's games. She gripped her thumb, twisted it against the wall. "Tell me what you know, you little bitch, or I'll break your thumb *and* sprain your wrist. Which means you won't be playing in any gold medal game."

Dani's eyes widened and there was an audible intake of breath that was sharp and sudden. Violence was not normally part of Eva's vernacular. On the ice, even after an opponent had run her over, or slashed her, or tackled her, or done any number of illegal and brutal things, Eva didn't retaliate. Not with violence. A goal or two, yes. It wasn't so much that she was a pacifist as a cold-hearted realist. She employed the kind of revenge that would, in the long run, hurt you the most. And in this case, she knew that keeping Dani out of the final game would hurt her the most.

Eva didn't see the kick coming, hadn't anticipated it either. But she felt the pain in her knee like a lightning bolt splitting a tree. It was pain so red hot that it put spots before her eyes. She crumpled to the ground. Dani's fading laughter was the last thing she heard before she blacked out.

CHAPTER TWENTY-EIGHT

Shutout

Niki glanced at her watch again, then tapped out a beat on the tabletop. It wasn't like Eva to be late. As it was, they were going to have very little time before Niki had to get back to the arena for a short practice. Her team would be on the ice for less than an hour and wouldn't do anything vigorous before tonight's game against Finland. It was more for a final few tweaks and for the players to warm up their legs, but it was imperative that Niki be there. Especially since she could no longer trust Lynn's coaching. For all she knew, Lynn would have them in figure skates. Or something equally stupid like put them through a bag skate, which would leave them exhausted for the game. Lynn had lost all sense lately.

Shit. Eva was really late now. What if something had happened to her while she was following Dani? Most troubling was that she had no way of knowing if anything had happened, and if it had, what the hell could she do to help Eva? She pulled her phone from her coat pocket. To hell with it, she'd text Eva, and if Eva didn't text back within minutes, she'd phone her.

The restaurant door edged open and in came a limping Eva who couldn't, by the looks of it, straighten her left leg. It was painful to watch her drag her leg, her jaw clamped so tight that even from a distance, Niki could see was in extraordinary pain.

"Jesus," Niki said, springing up from her seat and rushing to help Eva. She slipped an arm under her left shoulder for support. "What the hell happened?"

In silence they hobbled to the table, where Eva dropped into her seat with a grimace and a loud groan.

"Here," Niki said, pushing a glass of cold water toward her. She watched her drink it, saw every tendril of pain etch its way onto her face and made a decision. "I'm taking you to the hospital. Let's go."

"No." Eva latched onto Niki's wrist to get her to sit down again. "You have to get to your practice."

"No. I'll skip it."

"You can't." The note of desperation in her voice made Niki sit up straighter. "You have to be there to keep an eye on Lynn." She stopped to take a breath, closing her eyes tightly for an instant. Her face, Niki noticed, was as white as the tablecloth. "Something's going to happen with the game tonight."

"*My* game? Against Finland?"

Eva nodded.

"No. Finland's never beaten us. Even with Lynn trying her damnedest to screw things up, we should be able to beat them with one arm tied behind our backs."

Eva shook her head. "I don't think so, not this time."

"What? What are you saying? What did you find out?" Niki leaned closer. "And more important than all that, who did this to you, sweetheart?"

"Dani. I confronted her. She kicked me."

Dread, chased by anger, was like a fist in Niki's gut. She'd kill Dani Compton next time she saw her. Kick her twice as hard as she'd kicked Eva. Better yet, she'd get her biggest, toughest player to give Dani something to think about on the ice.

The server, a gorgeous Asian woman with the shiniest, blackest hair Niki had ever seen, asked if they knew what they'd like to eat. Eva shook her head, closed her eyes again, probably to fight nausea, if Niki had to guess.

"I'm sorry," Niki said. "I think we've had a change in plans. Just more water for now. Thank you."

"As you wish," the young woman said, never dropping her smile, before scurrying away.

"Honey, if she kicked you, we should call the police. Then get you to a hospital. She's obviously hurt you badly."

"I'm okay. And we're not calling the police."

"You're not okay."

Eva was biting her bottom lip, her skin white where her teeth connected. "I don't want to argue about this."

"You're right. Let's not argue. Tell me what you think we should do."

"You have to go to your practice. And you have to make sure Lynn doesn't do something to make the team lose tonight."

"Why would she try to pull off something like that?"

"I don't know. But Dani said none of this crap would matter after tonight. That USA will win the gold, all fair and square."

It had never occurred to Niki that Lynn would try to throw tonight's game, that Canada wouldn't make it into the finals. But it made a certain sick sense. Tanking the gold medal game against the US would be too obvious. But failing to make it into the final game, well, that would pave the way for Team USA to win gold against the inferior Finns.

"I guess that's as much an admission as we're going to get," Niki mumbled, her thoughts turning to how she was going to thwart whatever Lynn might be cooking up for tonight's game. It wouldn't be easy to let the Finns beat them, not without the players in on it, and Niki was positive that wouldn't happen. "All right. Here's what we're going to do. I'll go to the practice and I'll do whatever it takes to make sure my team wins tonight. But first I'm calling Kathleen and asking her to take you to the hospital for X-rays."

"I'll call Kathleen, I promise. You go."

"I'm not leaving you here, Eva. Not until you call her and I know she's coming."

Eva rolled her eyes, but she pulled out her phone and began punching in Kathleen's number. "Fine. You win."

Niki beamed. "I like winning."

* * *

"I'm so sorry," Kathleen said to Eva as the doctor, a burly guy who looked like a rugby player in his spare time, left the exam room with a promise to return shortly with a set of crutches for her.

"The bitch of it is that now that I'm hurt, Alison has a legitimate reason not to play me in the final two games."

"No." Kathleen's voice rose to an angry pitch. "The bitch of it is that you can't play hockey for at least twelve weeks. And worse than that, your playing career is probably over now. Dani Compton is going to pay for this, I promise you that, Eva. If it's the last thing I do, I'll—"

"No, Kath. I don't want you doing anything to anybody right now. And my playing career was going to be done after these Games anyway."

It wasn't a secret that her body couldn't hack the rigors of the game anymore. Anyone paying any attention to the way she played or who saw her limping and grimacing after games or practices knew this was her last serious attempt at any kind of championship. A hairline fracture to her patella, thanks to Dani, had sealed the deal. And yes, she was pissed off and disappointed, and she wanted to scream and hit something. But it wouldn't change the fact that she would leave these Games without a medal. Nor would it change the fact that she'd sacrificed and worked so hard the last few months for nothing. If it wasn't for the rekindling of her romance with Niki, she'd be truly desolate.

Calmer now, Kathleen said, "What are you going to do? And what can I do?"

"I'm going to wait and see if Niki finds out anything at practice. If she doesn't, I'm prepared to blow the roof off everything."

Kathleen's eyebrows shot into her forehead. "How?"

"By holding the biggest press conference these Games has seen so far. And I'll tell them everything I know." It was a bold step and one that could and probably would permanently destroy any future she might have with hockey on a national or even collegiate level. But it beat the hell out of watching a team cheat its way to victory. And it might give her a small measure of consolation for suffering through another injury, one viciously inflicted by her own teammate this time.

"You've got nothing to lose, I suppose. And it just might smoke out the rats."

"Will you help me, Kath? Are you willing to stand up there beside me and verify everything I'm saying?" It was asking a lot, and she wouldn't take it personally if her friend said no.

The doctor returned, knocking lightly before barging in with a set of crutches. "Two weeks with these, I'm afraid. And I have a prescription for you to help with the pain."

"No," Eva said before she had a chance to reconsider. "I don't need any pills, thanks. I'll be fine."

"Suit yourself. Take some over-the-counter NSAIDs. And see your regular doctor in a couple of weeks, okay?"

"I will," she promised, taking the crutches and placing them under her arms.

The doctor led the way, Eva hobbling behind him and Kathleen taking up the rear. There were reporters hanging around, the doctor had warned them, because of a downhill skiing crash earlier in the day involving a medal favorite.

"I can get you out a side exit," he said over his shoulder. "I had one of our receptionists call a cab for you."

"Thank you," Eva replied. "I appreciate all—"

"Hey, that's Eva Caruso."

Shit. From the corner of her eye she saw a video camera swing in her direction and a reporter, a woman with unnaturally blond hair and wearing expensive boots, rush toward her.

"No questions," the doctor said, positioning himself between the reporter and Eva.

Ignoring him, the reporter peppered Eva with questions: How had she been hurt? Did she have a broken leg? Was she out of the Games?

Eva shook her head and kept hobbling toward the exit. Outside, she turned to Kathleen. "Get that woman's card, would you? In case I need to talk to her later."

"You got it. And Eva? Of course I'll stand beside you if you need to call a press conference."

Eva nodded, too tired and too overwhelmed to smile. She was lucky to have good people in her life. And that was worth far more than a medal. If karma existed, people like Dani and Alison would end up miserable one day, if they weren't already. And someday they too wouldn't have hockey in their lives, except that they'd have no one to comfort them, nothing else to fill the void. She almost felt sorry for them.

CHAPTER TWENTY-NINE

Bar Down

As Niki stepped onto the ice for the practice, she caught sight of the team's two best players, a defenseman and a forward, sitting in the stands near the bench, dressed in their tracksuits.

She skated to Lynn, who'd preceded her onto the ice with the rest of the team.

"What's with Kennedy and Matthews sitting in the stands?"

"They're scratched for tonight's game."

"What?" Niki's stomached bottomed out. Both women were potential future hall of famers, and without them, tonight's game would be a much tougher undertaking. Kennedy was averaging three points a game and had more game-winning goals than anyone on the team. Matthews had the team's best plus-minus and was the quarterback on power plays.

"Nagging injuries. Kennedy's got a bad shoulder, Matthews had her bell rung the last game. Best to rest them tonight so they're good to go for the final."

"Doc Stevenson wouldn't clear them to play tonight?" She'd have received an email memo if that had been the case, but she wasn't about to let Lynn off the hook.

"Coach's decision." Lynn's tone made it clear there'd be no further discussion.

Lynn blew her whistle and directed the group to skate a few laps at an easy pace. Niki skated to the bench and called out to Kennedy and Matthews. "You two okay?" Judging from their sullen expressions, they were not.

Matching shrugs from both.

"Are you guys really not up to playing tonight?"

"Coach wants to rest us," Kennedy said, looking at her shoes.

"We can play," Matthews grumbled. "If she'd let us."

It was common practice that you didn't rest your top players in a sudden-death game unless they were at risk of injuring themselves a hell of a lot worse than they were. Infuriated, Niki stood along the boards, watching the players skate around, then drop to the ice to stretch their muscles. She knew Kennedy and Matthews were drilling hopeful, desperate stares into her back, willing her to do something about their predicament.

The backup goalie, a rookie, moved into the net to get ready to receive shots. Niki watched as their regular goalie, a proven winner and the team's unequivocal number one goalie, stood along the boards, watching the play, glancing at Lynn for the signal that it was her turn in the net. It didn't come. On and on the shooting drills went, with the backup taking all the shots. Unwilling to hold her tongue about yet another inexcusable blunder, Niki approached Lynn.

"Sutherland's getting cold standing over there. Why don't I take a group of players and work her at the other end."

"No," Lynn said. "Sutherland's not starting tonight."

Niki felt her fingers curl into fists. She had to grind her teeth to keep from exploding. With three of the team's best players sitting out tonight's game, Lynn had lost it for sure. Or Eva was right and Lynn was sabotaging the game. "And why is that?"

Lynn chewed her gum with exaggeration, trying to look comfortably authoritative, except she wouldn't meet Niki's eyes. "I want her rested for the final. Besides, Graham needs the work. She'll be fine."

"There won't *be* a final game for us if we lose tonight," Niki ground out. "You're taking some awfully big risks here."

"It'll be fine, you'll see."

"And what if it's not?" Could Lynn be any more obvious about trying to screw their chances of getting into the final? More to the point, what the hell did Alison have on her that would make her do such a thing?

"We can beat Finland in our sleep."

"Maybe, maybe not without our top players. If we lose tonight, you *do* realize you're finished with Hockey Canada. And maybe coaching anything but high school hockey."

The smallest flash of discomfort registered in Lynn's eyes. "You're overstepping, Hartling. Now go hit the showers and I'll see you at the game tonight."

Niki stormed off, despairing. It was a disaster to have a coach and an assistant coach at loggerheads. And it was going to be a bigger disaster to sit their three best players tonight. Clearly, Lynn was up to something while caring little for personal consequences. If she was willing to sacrifice her reputation, her future, then she was extremely desperate. But short of physically locking her in a room and taking over the bench or conducting some other means of a *coup d'etat*, there seemed little choice for Niki than to watch how things played out. She couldn't go to their boss and claim that Lynn was screwing with the roster, the lines, the strategies, because Lynn would simply argue she was exercising her right as head coach to make all the final decisions about every aspect of what the team did on the ice. Smolenski could and frequently did attend practices and games. If he had concerns, it was up to him to voice them.

She sat down in the locker room, buried her face in her hands. She'd never experienced anything like this before. Maybe it was naïve, but she expected players and coaches at this level to act professionally, to have nothing but the best of intentions, to work their hardest for the common good of the team. When someone didn't do those things, it was so anathema to Niki that it left her paralyzed with inaction.

What would Eva do in this situation? Strangle Lynn? Demand the truth or else...or else what? Call the troops together behind Lynn's back and quietly mutiny? Eva wouldn't sit idly and do nothing. And neither could Niki. She had not sacrificed the last six months of her life for nothing. She needed to come up with a plan.

* * *

Eva scanned the hallway before she knocked on the door of Niki's hotel room. She was staying in Niki's room, but only at night. She'd slipped out shortly after daybreak this morning to hide out in a café, not wanting the media—or Rory—knowing she and Niki were shacking up for what was left of the Games.

Rory opened the door, shock on her face as her eyes registered the crutches under Eva's arms.

"Oh my God. Mom! Eva's hurt."

"It's okay," Eva said, hopping through the door before closing it.

"But how can you play hockey tomorrow? And in the final game?" She looked about to cry, which mirrored how Eva felt.

Niki came up behind Rory and gave her shoulder a squeeze. "I'm afraid she won't be, sweetie."

"But, why? What happened?"

Rory's disappointment was a dart straight into Eva's heart. "I, uh, slipped on some ice, can you believe it?" She forced a smile. "And no, I didn't have skates on. It was outside. I've got a little crack in my kneecap." She glanced at Niki, saw the strain on her face. "So, yeah, I'm off skates for a few weeks."

"No," Rory said, shaking her head. "You can't miss the final game, Eva. You can't!"

"I'm sorry, Ror." Eva reached out and stroked the top of her head. "I hate that I have to miss it, but accidents happen."

The kid was really working at hiding her tears, swallowing them back until she began to hiccup. If she didn't stop it, Eva herself was going to start crying like a baby. She cleared the sand from her throat. "We're gonna watch your mom's team win tonight, right? We're going to cheer as loud as we can for her. And I'll buy you as much ice cream as you want."

"I don't want no stupid ice cream."

"That's very rude, Rory." Niki mouthed a silent apology to Eva. "You were looking forward to hanging out with Eva and your Aunt Jenny at the game tonight, remember? Nothing's changed with that."

Rory hung her head, crossing her arms over her chest. "I'm sorry," she mumbled.

"Me, too," Eva said.

"Why don't you go get your backpack, sweetie. And make sure your sweater's in there."

"It's not a sweater, Mom, it's a hoodie. It's not even going to be cold in there, and besides, I'll have my Team Canada jersey on too."

"Fine, whatever," Niki said, rolling her eyes behind Rory's back. "Go get your stuff, please."

Rory ran off, and Eva took the opportunity to cup Niki's cheek and kiss her.

Niki pulled her in tight. "Darling, I was so worried about you," she whispered. "You have a fracture?"

"Just a hairline. It'll be fine."

"I'm so sorry. I wanted—hoped—it wasn't as bad as it looked."

Eva rested her forehead against Niki's and looked into her eyes. "There's more important things than playing in that gold medal game, Nik. I know that now. You, Rory…Anything else is way down the list."

"But it's not right, dammit. And somebody's got to pay for this."

"Somebody *will*. Eventually. What happened at practice today?"

Niki summarized, none of it surprising Eva. Lynn was beginning to show her hand.

"That's amateur stuff," Eva huffed. "Sitting her two best players, playing the backup goalie. Not very creative of her."

"She's changed the lines all around too."

"So what? That's no guarantee the team's going to lose. Lynn's scared. She's supposed to tank the game or at least make it look to someone like she's trying to tank the game. I think she's desperate and doesn't know what the hell she's doing."

"Meaning?"

"Meaning if you squeeze her the right way, I think she'll cave."

"I'm not so sure. But I know one thing. I won't stand by and watch my team lose tonight."

"Do you have a plan?"

Niki shook her head lightly. "Not yet. But I'll figure it out."

Rory cleared her throat loudly, causing Niki to leap back a step.

"Sheesh, Mom. It's okay. I know you and Eva are all, like, in love and stuff."

The look on Niki's face—mouth open, eyes as big as hockey pucks—was adorable. And made Eva giddy with happiness. "You do? I mean, and you're okay with that?"

"Of course." Rory's gaze swung from one to the other and she grinned. "And you better not mess it up, Mom."

Eva erupted in a fit of laughter, though Niki looked much less amused. "Never mind, young lady. The only thing I'm going to mess up is you if you don't get going. Now remember, your aunt—"

"I know, I know. She's meeting us at the game. I'm not a little kid, Mom. I could even get there myself if I needed to."

"You'll do no such thing," Niki said, hand at her heart.

"It's okay," Eva said. "Don't worry, I won't let her out of my sight. Besides, she's going to be my popcorn fetcher."

"All right, you two. I'll see you guys after the game."

Eva leaned on her crutches and kissed Niki on the lips. "Good luck, sweetheart. I'll be watching. And I'll be with you every step, okay? No matter what."

"I know. Thank you. And I *will* need luck."

"Knock 'em dead, Mom."

"I just might need to," Niki mumbled.

CHAPTER THIRTY

Overtime

Niki paced at her end of the bench. The first period was drawing to a close, and still there was no score. Canada hadn't been held scoreless in the first period of a game yet in this tournament. Her team wasn't getting the puck cleanly out of their end, and when they had possession in their opponent's end, they played without confidence. Their usual strategies were in shreds, thanks to Lynn's constant tinkering. The lines were all mixed up, so that players suddenly playing together didn't intrinsically know each other's habits. The backup goalie was holding her own so far, but she hadn't proved herself under fire yet. Niki feared that as soon as Finland potted a goal, her goalie would mentally collapse.

As each minute clicked down on the game clock, Niki grew more and more worried. Her team should be dominating this game. They should be razor-sharp and hungry to get on to the next game against the Americans. They should be peaking right now, not diving head first into the toilet. If they managed to survive this game, they wouldn't last a period in the finals. The

Americans would steamroll them. And laugh the whole time they were doing it. If Canada managed to win this game, victory would be short-lived.

She glanced up into the stands, into the section where she knew Eva, Rory and Jenny were sitting. Kids like Rory adored their national team, whether it was Canada, the United States, Finland or Sweden. They looked up to the players, wanted to be like their heroes. Those kids, Niki thought with burning indignation, expected and deserved their teams to play their hearts out, to win (or lose) fair and square. The integrity of the game was at stake, and if Niki turned a blind eye to it, she was every bit as guilty as Lynn, Alison and Dani.

She raked her eyes over Lynn and shook her head, wishing to somehow, magically, knock some sense into her. The crowd was getting restless and cranky too; they were used to their team breezing to victory. Many had begun yelling their frustration at the referee and the team, while others had tuned out and were chatting with their seatmates or goofing around on their cell phones.

When the buzzer mercifully signaled the first intermission, Niki shot ahead down the tunnel and into the coaches' office, where she planned to ambush Lynn the second she walked in. She didn't have a script or even a plan, but she couldn't take this anymore. She'd have to wing it, and she'd have to calm down. And then an idea occurred to her.

Lynn marched in, looking distracted, a bead of sweat at her temple.

Quietly and without judgment, Niki said, "You're in trouble, Lynn. I know everything. And I want you to know that we can fix this."

Lynn swayed a little, rocking on her heels. "What are you talking about?"

"I'm talking about this game. About how you're supposed to do your damnedest to make sure we lose. And if by some chance we win it, the girls will be so rattled, so disorganized, that we won't have a hope in hell of winning gold on Saturday. It's all part of the plan."

Lynn collapsed into the worn leather sofa along the wall, and buried her head in her hands. The silence was painful and it seemed to stretch out forever. Clearly, she had no intention of admitting to anything. Or maybe she was in complete denial. In any case, there wasn't much time; intermission was only twenty minutes long. Seventeen now.

"I know the plan is to hand the Americans the gold. And to do it without making it look like that's what we're doing. We either don't get into the final against them, or if we do, we'll sufficiently play like shit and have no hope against them."

The sofa hissed under Niki's weight as she sat down next to Lynn, so close that their shoulders touched. She softened her voice, hoping, praying her bluff would work. "Dani told Eva everything, and Eva told me. I know about all of it, Lynn."

Lynn shook her head over and over, her eyes pinched shut. She might have been silently crying for all Niki knew.

She put her arm around Lynn's shoulder. They'd been buddies once, teammates through victories and defeats, grueling practices, tough injuries and even tougher coaches. She remembered an exhibition game, months before the Nagano Olympics, when she'd sprained her ankle after flying feet first into a goalpost. It was Lynn who'd skated to her aid first, helped her off the ice and practically carried her to the locker room. They grew apart when Niki stopped playing and became a coach and an associate professor, while Lynn toiled in a semi-pro league awhile longer, then became a coach too. The sacred alliance that had been nurtured and solidified in those early, formative playing years should have transcended time and distance. But it hadn't.

"We can turn this around. No matter what you've done or what you've agreed to, we can undo it, I promise. It's not too late to make this right."

Lynn began to sob. Big, chest-heaving sobs that shook her whole body. Tears gushed through the fingers covering her face. Niki held her silence, rubbed Lynn's back reassuringly. She couldn't afford to rush her, even though they were on the clock, but she silently implored her to snap to it.

Nearly inaudibly, Lynn finally muttered, "I don't know what to do."

"Tell me first exactly what you were supposed to do tonight."

"Nothing, I…" Lynn took a deep, shuddering breath. "Just what you said. I was trying to stack the deck against us. If we…if we lose tonight, all the better. If we don't and we make the final, it'll be nearly impossible to beat the Americans."

Niki took a moment to steady herself. She wanted to shake Lynn. Or worse, slap her. "Okay, well." There was little satisfaction in being right. "We can fix that. We can put Sutherland back in net. We can get the lines back where they were. It's too late to insert Matthews and Kennedy, but we can do this without them."

Niki knew she would need to take matters further, to Smolenksi and maybe to the public as well, to ensure all the guilty parties were properly rooted out and censured. Even if Lynn had good reasons for crossing over to the dark side, it wouldn't be right to let her off scot-free. But justice would have to wait; it was time to focus on the game. She tapped the inside pocket of her sport coat and the hard casing of her micro-recorder there, which she'd clicked on a few seconds before confronting Lynn. Backup was never a bad idea.

"If we don't lose the gold…" Lynn looked away. Disgust, fear, self-loathing were all over her face.

"What?" Niki pressed. "What will happen? What will Alison do to you?"

"Not just to me. To Dani too."

"What will she do to you and Dani? What does she have on you, Lynn?"

"She'll throw us both under the bus. We'll be sanctioned. Dani will never play again for her country and her NCAA scholarship will be dissolved. And I'll…" Lynn shook her head and barked a laugh. "And I'll never coach again. But I won't anyway, since I've been making such a mess of this team. What I can't figure out is why Dani confessed it all to Eva. She hates Eva with a passion."

Niki glanced at the clock. Six more minutes. "She didn't confess to Eva. Eva tried to get her to talk, and instead she kicked her and broke her kneecap. That's why Eva's out of the tournament."

It took a moment for the surprise to register on Lynn's face, and when it did, her jaw turned to cement. "You lied to me?"

"I'm sorry, but I couldn't stand by and watch what was happening any longer. It's wrong, Lynn, no matter how good your reasons. Those girls out there…" Niki gestured toward the locker room next door, her voice breaking. "They deserve our best. They deserve to earn their wins, or their losses, fair and square. Not to mention you're screwing with their future careers, their future earnings. But it's not too late, I promise."

Lynn stood, her eyes lifeless, her composure in tatters. Her defeat produced no joy for Niki. "You take over the bench for the rest of the game, Nik. I have a feeling I'm done after tonight anyway."

Niki stood too. "Wait. You never told me why you did this. Or why Dani's involved." As much as she was horrified and disgusted by everything that had transpired, a greater part of her needed to understand why.

"It started last spring. At the world championships…"

* * *

In her boxer shorts and T-shirt, Eva lay on the king bed in Niki's room, restlessly jiggling her good leg. With the television remote she cruised through channels as fast as flipping the pages of a magazine. Nothing on but news, a rerun of a curling match, infomercials on a popular face cream, the shopping channel. After several restless minutes, she settled on an old *Sex and the City* episode and glanced at the clock again. It was almost midnight. Niki's game had ended more than two hours ago, a 5-0 win over Finland. When Niki had taken over the bench to start the second period, Eva had watched with a relief so intense that it made her hands tremble. Looking every bit the poised and competent commander she was, Niki seemed to have to do little to get her players back on track. Her presence alone conveyed that order had been restored, and relief oozed from the players in every stride they skated and every shot they took. They were themselves again, playing spirited hockey and doing it with a smile on their faces. But it was killing Eva not knowing what had transpired between the first and second periods. She glanced impatiently at the clock again as the door opened and Niki quietly entered.

"Hi, sweetie," Niki whispered. "I thought you might be sleeping."

"Sleeping?" Eva blinked in disbelief. "Are you kidding me?"

Niki hurried to her, leaned down and kissed her slowly and thoroughly. Eva moaned, wanting the kiss to go on forever, but she also needed the reassurance of Niki's body beside her and in her arms. They were nearly at the finish line now, Eva could feel it, and though it was right to celebrate this latest victory, there was still some distance to go before this entire nightmare was behind them. With a wicked grin, she flipped Niki onto the bed beside her, turned into her and held her tightly.

"You feel so good," Niki mumbled against her neck, her breath warm. "I don't want to leave this room. Like, ever."

"Me either. And maybe we shouldn't. But I'm dying to know what happened. Tell me everything before I burst!"

The worry that had taken up residence in Niki's eyes and in the lines around her eyes was gone now. Or at least was much faded. In its place there was a light Eva hadn't seen in weeks.

"Lynn confessed everything. I secretly taped it all on my recorder in case she had a change of heart later, but she didn't. She agreed to accompany me to meet Dan Smolenski after the game and she came clean with him too."

"Wow. I didn't think she had it in her. What changed her mind?"

"I told her I already knew everything. That Dani had confessed to you. So that was definitely the turning point. But later she said something else had been eating away at her too. She said when she saw Rory parading around everywhere these last few days wearing her Team Canada jersey, it began to break her heart."

"Huh. I didn't think she had one."

"Everyone has one. Some simply lose it for a while, and sometimes they even have reasons for losing their way. I think Lynn couldn't stand the pressure she was under anymore."

"Well, Alison doesn't have a heart. And if she does, it's black and gooey and the size of a pea."

Niki laughed. "I won't argue with you there. But a few things happened along the way for Lynn. Things I was too blind to see because I was so wrapped up in coaching, in worrying about Rory and then with us. I didn't see how much she was struggling. Well, that's not entirely true. The signs were as big as billboards, but I didn't handle things right. And that's a failure on me, both as a coach and as a friend."

"Whoa, wait a second. You can't blame yourself for her misdeeds. She was on her way to tanking tonight's game, for God sakes! Not to mention spying for Alison, and whatever else she's been doing. I suppose she was behind that hot tub photo too?"

"Sorry, let me back up a few steps. Last April at the worlds, Lynn and Dani started an affair. It was—"

"Wait. What?" Eva couldn't believe it. Lynn was at least fifteen years older and not at all Dani's type. Although, come to think of it, she didn't know a damned thing about who was or wasn't Dani's type, mostly because she didn't care. But she would never have guessed a sexual relationship between the two.

"It's true. It was mostly sexual on Lynn's part. So she says, anyway. It only lasted a couple of weeks and she ended it right after the tournament. But—"

"Wait, are you sure Dani wasn't getting into her pants so she could tap her as a future source for information? Lynn was the assistant coach for Canada at the worlds, right? Maybe it was all part of the plan leading to what's happened here."

"Lynn swears Dani fell in love with her. Kept bugging her all summer, pretty much stalking her, asking to see her, begging to keep the affair going, buying her gifts, calling her and texting her and emailing her all the time. And maybe it was part of some big plan of Dani's, but Lynn doesn't think so. By your own admission, Dani doesn't seem that bright. Besides, at the time, there was no suggestion that Lynn was going to be selected to be the assistant coach for the Olympic team. That didn't happen until early August."

"All right, so if that's true, how did Lynn get sucked into conspiring with Dani and Alison against her own team?"

"Lynn said she knew she fucked up by having an affair with Dani. There's nothing technically unethical about having a relationship with someone on another team. It's not a dismissal clause in our contract or—"

"Good thing, or you'd have been fired weeks ago."

"True. It's only prohibited for coaches and players on the same team to have a relationship. The problem is that Dani's unstable, as it turns out. Lynn really couldn't have picked anybody worse to have an affair with."

"I'll say." Eva flipped onto her back, remembering the hate-filled expression on Dani's face as she kicked her, followed by the rapture at seeing how badly she'd hurt her. It made her knee throb all over again.

"In the fall, Dani threatened to cause a big public shitstorm about their affair if Lynn didn't come back to her. She had some kind of video she'd recorded on her phone of them having sex."

"Holy shit, really?" *Ew*, Eva thought, but kept her mouth shut.

"Really. A public airing of their affair would have been bad. That kind of scandal probably would have forced Smolenski to fire Lynn. Lynn wouldn't go back to having a relationship with Dani, so Dani blackmailed her into feeding her information about the team. Simple stuff like strategies, lines, who was injured at any given time. Things that would have annoyed the shit out of me, but that we could have overcome."

"But?"

"But then Dani bragged to Alison that she had inside knowledge. Mostly because Dani was a bubble player who feared she'd be cut from the team before ever getting to the Olympics."

"Well, that part was true. I couldn't figure out why in hell Alison kept her on the team. She wasn't good enough." Eva shook her head. "Now I know why. So let me guess. Alison got carried away. Kept Dani turning the screws on Lynn if Dani wanted to be kept on the team."

"I think things escalated quickly, from trading information to trying to throw a game. Both Dani and Lynn got in way over their heads. And the hot tub photo?"

"My money's on Dani."

"You're right, it was her. Lynn, if she's to be believed, tried to stop Dani from using it. But I think Dani got some kind of perverse pleasure in watching Lynn squirm under the pressure. She's sadistic, that one. And I think it's time you filed a police report on her assaulting you. We can't and shouldn't protect somebody like that."

"You're right, but shouldn't I wait until after the gold medal game?"

Niki's eyes were sharp and uncompromising. "No, honey. Tomorrow. It's time to blow the lid off what's been happening. My ass is already out on a limb, and I don't want to be alone out there."

"But won't charges against Dani now be a huge distraction? It'll put the game, hell, the whole sport, in a negative light and right on the biggest stage in the world."

"It's already going to be a huge distraction for our teams, especially once the shit really hits the fan tomorrow with Hockey Canada and USA Hockey. I expect some pretty big announcements. We've got to see this through. And we have to shed light on the darkest corners of our sport if we're going to keep it clean."

Niki was right, of course, but so many people had sacrificed for so long for the chance to win gold. Now there was a chance that in less than forty-eight hours the game could be forfeited. Or worse, women's hockey might suffer under a cloud of suspicion and contempt for years because of this. A black eye for the sport didn't simply mean losing a few fans, it meant losing scads of financial backers, which could set development of women's hockey back decades in North America.

"Jesus," was all Eva could manage. The magnitude of the consequences was almost too much to fathom.

"Dan's called an emergency meeting for tomorrow between himself, the brass at Hockey USA and the International Ice Hockey Federation. The wheels are already in motion for this, there's no going back. Oh, and I told Dan that sweeping any of this under the carpet isn't an option, because you're filing that police report tomorrow, which will all be a matter of public record."

Eva's eyes widened in surprise. She had no idea Niki was capable of such brutal toughness. But then again, it shouldn't have come as a surprise. Her spirit had been forged in the fires of grief and single parenthood the last few years. She was a survivor. "You're really holding their feet to the fire on this, aren't you?"

"Yes. There's no other way. And I don't want to be part of a sport that doesn't hold people's feet to the fire. Nor do I want my daughter or my lover to be part of a sport so corrupt."

Eva grinned. "My girlfriend the whistleblower. Has a nice ring to it, as a matter of fact."

Niki grinned back at her. "It does, does it?"

"Yes. And it turns me on." Eva moved on top of Niki, inserting her good leg between Niki's thighs. Her hands got busy unbuttoning Niki's shirt.

"Well, you were in this with me right from the start. In fact, the whole whistleblowing thing was really your idea. So you know what that means?"

Eva pushed Niki's shirt and bra aside, licked her lips at the rigid nipple awaiting her mouth. "No, what?"

"It means I'm as turned on as you." Niki's hand slipped between their bodies, cupping Eva between the legs, sending her desire into overdrive. "Which also means the night is still young."

Eva glided her tongue over Niki's nipple. "Yes, it certainly is, my love."

CHAPTER THIRTY-ONE

Slap shot

Niki could only imagine what was going through Lynn's mind as she watched the nervous drumbeat of her fingers on the surface of the massive chrome and glass table in one of the hotel's conference rooms. Chief among those thoughts, Niki hoped, was regret.

"I'm sorry," Niki said to break the silence. And she was sorry, even though she was not responsible for any of this. But she was sorry her friend hadn't the fortitude to stop things before they'd gotten so badly out of hand, that she hadn't made better choices, that she hadn't sought help. Lynn's coaching career was forever finished. If she was lucky, though, she wouldn't face criminal charges.

Lynn's face was a blank page, but her voice—cool, disdainful—hinted at her feelings. "You didn't do anything wrong. If anything, you'll be the hero when all this is said and done, Nik."

"You sound like you despise me." Niki tried to keep her anger in check. "What did I ever do to you?"

Lynn's gaze traveled to the ceiling, down to the far wall and back to Niki. Her eyes were moist and there was the tiniest tremble in her chin. "I don't. I always wanted to *be* you, Nik. But I was never as good as you. Not as a player and certainly not as a coach. For a few minutes I fooled myself, thought I could actually figure out a way to coach this team to a gold medal. But Alison would have never let that happen. I got played. And I deserved it."

"Alison didn't *make* you do anything. You could have told her to fuck off. You could have gone to Dan. Or to the police. Or to the media." Niki boldly reached for Lynn's hand and was glad when she didn't pull away. "You could have come to me. We could have figured this out together before anyone got hurt."

"I know." Lynn shook her head in self-admonishment, her gaze slipping from Niki's. "At first I thought I could handle things. And then I think I got seduced by the power, by the prospect of finally making head coach of this team. I...Shit, I don't know anymore. Just don't hate me, okay? I know you didn't deserve any of this, and I know the team didn't either."

It was as much of an apology as Niki was going to get. "What are you going to do after this?"

"I don't know. Try to stay out of jail." Lynn's laughter rang hollow.

The door pushed open, and through it strode Dan Smolenski and Megan Reed, the organization's lawyer. Both carried bulging briefcases and expressions that looked as though they were about to sign someone's death warrant.

"Please," Dan said gruffly to Lynn and Niki, "don't get up." He and Megan took seats at the table, both, Niki noticed with interest, joining her side of it, leaving Lynn very much alone and looking dejected. "Things are moving quickly. And so they should. We only have thirty hours before the gold medal game. Megan?"

The lawyer removed a couple of pages from her briefcase and set them before Lynn, along with a pen.

"So the game is going ahead?" Niki asked.

"Of course it's going ahead," Dan said, his eyes as hard and as cold as the ice cubes in the pitcher of water before him. "I'd sell my firstborn, actually both kids, to make sure this game proceeds. My wife will be glad that won't be necessary. You..." A terse nod at Lynn. "...need to sign the statement and the apology in front of you. We'll disseminate it to the media at the presser we're jointly holding with USA Hockey later this afternoon."

Lynn's face slackened. "That's it?"

Dan's lip curled up condescendingly. "Oh no, that's just the start for you. You're fired with cause, of course, and suspended from working with Hockey Canada and any of its programs and players anywhere in the world for the next ten years. You'll also forfeit the last three months' pay. And that, believe it or not, I consider getting off lightly. It's only because our organization doesn't want the embarrassment of this ending up in the courts that you're not being charged criminally. Megan will have more papers for you to sign. You can expect a lengthy suspension from the International Ice Hockey Federation, I'm sure, if not a lifetime ban. As well..." His jaw clenched and unclenched. "I want you away from here, out of the city as a matter of fact, before this press conference in two hours. You are to have no further contact with any of our players or staff from here on."

Lynn nodded, her face red and her eyes puffy as she stared into her lap. Niki knew she shouldn't, but she felt sorry for her old friend. Greed, fear and ego had put her where she was today, had ruined a good piece of her future. She knew with certainty she'd never have done what Lynn did, but that didn't mean it was up to her to be the judge, jury and the executioner. She held her hand out across the table to offer a handshake. She had more to think about right now than how Lynn had fucked over both her and the team.

Lynn looked up in surprise, nodded once at her and shook her hand. She scribbled her signature on the papers like she couldn't wait to get away, then rushed out the door without a look back. Niki knew she'd never see her again.

Dan leaned back in his chair and sighed as though he had the weight of the world on his shoulders. "What a fucking nightmare," he mumbled. He stared, unblinking, at Niki. "I regret what's happened, Niki, but now's not the time to have a debriefing on it. We've got a gold medal game to play tomorrow."

A flutter came to life in Niki's stomach. So much had been happening that she hadn't had a chance to turn her mind to tomorrow's game. And yet making it to the final was the sole reason she came onboard to coach this team in the first place. It was the reason she'd sacrificed time away from her daughter, from her job at the university. It was the reason why Eva was on crutches and would, no doubt, never play competitive hockey again. That medal, she knew with razor-sharp awareness, still meant everything. Still meant all the sacrifices had a chance of being worth it. She wanted it.

"What do you want me to do?" she said.

"I want you," Dan said as calmly and as matter-of-factly as if he were talking about the weather, "to coach this team to a gold medal. I'll join you on the bench to be your assistant. It's your baby." His gaze turned apologetic for the briefest moment. "As it should have been all along. Now. Let's get to work."

* * *

Eva's good leg tapped an erratic beat on the floor, but it was her stomach that was doing cartwheels. Hockey USA's president and vice president of operations had moments before explained that Alison was on a plane back home and that the team, badly in disarray, needed strong leadership heading into the final game.

"And that leader is going to be you," said Jim Betts, the VP of operations. He was all but pointing a finger at Eva. "You're now Team USA's head coach."

"Me? But I'm not a coach." The shock of Betts's decision quickly morphed into disbelief. She'd expected that out of courtesy and because she was still technically the team's captain and, more to the point, because she'd played a role in uncovering Alison's unscrupulous and heinous actions, she'd be kept apprised of what was happening, maybe even be put on the game roster for ceremonial reasons. But to be named head coach? What did she know about coaching? She searched her mind, drawing only blanks, then searched for a way to wiggle out of it.

"Look," she said with a polite smile. "I'll do anything you ask. I'll assist on the bench. I'll be the team's number one cheerleader. But I can't be head coach of this team."

"You can." The organization's president, Bob Smithson, sat back in his chair with a lazy grin that was in stark contrast to the tension in the room. "And you will."

"I'm a complete novice at this. Worse than a novice. And this is the biggest game on the planet. I can't—"

Betts leaned forward, looked her in the eye and gentled his voice. "In all the years I've known you, Eva Caruso, I've never once heard you say 'I can't.' I want you to think about that for a moment."

It was the wake-up call she needed because it was true. "I can't" was not part of her vocabulary, had never been part of who she was. She'd played the game so hobbled at times that she could barely walk, had urged her teammates on in games she knew were nearly impossible to win, had many times skated through five defenders to score a crucial goal. Of course she could do this if she wanted it badly enough. "You're sure about this?"

"We're sure," Smithson said. "You're the logical choice. The only choice."

"What about Amanda Fox?" Amanda had been Alison's assistant coach for the last couple of years.

"Amanda's gone too. We need a clean slate. There was no indication of any impropriety on Amanda's part, but many people will assume she was part of it, and we can't have a cloud of suspicion over this team."

"You see," Betts weighed in, "you're the only one who comes out of this looking honest, clean. You saw wrongs and tried to right them. That's something fans, the team, the whole country can get behind. You alone can turn what's very much a bad news story into a good news story for us."

Eva understood their point, although it didn't escape her that they were using her as the quickest and most dramatic way to show the hockey world that Alison and Dani were aberrations, bad apples that had been excised from the team, and that in her hands, the good ship USA was back on course again.

Slowly, Eva said, "I very much have reservations." Which was the understatement of the year. "But you're right. We have to try to make things right, to show the world that we want to make things right. But mostly why I'll agree to do this is because of my teammates. They deserve a real chance out there. And they deserve to prove that they're honest and hardworking. Now," she added, "what about my assistant?"

"We have a few candidates in mind," Smithson said. "Do you have any suggestions?"

Eva didn't need to think about it. She wanted the one person associated with the team that she could trust absolutely. "I want Kathleen Benson."

"B-but she's an athletic therapist," Betts said. "You need an experienced coach at your side, someone—"

"No," Eva said flatly. "Benson is my price."

Smithson sighed as though granting her a huge favor. "All right, all right. Whatever makes you comfortable. And it goes without saying that when this is over, we'd very much like to consider moving you full time into the national coaching ranks. Maybe start at the under-18 level."

Eva stood up, reaching for her crutches. She didn't need to think twice about her answer. "Thank you for your confidence. But after this is over, I'm retiring in all capacities from the national program." Hockey as a job, as a way of life, was over for her.

Both men looked at her with raised eyebrows. But hell, could they blame her? After everything that had happened? She smiled to herself. *After all this, I deserve a month-long vacation on a hot beach with a cold drink in my hand. With Niki at my side.*

Slowly Eva began hobbling away. "Excuse me, gentlemen," she said over her shoulder, "but I've got a big game to prepare for."

With the door closed behind her, Eva sagged against her crutches. What the hell was she going to do now? More to the point, how the hell was she going to coach her team to a gold medal? The worse thing about it was that the one person she wanted advice and support from, the one person she needed to lean on, was the person she would be going head-to-head with for the game's biggest prize. *Oh, Niki,* she thought with quiet desperation. *I need you more than ever right now. And I can't even talk to you about it.*

CHAPTER THIRTY-TWO

Hat Trick

As the two captains skated to center ice for the ceremonial puck drop, Niki glanced at Eva on the opposite bench. She was standing as straight and as poised as she could, given her injury. She leaned slightly on one crutch, her dark wavy hair cascading behind her, her navy blue sport coat and slacks pressed to military perfection. A crisp white collared shirt and a red scarf at her throat completed her wardrobe. *Nice touch wearing the country's colors*, Niki thought with a prideful scratch in her throat that threatened to erupt into a sob if she didn't keep control.

It had come like lightning out of a blue sky when Kathleen texted her late yesterday afternoon to say Eva was about to be announced as Alison's replacement. She apologized on behalf of Eva, explained that team policy prohibited the two from communicating until after the gold medal game and that she'd discreetly send someone around to collect Eva's things from her hotel room. Seeing Eva now, on the world's biggest stage, with twenty thousand people in the stands and millions more at home watching the game on television, was almost more than Niki could handle.

She squared her shoulders and tried to force her attention to the task that lay ahead. She was confident Eva would handle herself and her team just fine. Nobody knew the game, or her team, better than Eva. And nobody understood pressure—and succeeded under that pressure—better than Eva did. But it didn't mean Niki wasn't nervous for her lover, because in spite of Eva's calm and authoritative demeanor, she was undoubtedly quaking in her hand-tooled leather boots. Niki smiled. She was proud of Eva, though there wasn't a chance she would take it easy on her. And anyway, Eva wouldn't want her taking it easy on her. Today it was war, and they'd both been around the game long enough to understand that the gloves were off. Exactly as it should be.

As the players lined up for the center ice faceoff, Niki looked one last time at Eva and was rewarded with a confident wink. Niki responded with the thinnest of smiles. She wanted Eva to know that she was in for a dogfight. Bring it, a slight lift to Eva's chin said.

"Okay, ladies," Niki said to her charges on the bench. "This is the game we've been working toward since last summer. There's no tomorrow. There's only now. Let's do this!"

Her heart beat wildly in her chest as the Americans won the faceoff, sent the puck back to their defense to regroup, then raced to spread out. It was clear they would use their speed to force Canada to play man-on-man coverage and then try to slip behind that coverage. Which wasn't unexpected. Niki's players were good at covering their man.

"Make sure you close down the passing lanes," she yelled down the bench. "Don't let them pass. They want to skate, let them skate. Just make sure they've got nobody to pass it to." If the Americans broke out of their coverage and skated with the puck, Canada would simply close down the zone. It was nothing they'd hadn't worked on and perfected during countless hours of practice. But if the Americans broke from their coverage *and* got their passes through, Canada was in tough. "Stick to the plan, ladies. Stick to the plan!"

An American forward's pass was intercepted by one of Niki's wily veterans, who broke away with the puck on the end of her stick. A speedier defender caught up to her before it became a true breakaway, but the Canadian managed to get a shot off. The rebound skittered to the corner as the crowd emitted a collective groan. *It's okay*, Niki thought. *We'll get more chances.* She gave a reassuring pat on the shoulders to the players in front of her, before casting her eyes up at the boisterous crowd. It was a sea of red and white jerseys. And flags. And pompoms and hand-painted posters urging Canada on. There was nothing like playing in front of a home crowd. The energy was contagious. It was that kind of lift to the team's spirits that made the players' legs feel light as feathers and their lungs strong as iron. The crowd, Niki knew from experience, was like a seventh player on the ice.

Another shot from Canada that missed only by inches. The crowd banged on the glass, demanded a goal. Niki drew in an exultant breath. Somewhere in that clamorous crowd was Rory, in her Team Canada jersey that had dutifully been signed by all the players. She'd been so excited this morning, barely able to eat any breakfast and wanting her aunt to make sure they were at the game two hours early. It was at the breakfast table that Niki caught a glimpse of blue and white beneath Rory's jersey.

"What have you got under there, honey?" She'd demanded with a raised eyebrow, already having a pretty good idea what it was.

"Nothing," Rory answered sheepishly. "Just a T-shirt."

Niki could always tell when her daughter was fibbing or being coy. She reached over and tugged Rory's jersey up, biting back a smile at the USA Hockey T-shirt. "What are you doing wearing this?" she said in the most reprimanding voice she could muster. Which wasn't much.

Rory's face colored. "Nothing, Mom. It's just a shirt."

Niki shook her head before wielding a grin at her daughter. "I'll let it go this once, sport, because I know you want to support Eva. But after this, we're back to our number one rule."

"I know, I know," Rory mumbled. "No wearing the enemy's colors on game days."

Niki's attention was drawn back to the game as Canada chased down a puck in the offensive corner. Her player scooped it on her stick and with a no-look pass dumped it out to the high slot, where a teammate was cutting across. With a quick flick of the player's wrist, the puck was in the back of the American net. As the crowd erupted, Niki let out her breath in a whoosh. Getting on the board first was her main priority. It would allow her team to set the tone, to put the Americans in the unenviable position of chasing the game.

"Well done, women, well done!" she shouted to her players, who were still high-fiving in front of the bench. "They'll be out for blood now, so let's keep shutting them down!"

* * *

Eva didn't dare let her disappointment and fear show as she entered the locker room minutes before the second period was to start. She knew what it meant to be chasing the game. Knew too what it meant when the opposing goalie saw every shot and stopped every puck as though it were a beach ball and not a small rubber disc. Her stomach had dropped to her shoes when the Canadian goalie stretched to the far post at the very last second to kick away a shot that was about to sneak in. Ditto when she reacted with lightning speed to get a pad on a puck that had ricocheted off a skate and was headed for the back of the net. The American bench was left wondering what other magic the goalie had up her sleeve. And how the hell they were ever going to score on her. On one power play alone, Eva's team had peppered the Canadian net with eight shots, none of which went in.

The locker room was as quiet as a church nave. Heads were bowed, shoulders were slumped. Maybe they were praying, because everything about their body language told Eva they'd given up already.

"Okay, women, listen up." Eva drew herself up to her full height, tilting slightly on her toes with the assistance of a single crutch under her armpit. "It's only been one period. And we're only down a goal. If you've already lost this game in your mind and in your heart, then there's no sense in going back out there.

You might as well hit the showers now. Is that what you all want? You all want to give up?"

Two players looked up at her in challenge. Another set of eyes, then another and another, rose to meet her gaze as well. The players were looking for leadership. Looking for someone— some *thing*—to get them going again. And Eva would have to be it.

"We didn't work this hard," she said, looking at each player in turn, "come this far, or go through all the shit we've gone through the last couple of weeks to give up now. Have we?"

"No," a few players chimed in.

"Good. And there's something I want you all to remember. And not just for this game, but always, no matter what happens to you in your life." She cast her eyes around the room, waiting until she had everyone's attention. "When you've been disappointed, when you've screwed up, when you've fallen short or when unfair shit happens to you, you have two choices. You can either wallow in it and stay in that miserable place full of regret and self-pity, or you can move on and do something. You can't change the past, but you *can* move forward. You can start again. You can make your own future."

She thought for a moment about her own failings and missed opportunities, both on the ice and in her personal life. She'd spent her fair share of time wallowing in regret and self-pity. And many times in denial. In the end, it had gotten her nowhere. If anything, those times had set her back, stalled her journey, made her miss opportunities. She'd been lucky to get a do-over with Niki. Damned lucky. But it was a rare thing, something that could never be anticipated or counted on. She should have taken her future with Niki by the balls twelve years ago instead of waiting on the fickleness of fate. She'd never make that mistake again, and she didn't want her players making a mistake like that either.

"You have a choice," she continued. "Right here. Right now. So what's it going to be? Are you going to take control of events or are you going to let events control you?"

The players sat up straighter, their resolve hardening before Eva's eyes.

"Not going to quit," said one.

"We're gonna go out there and win," shouted another, to the eruption of cheers.

Eva nodded. She didn't have the experience or the skills of a great coach, but she knew herself and this game really, really well. And that would have to be enough.

"All right, good," she said. "But desire alone is not enough to win. You need a plan. So let's figure out how we're going to beat this team." She limped to the large erase board that was shaped and marked up like an ice rink. She picked up a dry erase marker and began scratching out a new breakout strategy.

"And we're going to keep peppering them with shots," she said over her shoulder. "Something's bound to go in because one thing is for sure. If we don't put shots on net, we're guaranteed that nothing is going to go in."

She turned and looked at her charges once more and the twenty sets of hopeful eyes that stared back at her. Leading these women was an awesome responsibility and one she'd never fully appreciated until now. *We may not win*, she thought, *but we're going to live or die through this thing together.*

As she and Kathleen followed the players out of the tunnel, she wondered what Niki's locker room advice had been. And then it occurred to her that win or lose tonight, the thing she wanted most was for Niki to be proud of her.

* * *

Niki didn't have to work particularly hard to keep her players focused on the present. Most of them were experienced enough to know that a one-goal lead was hardly enough to allow them to rest on their laurels. Though with the way their goaltender was playing, their one goal might actually be enough to win. That was something Niki wouldn't share with her players. If they stopped playing and let their goalie do all the work, one lucky shot would change everything.

Staying calm was the best thing she could do for her team, even when a second-period point shot from a US defender nearly snuck through to tie things up. She didn't need to flick a glance at Eva to know that she too would be the picture of calm. As a player, especially in more recent years, Eva rarely let herself come unglued on the ice, and Niki knew that would bode well for her as a coach. Oh, how she wanted Eva to have success. In her heart she cheered for her, but not as deeply as she cheered for her own team. She didn't want Eva's success to come at the expense of this team. There were no torn loyalties about that. Winning was what Niki and her team were here to do, and if she didn't wholeheartedly believe that, then she had no business coaching this team. Eva would feel the same.

Niki watched the faceoff deep in the American zone. She watched, leaning over the bench, up on her toes, as her player won the draw and passed it quickly to a teammate in front of the net who then shoveled it past the goalie.

"Yes!" Niki did a fist pump. Up two goals with only a period to go. She couldn't ask for much more.

As the clock wound down on the second period, she snuck a look at Eva. Eva hadn't given up, and that made Niki smile. Eva was gently slapping the shoulder pads of each player on the bench, whispering instructions, urging them to keep trying. *That's my girl*, Niki thought, *fighting to the end*. She wouldn't love Eva if she were any other way.

* * *

With only minutes left in the game, Eva pulled out all the stops. She stacked her lines, shortening the bench to four defensemen and six forwards. She didn't need to urge her players to try harder; they were playing with all the desperation they could. They rained down shots on the opposing goalie and somehow found another gear when it came to moving the puck down the ice with speed and accuracy. And still it wasn't enough. With a little over a minute to go, Eva resorted to the ultimate coaching act of desperation: she pulled the goalie in favor of another skater.

Tears caught in her throat as she watched her team battle against a losing cause. The crowd was collectively on its feet, clapping, chanting, "Let's go Can-a-da!" It was so deafening, so raucous, Eva couldn't hear herself think.

As the seconds ticked down it became starkly clear that her coaching debut would end in a loss while her team would walk away with silver—again. She wasn't sad for herself but for her team. They'd battled hard, had put all the distraction of the last few days and weeks behind them, had given their all. No matter what color their medal, to Eva they were winners.

Jocelyn, a long-time forward who'd played in the last Olympics and beyond, used the blade of her stick to flip the game puck to Eva, who caught it one-handed.

"What's this for?" Eva asked, staring at it as though it were a foreign object.

"Something for you to remember the game by. A coach should always have the game puck from her first game." She was grinning through her tears.

Eva nodded and tucked the puck into the pocket of her sport coat. She knew who the puck belonged with, and it wasn't her.

"Come here, women, gather around," she said to the long faces before her. They had to huddle close to hear her words, as the Canadians and their fans continued to celebrate.

"No matter how sad, how frustrated you feel about losing this game, I want you all to remember one thing: you're not losers. You're winners, okay? You got here because you worked hard, because you've got what it takes to be here. You all fought through a lot of crap the last few days and weeks, more than anyone should have had to face. And you fought through it with dignity, with dedication and with discipline—all things that will serve you well as you go through life."

For the briefest of moments she thought of Dani Compton, who was cooling her heels in a jail cell until a bail hearing tomorrow. Dani would never be a winner in life, because she didn't know how to be honest, how to work for what she wanted and, mostly, because she didn't know how to respect anyone, including herself.

The women threw their arms around each other, some in tears as they listened to Eva.

"And remember this," Eva continued. "All of us here, because of what we've gone through, will always be teammates. We'll always have each other's backs. So I want you to hold your heads high, because you're all winners tonight." She looked each woman in the eye, then smiled, even though she wanted to cry. "Now go out there and shake hands with the winners and congratulate them. Tonight they were the better team, nothing more and nothing less."

Eva left her crutches behind and, leaning against the arm of Kathleen, followed her teammates to center ice, taking the last spot as they went through the victors' lineup. Her team shook the Canadians' hands, congratulated them, chose sportsmanship over bitterness. Eva drew in a ragged breath as she came to Niki, and her knees, for the first time all evening, nearly quit on her altogether.

Niki immediately crushed her into a hug. "Oh, my darling, I'm so sorry," she rasped. "You were wonderful, you did a fantastic job, Eva. Congratulations. I was so damned proud of you, sweetheart."

A sob burst from Eva's throat and she cried into Niki's shoulder. What had once been spinning came to an abrupt stop. Even the noise around them stilled, and it seemed everyone, crowd and players alike, were keenly aware of this moment where her and Niki's love and support for one another incontestably transcended the game. Sport was war, but only on the field of play. And to Eva, sport was only a small part, and the least important part, of her life now with Niki.

When she could finally speak, she whispered, "Congratulations, my love. You deserved to win. You did a tremendous job and I'm so happy for you." She carefully wiped a tear from Niki's cheek, then one from her own.

Niki smiled through fresh tears. "I'm sharing this medal with you, so you know. I wouldn't have been coaching this game if it hadn't been for you."

"Hmm. My only regret is I would have liked my team to kick Lynn's ass tonight."

"And I would have liked *my* team to kick Alison's ass."

Eva laughed. "I think those two have sufficiently had their asses kicked, because they'll never be around this game again. Now. I think we might be holding up the medal presentation." She glanced around, saw that the teams had begun assembling on the blue lines, facing each other. "But there's one more thing." She pulled the puck from her pocket and slipped it into Niki's hand. "Your game puck. You won it. You deserve it."

Niki turned it over in her hand, rubbed it between her thumb and forefinger. "No. It's *our* game puck. We're sharing this one. Now let's go get those medals, shall we?"

CHAPTER THIRTY-THREE

Delay of Game

The celebration went late into the night for Niki and her team—champagne in the locker room and later, after the lights over the ice had been dimmed, she and the players snuck out to center ice to snap more photos and smoke celebratory cigars. The players' gear was soaked and sweaty, their hair stringy from the champagne spray, their cheeks stained with tears, but none of them could stop smiling.

Niki had brought Rory down to the locker room, but only long enough for a few autographs and photos. The salty language, the ribald humor and the abundant alcohol was no environment for a kid. Of course Rory wanted to stay longer. And of course Niki said no, eventually bribing her with the promise of a championship hat signed by the entire team.

It was two in the morning before Niki, half drunk, more exhausted than she'd ever been in her life, dragged herself back to her hotel room. She flicked on the light, only to stumble in surprise at the sight of Eva curled up on her bed, still clothed and lying on top of the bedspread. She was fast asleep.

Niki bent and softly placed a kiss on Eva's cheek. She hadn't expected her tonight, and they hadn't talked since the handshake lineup following the game. She sat down on the edge of the bed, waited for Eva to stir and finally to sit up and rub the sleep from her eyes.

"Hey," Niki whispered.

"Hi, Goldilocks. Or would you rather I call you Golden Girl?"

"How about just 'sweetheart'?"

"That'll work." Eva flung her arms around Niki and kissed her on the lips. Her fingers snaked up to the gold medal draped around Niki's neck. "You look great in gold, sweetheart."

"You look great in gold too, you know. Your Nagano gold medal."

"Yeah, don't remind me. The only Olympic Games we've been able to beat you guys."

Niki lay down on the bed beside Eva and rubbed her eyes, which still stung from the champagne. She could smell herself, and it wasn't good. "Jesus, I need a shower."

"Only if I can join you."

Niki grinned at her lover. "You know you have an open invitation to that."

Eva began to crawl off the bed, but Niki sat up and pulled her back. "Wait, honey. I want us to talk first."

"Okay." A look of panic flashed across Eva's face, and Niki could feel the weight of those soulful brown eyes on her. "Are you going to dump my silver ass?"

Niki laughed, playfully brushing Eva's chin with her fingers. Simply touching Eva melted her, turned her into a quivering, needy fool. "No, I most assuredly am not dumping your cute, silver ass."

Eva relaxed beside her. "Then I'm all ears."

The discussion could have waited another day, of course it could have, but Niki had crossed a threshold with the gold medal win. She'd coached her team to the biggest prize there was, had gone through an emotional gauntlet these last few days, had put her life aside for months to reach this moment. And now it was over. Worth it, but over. She had nothing left to prove, nothing else to give. It was time to exhale. It was time, finally, to figure out how she was going to live the next fifty years of her life.

"I need to tell you about Shannon."

They each fluffed their pillow and sat back against the headboard. Eva reached for Niki's hand and held it.

"You asked me once," Niki continued, "if I loved her. And I did. Of course I did."

"I know. That was a stupid question."

"No. It wasn't." Niki swallowed against the roughness in her throat. "You see, Shannon was everything I wanted—needed—in my life when she came along. She was…" Niki pictured her wife's calm, even brown eyes, her gentle smile that wasn't quick but was as deep as her heart. "She was stable, reliable, loyal, predictable. God!" Niki pinched her eyes shut for a moment. "I sound like I'm describing an old farm horse."

"You mean," Eva said quietly, "she was everything I wasn't."

"At the time, yes."

"Okay. I deserved that."

"But that was also the problem."

Eva's eyebrows shot into her forehead. "Meaning?"

"She wasn't you." Niki shook her head in self-condemnation. She'd beaten herself up so many times over this very thing, but she'd never verbalized it to anyone. And she needed to before it damaged another relationship. "I could never quite give all of myself to her, because I'd never gotten over you. I mean, do you have any idea how that felt? What that did to me, to her?"

"Oh, man. I'm so sorry, Nik." Eva threw her arm around Niki's shoulders and gently pulled her against her. "I'm so sorry I hurt you. If I could take it back, I—"

"No," Niki said sharply. "It's not all on you. It never was. If anything, most of the blame rests on me, because I tried so hard to love Shannon, to convince myself and her that I loved her completely. And I did love her, but my heart wasn't being fully honest."

"Do you think she knew?"

"Yes. You don't live with someone for years, raise a child together, and not know there's something wrong. Something missing. But I couldn't tell her. I just couldn't hurt her like that.

And I thought that with more time…" Niki wiped a tear from her cheek. There hadn't been more time, and Shannon had died before Niki had ever completely fallen in love with her. And that was what continued to haunt her.

"Hey," Eva said, squeezing her shoulder. "Like you said, you loved her. She had to know that, and that's the most important part. You looked after her when she got sick, right? And now you're raising her daughter. There's nothing more loving than those two things. Sweetheart, you did more and you gave more than most people could humanly do."

Niki sniffled against more tears and thought about that. If she hadn't been able to give Shannon all of her heart, she prayed that what she'd given her was enough.

* * *

Slowly, like a hammer chipping at a rock face, Niki's guilt broke Eva's heart. Niki was the best person she knew. The most generous, the most loyal, the most loving. She kissed her temple. "Shannon was lucky to have you, and I'm sure she knew that. And Rory is super lucky to have you as a mom."

She could feel Niki smiling against her neck. "I'm the lucky one. I've had all these great women in my life."

Eva tilted Niki's chin until their eyes met. "You've had great women in your life because *you're* great. And now that I've found you again, I'm not letting you go. Ever."

"I don't want you to ever let me go again. But I do need to ask how you feel about being a stepmom. And about moving to Windsor to be with Rory and me."

Eva's heart was a feather fluttering in the breeze. She'd never felt so free and so anchored at the same time. She wanted nothing more than to make a family with Niki and Rory. To plant her feet in one spot. To make a life with the most special people in the world to her. She wanted to laugh and yet she found herself crying.

"Oh, honey," Niki whispered, clutching her closer. "I didn't mean to make you cry."

"Well, you did," Eva sputtered, coughing. "But it's a good kind of crying."

"Is that a yes?"

"Yes, that's a yes." Eva laughed. "Are you kidding me? You've made me the happiest woman in the world."

"Then kiss me and make *me* the happiest woman in the world."

With gentle determination, Eva traced the outline of Niki's lips with her tongue. They were so soft, so satiny, so delicate, so delicious. A moment later, she kissed her with a tenderness that soon hardened into fervent longing. Desire unfurled in her belly, blotting out her thoughts. She wanted Niki more than she'd ever wanted her before.

"Wait," Niki ordered between quick breaths. "Shower first."

"Oh, right. Shower. Except I can't wait the ten or fifteen minutes the shower's going to take. So prepare yourself for shower sex."

"Ooh, shower sex. My favorite!"

Eva carefully extricated herself from the bed and playfully swatted Niki's thigh. "Come on, you. Shower and sex await."

"Wait, there's one more thing." Niki fingered the medal at her chest and its blue fabric lanyard and quirked a teasing smile at Eva. "Just so you know, I'm bringing this in the shower with us."

Gingerly, because her knee still screamed at her, Eva chased Niki into the bathroom as best she could, both of them giggling all the way. With the medal pressed between them and Niki backed against the tile wall, Eva kissed her senseless.

EPILOGUE

April, 2010

Niki dug her toes into the warm sand with each stride, the green of the ocean momentarily blinding her as the sun rode each cresting wave. The sky was a wide, clear canvas of blue, unblemished from clouds or even, surprisingly, the vapor trails of passing jets. She, Eva and Rory gaped at the tableau before them, and it was perfect. None of them had ever taken a winter vacation to the Caribbean before. Hockey precluded winter vacations that didn't involve a rink nearby. And while it wasn't technically winter anymore, April in Canada was close enough.

"Mom, can we do this again next year?" Rory asked, slipping one hand into Niki's and the other into Eva's.

"That depends on you, sweetie."

"What do you mean?" Rory asked.

"Well," Niki answered patiently. "Next winter you're moving up a level with your hockey. So there'll be more travel, more games. It depends on whether you want to take a break from that or not."

"What about your hockey?" Rory asked. There was only curiosity in her tone, but Niki wouldn't blame her if she was feeling her out. Niki's hockey career had almost always come before everything else, save for the three years before the Vancouver Olympics.

"Sweetie, I'm not coaching again anytime soon. Not next year and not the year after that either. We talked about this, remember? It's time for me to be at home more."

"I know, but I didn't think you were serious."

Niki smiled. She wouldn't change her mind, well, unless it was to coach Rory's hockey team. It was time to enjoy the important things in her life, the things that mattered most to her now: Rory, Eva, her teaching job at the university. Hockey would always be one of her favorite things, but from now on it would be much, much farther down the list.

"What about you, Eva?" Rory said. "Are you really not gonna play anymore?"

Doesn't this kid believe anything anybody says? Well, Niki thought, she couldn't blame her if she didn't. When Shannon was dying, Niki had vowed she was finished coaching at the highest levels, and yet she'd broken her word. Rory had forgiven her, had actually encouraged her to do it, but now it was time to give her daughter a stable home life.

"Nope," Eva said. "My playing days are done. My knees have sealed that deal."

Eva would need another surgery in the summer. Her final one, they both hoped, until it was time for a full knee replacement a few years down the road. Playing high-level hockey again was definitely not an option.

"Will you coach my team next year? Please? I want both of you to coach me."

Rory had been playing this little game of trying to pin down commitments and plans from Eva in the weeks following the Olympics. It couldn't be more obvious that she wanted Eva's presence in their lives to be permanent, and she'd continued to bait them both.

"Actually," Eva said, stopping their progress and turning to face Niki and Rory. "There's something I want to ask both of you. Well, your mom mainly, but it's something you both have to answer."

Oh shit, Niki thought, her throat suddenly as dry as the sand beneath her feet. She'd suspected in the deepest part of her soul that this moment would come eventually, but she hadn't expected to feel so nervous, hadn't expected it to happen *now*. She wanted this, of course she did, but the idea scared the living hell out of her too.

Eva dropped slowly to one knee and reached for Niki's left hand. Her eyes were moist, resolute with determination, but there was a tiny amount of fear there too.

"Niki Hartling, will you do me the honor of becoming my wife?"

She heard Rory's intake of breath, but she couldn't peel her eyes from Eva's. "I, I…" Her mouth was full of cotton, sucking back her words, leaving them there. Eva waited. She was patient, but her eyes widened in disbelief with each passing second.

"Mom!" Rory squealed.

"Honey, this is between Eva and me. Well, you too, but—"

"Niki, it's okay," Eva said, her voice quavering, her tone flattening out. Carefully, she pulled herself to her feet, and Niki wanted to cry, wanted to tell her to give her a minute, but she couldn't speak.

"It's…I'm sorry," Eva said, her voice sounding like it was under water. It pierced Niki's heart. "It was a bad idea. I understand if you think it's way too soon." Eva was in the midst of closing down her Traverse City business and would be moving in with Niki and Rory in the next month. It was a big step, one they'd talked about and were comfortable with. But it was the only step they'd talked about until now.

"No," Niki said, holding up her other hand. "It's not. Just… Everybody just wait." The flow of heat from Eva's hand in hers calmed her, reduced the shock of her proposal, which shouldn't have been a shock at all, but it was; the actual words absolutely were. She never expected to marry again, even though Shannon had tried to get her to promise she would if she met someone deserving.

That day, in the hospital, came rushing back to her. Shannon was hours from death, in and out of consciousness. She was so pale, so thin, lying against those stark white sheets, bones jutting out like little tent poles. The room was quiet but for the beeping of the heart monitor machine—the only thing at times that told her Shannon was still alive. And then Shannon opened her eyes, looked straight at her and told her she had to promise she wouldn't spend her life alone. That she would find love again.

Niki hadn't been able to promise it, hadn't wanted to promise it, and so she'd left Shannon hanging. Now she looked at Eva and Rory, both of them expectantly gazing back at her. She swallowed, told her pounding heart to settle the hell down enough to let her get the words out.

"Eva, I love you. And I do want to spend the rest of my life with you."

"But?" Eva said quietly.

She didn't want to say certain things in front of Rory. But Rory was a smart kid; she'd been through more pain and heartache than any kid her age should have to bear. "Marriage doesn't…It…Bad things can happen. Things beyond our control."

"I don't want to lose another wife" is what she wanted to say but couldn't. Not in front of Rory.

Eva smiled through her tears. She squeezed Niki's hand. "Good things happen too, Nik, whether we're married or not. And I'm willing to gamble everything on more good things happening than bad. And you know what?"

"What?"

"Whatever happens in the future, it's a hell of a lot easier if we face it together. As a married couple." Eva stepped closer, brought her hand to Niki's chin and raised it. "I'm an all-or-nothing kind of gal, you know. I won't live in sin with you forever. I want you as my wife. And I want Rory as my daughter. My legally, adopted daughter. Anything less than all of that… What can I say. It's a deal breaker."

It had never felt so good giving in. This was Eva asking her to marry her. Her first love. The woman she was meant to be with. The woman who would make a fantastic stepmother to her daughter. "You drive a hard bargain, lady."

Eva laughed, relief in her voice. "It can be a long engagement, you know. Or is that showing my hand too much?"

Rory stepped between them. "Are you two getting married or what?"

Eva's eyebrows rose playfully. "Well?"

"Yes! Yes we're getting married." Above Rory's head, she kissed Eva on the lips.

"Now that," Eva said, "is better than any medal. Gold or silver or even bronze."

Rory threw her arms around them both, and the three of them huddled in a long group hug. After a moment, Niki caught Eva's eye again. She wanted to freeze-frame this moment forever. But since she couldn't, the next best thing was to continue having moments like this. For as long as she could.

Bella Books, Inc.

Women. Books. Even Better Together.

P.O. Box 10543
Tallahassee, FL 32302

Phone: 800-729-4992
www.bellabooks.com